Her mind whirled with unanswered questions

What should she do now? The situation was beyond her experience. Corey knew she had better get word to Professor White who would know what they might do to save the eggs if the falcon abandoned them.

Corey hiked down the slope to the tent and ducked under the canvas flap. "What—?"

She saw the tip of an army boot too late. She tripped and sprawled forward on the tent floor. The next instant her arms were pinned at her sides and her head and arms rolled up in a small rug.

She fought and tried to scream, but choked from lack of air.

A suffocating sensation sent all air back down her throat. In a few seconds, she was as securely confined as the tiercel had been in the mist net.

ABOUT THE AUTHOR

Leona Karr, a native of Colorado, lives in a
suburb of Denver near the front range of the
Rocky Mountains. She has pursued a career
as Reading Specialist, raised four children
with her husband, Marshall, and is currently
enjoying the excitement of a writing career
and eight granddaughters.

Books by Leona Karr

HARLEQUIN INTRIGUE

120–TREASURE HUNT

Don't miss any of our special offers. Write to us at the
following address for information on our newest releases.

Harlequin Reader Service
901 Fuhrmann Blvd., P.O. Box 1397, Buffalo, NY 14240
Canadian address: P.O. Box 603,
Fort Erie, Ont. L2A 5X3

Falcon's Cry
Leona Karr

Harlequin Books

TORONTO • NEW YORK • LONDON
AMSTERDAM • PARIS • SYDNEY • HAMBURG
STOCKHOLM • ATHENS • TOKYO • MILAN

With deep affection to my special daughters,
Cynthia K. Karr
Patricia H. Karr

Harlequin Intrigue edition published August 1990

ISBN 0-373-22144-4

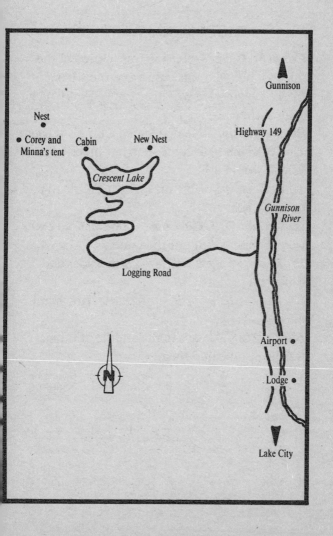

CAST OF CHARACTERS

Corey McCalley—Her job was to protect the falcons, but who was going to protect her?

Ross Sinclair—He was in a secret, deadly race against time.

Prince Amund—He demanded a king's ransom.

Zaki Kashan—He could help or hinder Ross. Which would it be?

Trudi Cochran—She was everyone's friend and no one's enemy.

Delvin and D. J. Cochran—The Cochran twins were identical, but not the same.

Professor Richard White—Team leader and expert on raptors.

Chester Carlson—The professor's right-hand man.

Bill Collins—Always in the middle of things, was he also behind them?

Prologue

The dark, official car moved slowly through the narrow sunbaked streets of Kasardi, Arabia, like a black creature in search of its prey. The veiled woman walking close to a high wall heard the warning hum of its engine and turned around. Her heartbeat quickened, and she drew the three-year-old American boy closer to her side. An apprehension that defied identification surged through her. The car was following. Slowly. Purposefully.

"Can I have some sweets, Nana?" the blond, curly-headed boy asked.

"Some dates when we get home, Robin." Her voice was tense.

"I'm tired, Nana," he whined.

"I know, child, but we must hurry. Your father will be home soon."

His blue eyes brightened and he quickened his childish steps.

She sent another look backward. The car was still coming. The woman had first noticed the dark sedan when she and Robin crossed the square to enter the market. The black car was parked in the square, its engine idling. Now it was moving slowly behind her.

She must get Robin home safely. The boy had been in her charge ever since his frail American mother had died three years before and she had been hired as his nanny. She didn't know what enemies his father might have made during their stay in Tasir Province.

"Hurry, Robin!" She pulled the boy into a faster pace.

The car accelerated and lurched forward. The woman shrieked and pressed the child up against the wall as the car door flew open. Two men in palace uniforms dragged them into the car.

ROSS TOOK THE STEPS up to his apartment two at a time. It had been a long hot day, and he was ready for a cool drink and games with Robin. His son's childish laughter was the tonic he needed to forget the frustrations of developing an irrigation system for His Royal Highness, Prince Amund.

"Hello. I'm here," he called as he stripped off his tie and jacket and tossed them onto a hall rack. The interior of the house was cool and filled with lingering shadows. He peered into the living room and then went down the hall to the kitchen. "Robin? Nana?"

No one answered. The kitchen was empty. He frowned. No sign of his dinner being prepared. No rich aromas floating in the air. The first flicker of anxiety touched him. Robin and his nursemaid were always waiting for him with eager smiles and complicated little-boy stories about the day's happenings. Where were they?

"Robin. Robin!" Usually when he arrived home, his son squealed and leaped into his arms like a rambunctious kangaroo, and Ross silently thanked God that Elaine had safely delivered his son before she died.

Ross went back to the front of the house. With every step, the silence grew like an ominous, invisible cloud. "Robin!" His voice became strident as he went through the apartment.

"Nana. Where is everybody?"

Ross checked the bedrooms and then came back to the living room. He froze when he saw an official envelope on the small living room table. He grabbed the royal stationery and tore the letter open.

"I have taken your son. Prince Amund."

MINUTES LATER, he strode into the royal palace's outer court with his hands clenched and eyes as hard as polished blue steel. Water spraying from numerous fountains seemed gentle and quiet, but the night's stillness was one of waiting, not of peace. Rounded domes with sharp spires still held warmth from the Arabian sun, and a hushed, languid breeze moved through the open corridors.

His quick-moving figure made a lean shadow against alabaster-white pillars, and the sound of his hurrying footsteps on the wide marble stairs was an intrusion on the mosaic-tiled floors. As Ross passed under high arches and entered the main hall, two guards stepped forward to intercept him. One guard leveled a rifle at Ross's stomach, and the other methodically searched him for weapons. When the thorough check did not reveal even a pocketknife hidden on his slim, hard frame, the guards stepped back.

"Now take me to Prince Amund," Ross ordered through tight lips.

Ross had been to the palace on numerous occasions during his stay in Kasardi. He had supped with Prince Amund, hunted together with falcons in the desert and had escorted the royal ruler around the irrigation project that Ross's U.S. company was developing in his province. They had always met on congenial terms, but this night Ross's blood ran hot with the fury of an explosion. He didn't know how he could keep from grabbing the prince's thick neck and squeezing the life out of him. He only knew he must keep his head. This was a moment when cold, deliberate reasoning must rule his actions.

Flanked by the two guards, Ross was ushered past numerous corridors and luxurious chambers into the inner recesses of the palace. When they reached a pair of gold-embossed doors, an order from one of the guards admitted them into a long reception room hung with luminous chandeliers and covered with deep crimson carpeting.

The air was redolent with distinctive odors that flared his nostrils: cardamom-flavored coffee, sweet mint tea, poignant incense and body perfumes. Robed men sat in numerous gold brocade armchairs that lined the walls. At the far end of the room, seated in a crimson velvet armchair was Prince Amund. His smiling face was like the wave of a red flag in front of Ross's eyes, but he forced himself to move in a nonthreatening manner across the vast chamber, controlling the raw fury exploding inside his chest. He clenched his jaw tightly and took a deep breath to settle the rage. He would need to be calm if he hoped to help Robin.

Both guards stayed at his side, and Ross was aware of robed figures on the edges of his peripheral vision, but his gaze remained fixed on Prince Amund. The Arab was a thick, heavy-boned man whose girth was increased by flowing white robes and the folds of the traditional *kaffrieh* on his head. Prince Amund raised his hand to indicate to Ross that he was close enough, and instantly two guards restrained him from moving closer.

Ross knew the polite ritual *Salam 'alaikum* and the responding *Wa 'alaikum as-salam*, wishing his guest peace, but the greetings were a mockery in this situation. Ross couldn't bring himself to utter them. He fixed his eyes upon the potentate. "What have you done with my son?"

"*Salam 'alaikum.* No harm will come to your son, my friend," Amund responded smoothly.

"Friend! What friend would take away my three-year-old son and his nurse and leave a cold message for me to pay His

Highness an audience? In my country this is not called friendship—but abduction.''

"Ah, yes, but this is not your country, Mr. Sinclair, and there is a little favor I have to ask of you. I wanted to insure your cooperation. You know of my interest in raising the best hunting falcons. I am determined to add the North American peregrine falcons to my collection. Unfortunately, my offer to pay a hundred thousand dollars for a breeding pair has not brought any of these magnificent birds into my possession.''

"It is illegal to take them out of the United States! The peregrine falcon is an endangered species, and the U.S. government has passed laws to protect them. Remember, I told you about programs designed to put more peregrines back into the wild—'' Then he stopped himself. What a fool he'd been!

The prince smiled benignly. "Exactly. I was very interested in what you had to say and have decided I would like to try the same kind of breeding program. It would be most interesting to raise our fierce hawks with the more refined and graceful peregrine. When I heard you were going back to your country for a brief visit, I decided that you should bring me a pair.''

"Smuggling falcons is not in my line of work!''

"I know,'' said Amund softly. "But you are a good falconer, Mr. Sinclair. I have watched you on our little hunting trips. You are quite capable of handling this special request while your son remains safely in my custody. There is no offense intended, just a gift between friends.'' His smile did not reach his eyes but twisted on his fat lips like a challenge. "Your son will spend his holiday under my protection while you return to the United States and arrange for my gift. You will have one month.''

"It's impossible!'' A vein pulsated angrily in Ross's bronzed forehead. "I'd have to find the birds, steal them and then smuggle them safely out of the country! What if I'm caught?''

"Alas, such a disappointment for all of us. It saddens me to think that a boy who lost his mother at birth might also be deprived of his father. Yes, you must make certain you are not caught, Mr. Sinclair. That would be most unfortunate...most unfortunate." He gave a flicker of his fat finger.

A guard jerked open a door at the far corner of the room, and Ross's eyes widened with anger.

"Daddy!" called a curly-head boy as he struggled in the arms of a soldier who held him in the doorway.

"Robin!" Wild rage raced through Ross. His muscles flexed, but the two guards at his side tightened their grip, and the prick of a knife at his throat immobilized Ross before he could move. A razor-edged tip sank into his flesh, and he felt a warm flow of blood trickle down his neck.

"Don't be foolish," warned the prince.

"You can't do this!" swore Ross. "Let my son go!"

The prince only smiled. He gave a wave of his hand. The door closed and Ross's son was gone.

"If you hurt him," growled Ross. "I'll—"

"Silence!" The prince's jeweled hand sliced the air. "I am the one issuing the warning, Mr. Sinclair," snapped the prince imperiously. His eyes were as cold as his voice. "I suggest you spend your energies carrying out my wishes. As you well know, I am not a patient man. And I don't like disappointments."

"It's impossible! There's no way that I can smuggle a pair of falcons out of the country."

"You will find a way, Mr. Sinclair." He motioned for the guards to take Ross away.

"My son—!"

"He will be safe...for the period of one month."

"A month! That's not enough time."

"It will have to be. One month, no more. If you fail in your quest, do not come back to my country, Mr. Sinclair. There will be nothing here for you but the same unfortunate fate as can befall your son."

Chapter One

Corey heard the "kaa,kaa,kaa," of the male peregrine falcon as he circled high above the aerie where his mate waited. He had left the nest just seconds before, and she knew that this relentless provider had gone to forage for prey on the flat area just above the cliff. Through her binoculars, she watched the bird's swift upward flight. As a member of a research team from the University of Colorado, she was spending the summer in the Uncompahgre National Forest wilderness area in the San Juan mountains.

Corey and her partner, Minna Gibbons, had found this aerie near the top of a bleak, sheer cliff, and by climbing up to the ledge, they had determined that four eggs were being incubated in the nest. As aerie wardens, it was their job to closely observe and record the hatching and later to band the young fledglings and adults so data could be collected from year to year.

Corey tipped her blond head back and watched the male falcon, which was called a tiercel, rise with quick wing beats and then glide in leisurely turns, soaring in a wide circle. A beautiful bird, she thought. His proud head was a black helmet; strong blue-black wings stretched widely away from a trim body. The white feathers of his underparts contrasted with an overcast afternoon sky darkening with the promise of rain. She knew his sharp eyes could see farther and more clearly than a human's. At that moment, the bird suddenly plunged downward in a dive that Minna had informed her was called a stoop.

The tiercel must have seen prey on the flat ground above the ridge, Corey thought. She kept her binoculars fixed on the spot of its disappearance, expecting the falcon to rise in the next instant with his booty fixed in his talons. She knew he killed only to eat and that his kills were quick and sure. She had watched the tiercel hunt many times before, and he usually brought the prey right back to the nest like the dutiful mate he was. But this time the peregrine did not launch back up into the air again. Instead she heard a frantic falcon's cry, "Kaak! Kaak! Kaak!"

The bird was in distress!

For a moment Corey didn't know what to do. Every precaution had been taken so that her presence on the ridge was one of quiet concealment. She and Minna had hidden with their zoom lens telescope behind a blind built of branches, wood and canvas, so they could observe without causing anxiety to the mating birds. Corey knew that any hint of human aggression might cause them to abandon the incubating eggs. To rush out could easily betray her presence and perhaps flush the female off her nest. In all the briefing sessions, no one had instructed her on how to proceed in this kind of contingency. Professor White might be furious with her, but she had no choice. She couldn't ignore the tiercel's frantic screeching. It was as poignant a cry for help as she had ever heard.

Corey whipped the binoculars off her head and left her concealed position behind the screen of wood and twigs. Quickly she surveyed the cliff that rose straight up. Somewhere on the high ridge, the tiercel was still screeching.

Her eyes quickly scanned the layered rock. The surface was irregular. Would the narrow shelves of stone provide safe footing? Her gaze moved from one ledge to the next in a zigzag path to the top. She shoved aside the ever-present danger of crumbling rock caused by the weight of her body. Climbing the face of the cliff was the only way up. One false step—!

Her mouth was suddenly dry and her heart raced wildly. It would be a precarious climb but not impossible. At that moment caution seemed a commodity she couldn't afford. The tiercel's cries were fading, becoming hoarse and weak.

Corey darted to the first ledge in the cliff. A screech from the female falcon told Corey that the bird had seen her. With a rush of wings and a high-pitched "Kaak...kaak... kaak..." the falcon came swooping off her nest. Protective of her eggs, the frantic female darted at Corey, beating her wings, cutting the air with her sharp-edged cry as the falcon instinctively tried to drive this intruder away.

Corey knew that nesting falcons would viciously protect their nests. During the months of May through July, wildlife biologists wore riot gear of helmets and protective vests when they tried to band chicks or remove eggs. Corey never dreamed she would have need of such protection, but as the falcon swooped around her, razor-sharp talons were only inches away from her bare head, and she would have given anything for a motorcycle helmet.

She shut out the cacophony of screeches and whipping wings as she clawed up the first shelf of rock and centered her attention on moving cautiously from one narrow ledge to the other. Her nails bit into the jagged crevices. She tested each slab of rock before she stepped onto it. When one broke off, she tried another. Slowly she made her way upward toward the lip of the precipice where the tiercel had disappeared. The cries of the tiercel on the promontory above were faint now and drowned out by the abrasive screeches of his mate, who swooped around Corey's head.

Corey knew that one swipe of the falcon's sharp talons could lay her skull open, but at the moment, falling from the cliff presented more danger than the bird who frantically screamed and darted at her.

Corey didn't know what damage had already been done by scaring the female off her nest. They had taken extreme precautions to stay hidden so the normal pattern of behavior of the falcons would not be disturbed. Even if she found the tiercel safe, her presence so close to the nest might frighten the pair away. If only her tent mate hadn't decided to fish the upper stream this morning, thought Corey. Minna might have heard the uproar from their tent at the bottom of the rocky talus, but it would be afternoon before the Texan returned to take her shift. The rest of the research team were scattered, either searching for peregrine aeries or remaining as wardens observing identified pairs. It was no use expecting help from anyone. Whatever happened, Corey knew she was on her own in the present crisis.

Loose pebbles gave way under her, and more than once she almost lost her footing. Overhead, the sky was darkening. Shadows fell upon the cliff's face as fast-moving rain clouds blanketed the sun and moved lower along the mountainous ridge. A driving need to hurry kept Corey climbing at a breathless pace.

The female falcon gave up screeching and flew back down to her nest. Thank heavens, breathed Corey. A faint "kaak...kaak..." gave her new assurance that the male falcon was still somewhere above. This heartening knowledge made the last few feet of the climb the easiest. She swung herself over the lip of the cliff and was on her feet almost in the same movement.

An expanse of tawny wild grass and junipers spread across the high ground, which was dotted with drifts of low-growing cedar and pine trees. Corey had watched the tiercel frequently fly over this elevated plateau, and she reasoned that he must have seen something to make him dive a few minutes earlier. Her frantic gaze swept over the mountain terrain. No sign of the falcon, but she could still hear him.

She bounded over the rough ground like a sprinter taking hurdles at a race. A cold drop of rain touched her face. She'd never find the bird in a rainstorm. The sun was only a smudge of light behind dark gray clouds now, lowering like a shroud down the mountain slopes. The falcon's cries were coming somewhere to her right. She spurted in that direction.

As she ran, her feet scattered loose rocks and crunched dead leaves. This noise drowned out the tiercel's faint cries. She stopped. Listened. Nothing. Only the sound of a rising wind bending grass in waves and whining through needled branches. Had she been mistaken? She couldn't be sure now where the cries had been coming from.

Corey plunged through a band of straggly cedars. In her anxiety she was oblivious to nettled branches biting into her flesh and pungent sticky sap coating her hands. As she came into a small clearing, she gasped with relief.

There he was!

She couldn't believe her eyes.

In an open space, rimmed by a thicket of conifers, the bird was thrashing hopelessly in a mist net, a trapping device of loosely stretched mesh with strong threads so that the more a victim struggled the more hopelessly bound it became. The tiercel's valiant fight had maliciously rolled him up in the net like a bird trussed for marketing. At the moment he wasn't in any mortal danger but merely a prisoner held securely for his captor. Corey felt a rush of hot fury at the sight—someone had deliberately set a trap! She saw that a pair of pigeons had been tethered there on short leashes, and the minute the falcon had seized one, he had flown right into the net. She started toward the flapping bird, but a sound behind her made her stop. On the edge of her peripheral vision, she saw a shadow rise from behind a needled thicket, and Corey realized that she was not alone. She swung around, but too late. She cried out as pain exploded on one side of her skull just above her right ear. She wavered from the blow, her knees gave way, and blackness enveloped her as she hit the ground.

COREY FOUGHT HER WAY through spinning layers of deep gray. Soft rain was beginning to bathe her face. Her eyes fluttered open and focused on fast-moving dark clouds above her. Pain thumped in her head, and she realized she was lying flat on her back on the ground. The knowledge was detached and floated around in her mind without comprehension. She struggled up to a sitting position, gingerly touching a large knot on her head. Then she remembered. Everything came back in a flash. The tiercel!

Her eyes darted swiftly to the small circle of open ground. The bird was gone. Only a few scattered white feathers remained to verify the place where the trap had been set. Anger brought Corey swiftly to her feet, but she wavered unsteadily in a wash of vertigo. She must not have been out very long, she reasoned, for the rain was just beginning.

A loud rolling boom of thunder vibrated in her ears as thunderheads amassed against the Continental Divide. Overhead, lightning forks pierced the blanket of storm clouds. Corey knew she had better find shelter before the storm hit. It would be suicide to climb back down the face of the cliff the way she had come. Better to go in the direction of a small lake that lay beyond the cliffs. A rocky draw sloped down at one end of its crescent shape, and she could double back from there.

Her legs floated away under her in a weird detachment, and more than once she fell to her knees on the rough ground. The blow near her ear must have affected her equilibrium, she thought hazily. Another crash of thunder, and the first heavy pelting of cold raindrops hit her face in warning.

Confused thoughts tumbled in her head. Someone had trapped the tiercel. The thief must have been there ready to claim his booty when she came over the lip of the cliff. She had passed him as he hid in the thicket, and she'd only glimpsed a movement before he struck her.

A steady rain began to beat down on her. Her hair and clothes were drenched by the time she reached a rocky hillside that sloped down to the lake. Through a thickening downpour, she glimpsed snatches of white-ruffled water. The lake nestled between steep mountain slopes and bore the name of its shape, Crescent Lake. Taking careful steps down the slippery ground, Corey cautioned herself that she'd have to watch her footing unless she wanted to roll to the bottom of the hill and into the lake. A barrage of booms like cannon fire vibrated down the canyon, coming closer and closer like invading artillery. Corey quickened her pace, nearly going down on her knees several times. When she was almost to the bottom, she wiped away beaded raindrops on her lashes and peered ahead.

Her heart lurched to a stop. The figure of a man was etched darkly against rounded gray boulders just below her. With his back to her, he was turning his head and peering across the lake. Was he waiting for someone to pick him up in a boat? On the ground beside him was a satchel—the right size for carrying a captured tiercel.

He must have been the one to hit her on the head and take the bird. He'd come down to the lake ahead of her, she reasoned. Fortunately, her stumbling, sliding descent had been muffled by the peals of rumbling thunder. She couldn't believe her luck. The smuggler seemed unaware that she was behind him.

Corey's heart leaped with excitement. She had a chance to get the bird back. She'd never thought herself capable of physical violence, but the vision of her beautiful falcon trussed up inside that hamper fueled her anger to a near-violent rage. She reached down to the wet ground for a rock. When she found one that fit into her hand, she stealthily moved forward.

He turned enough for her to see his profile and dark hair.

She froze.

For a moment, she thought he was going to turn completely around and face her, but he returned his gaze to the lake.

She eased out the breath she had been holding and moved forward again. Just as she reached the thief, her unsteady footing caught on a rough stone and the sound brought him lurching around. The blow she struck was off balance, and the rock only grazed his lean cheek. She had an impression of ice-blue eyes in a tanned bronze face as his muscular arms engulfed her.

Fighting wildly, she twisted, kicked and raised her knee to his groin. It connected in an effective jab, and for an instant he lessened his grip.

She jerked away, darted around the rocks and ran as fast as she could along the lake's edge. Her only chance lay in concealment. But where to hide? Her gaze fastened on a band of trees reaching almost to the lake's edge. The hope of reaching them was knocked out of her head, along with her breath, when a pair of arms grabbed her from behind and threw her to the ground in a flying tackle.

They rolled almost into the water.

"Let me go." She struck out. Her hands pelted his face and chest.

He swore and tightened his grip.

She struggled to get free, but his hold on her was too strong. Steel-hard hands were like a vise. He grabbed her arms and pinned them at her side. Securing her body with his weight, he pressed her down into the mud, holding her

flat on her back. Even though she writhed, it was hopeless.
She couldn't get free. He had made her as helpless as the
tiercel.

Rain stung her face so that she couldn't see him clearly.
Thatched dark hair drifted over his face. Mud and pouring
rain distorted his features. His hands were like grappling
hooks as he jerked her to her feet. In one swift motion he
lifted her up bodily and swung her over his shoulder.

Her head dangled downward, bobbing dizzily as he strode
over the rough ground. She pounded on his back and gasped
her protests. He was indifferent to her struggle as she
bounced against his back with every step.

At first she thought he was going to dump her into a boat,
because water splashed around his feet, but in a few moments he veered away from the lake's edge. Her upside-
down view gave her glimpses of rocks and mud. Where was
he taking her? Blood rushed to her head. Throbbing pain
scattered into jagged sharp pieces.

He kicked open a door that creaked loudly above the
clamor of rain. The air inside was warm and dry. He
dumped Corey down onto a narrow cot at one end of a small
cabin and then stood over her. She saw his face clearly then
for the first time. Her blow with the rock had grazed his
cheek, and an ugly scratch ran from a dark eyebrow down
to a full mouth twisted in anger. His eyes were arctic blue,
and yet they smoldered hotly as if deep in their depths was
a raging fire.

"Who are you?" he demanded. He wiped his cheek where
the rock had grazed him. "Why jump me like that?"

"You know why!" She would never have been foolish
enough to try to attack him if he had been standing level
with her when she first saw him. He stood well over six feet,
and she guessed him to be somewhere in his thirties. Rain
and mud plastered down his hair and ran in ugly rivulets

over his lean face. The glower in his eyes was clear and sharp and threatening.

"I asked you a question. What is this all about?"

"As if you didn't know." She glared at him and firmed her chin. "I know you trapped the falcon in that mist net. And I want him back." She had to admit that jumping this guy hadn't been the smartest thing she'd ever done. Now that her anger had cooled, she was just a little bit frightened that her bravado had put more than the tiercel in jeopardy.

His eyes shuttered. "You're not making sense."

"I saw you behind me—before you knocked me out and ran off with my tiercel."

"Your tiercel?"

"Well, my responsibility, anyway."

"Would you mind telling me just who you are?"

Her chin came up. "I'm a member of the University of Colorado research team. An aerie warden. I was watching the nest when the tiercel left it. He disappeared on the cliff above and I heard his frantic cries. I climbed the cliff and saw him in your net." She touched the bump on her head. "You know the rest."

"I'm not sure I do. Enlighten me." Ross studied her. Even with wet blond hair framing her face, she was something to look at. Wide eyes the color of azure-blue lapis stones, a full mouth, firm and yet provocative in anger. Her chin was jutted out as to belie any fear she might be feeling. She was tensed, ready to spring at him at the first opportunity. Not an easy woman to handle under the best of circumstances, thought Ross, but definitely well worth the effort. He wondered if she was always so fearless—and foolhardy.

Before she could react, he reached down and jerked off her walking boots and cotton socks. She feared her jeans might go next, but he stepped away from the cot before she could take a swing at him.

"All right, Tiger. Take a little time to cool off. If you try to bolt without your shoes, your bare feet will be ripped to shreds on the rocks, and I'll catch up with you before you've gone ten yards. You'll have nothing to show for your foolishness but a pair of bloody feet." With this dire warning, he turned and grabbed a rain poncho hanging from a pair of antlers pounded to the wall for a hat rack.

"What are you going to do? Where are you going?" she demanded, clenching her fists.

Without answering, he disappeared through the door and slammed it behind him.

He's going after the satchel with the tiercel in it, she thought with new hope. She still had a chance to get the peregrine back.

Chapter Two

Gingerly Corey sat up trying to get her bearings. Muted light came through a small window at the back of the cabin. Although the peppering of rain on the roof was steady, the hollow boom of thunder sounded distant. The cloudburst was over. Her mother called these Colorado storms "goose drowners." Corey sighed. This wasn't the right time to think about her parents. She knew they were bewildered by her need to get off by herself and to decide what course her future was going to take. Having received her law degree in the spring, she had surprised her father by not falling in with his plan for her to join his law firm. She didn't want to disappoint her parents, but she was stubborn enough to want to be in control of her career. She had graduated with honors, and many options were open to her as a young, bright lawyer. Much to the surprise of everyone, she had taken this job in the Colorado Rocky Mountains instead of rushing into a career commitment. Money and prestige had never rated very high with her, and she needed goals that were more satisfying than those offered by her father's prosperous law firm. There was no rush, she had told herself. Her whole life stretched in front of her, and she hoped to find the right pattern for her future during the summer of leisurely solitude. Watching two beautiful birds nesting in the high cliffs would give her the chance to get in touch with her deep feelings, she had thought, never expecting such a job would plunge her into a life-threatening drama that was anything but peaceful.

She groaned as she wavered to her feet, putting her hands on both sides of her head and holding it tightly. The sharp pain had receded, leaving a dull ache that intensified when she moved too quickly. She took a deep breath to steady herself. Her eyes traveled over the crude furnishings. Gingerly she moved away from the cot to a roughly hewn table set in the middle of the floor. With both hands gripping the table's edge, she turned her head slowly and looked about. She had to find some kind of weapon before her abductor returned with the falcon.

The cabin was probably an old miner's shack, she thought. Only one room with two narrow windows, one in front and one in back, and one front door. A camp stove for cooking stood at one end of the room and a stone fireplace at the other. Someone had recently caulked the gray-bleached logs and repaired the floor, she noticed, but it still looked like something belonging in a Colorado ghost town. Rainwater dripped through the roof in several places, making light plopping noises on the floor. Her abductor must not have been living here for long, she reasoned. She saw no personal belongings of any kind. A hurricane lamp stood on the table, but the wick was not heavily singed nor the level of oil down very much.

Why had he brought her here? She knew that unscrupulous smugglers of raptor birds were worldwide, and one gang in the United States was reported to have sold hundreds of thousands of dollars' worth of falcons over a two-year period. Professor White had warned his research team that last year an aerie warden had been killed in Idaho when several pairs of birds were lifted from that state.

A sense of panic drove her. Not only did she have to try to save the falcon, but her own life was in danger. The man would be back any minute. Leaving the table, she wavered unsteadily across the room, looking for some kind of weapon. On the camp stove, one small blackened pan with a weak handle promised little striking power. Her frantic gaze around the kitchen end of the room failed to identify anything that would serve as a weapon. She wavered over to the small fireplace. No tongs or poker. Nothing but a few pieces of stacked wood. One of them would have to do. She reached down and picked a chunk of wood. The roughly split log was thick and clumsy to hold. Her small hands could barely grip it, but it was the only choice of weapon that she had.

The rain had stopped now. The soft plop of water off the roof was only intermittent. Corey's ears strained to pick up any sound of approaching footsteps outside the cabin as she staggered across the room to the door, dragging the chunk of wood. She'd only have a split second to strike as he came through the door.

Corey leaned against the wall and waited, straining to hear his approach. The club was too heavy to hold over her head until the last minute. She would have to depend upon one final burst of strength to raise the heavy piece of wood and bring it down with all the force she could muster.

ROSS TOSSED the woman's boots into the bushes and made his way back to the lake. He had been watching a man rowing a boat on the lake when she'd jumped him from behind. From what she had said, he knew that someone ahead of him had trapped her falcon. What foul luck. Another smuggler in the area made his position more precarious than it was already. It had taken him more time than he'd planned to reach the San Juan Mountains of Colorado and to find a location that would provide him with the birds he needed. The month that Prince Amund had given him was passing at a terrifying rate. And now this. He couldn't afford any more delays. Every day that passed, his anxieties over Robin increased. Ross knew that the little boy's security was centered in his daddy's love and attention. Since he had taken the newborn infant from the hospital after his wife had died in childbirth, he had never been separated from Robin for more than the working hours of a single day. Being both parents to the boy had made them closer than most fathers and sons, eating and playing together, and sleeping in the same room. Except for the Arabian woman who was Robin's nursemaid, the three-year-old boy had been raised in isolation in the foreign country. Robin had actually become ill one night and was gasping for breath when Ross was unavoidably detained by a road blockage and unable to reach home until after midnight. Ross called the doctor and had been told that Robin was slightly asthmatic, a condition that was often triggered by stress. Sometimes his little chest was racked with a cough so deep that it sounded like a seal's bark.

What was happening to Robin now? Did he think his father was gone forever? Was he ill? Worry over his son drove Ross with relentless fury. He had to get back to Robin with the falcons that would ransom him—before the time limit ran out. Ross knew that the malicious Arab wouldn't hesitate to have the boy killed if the ransom was not delivered on time. Less than ten days remained. Sweat broke out on his forehead. He had to snatch the falcons within the next week if he was to make it back in time to save his son.

He had come to Colorado because he knew the area. His friend Paul Hines, who had a guest ranch in Lake City, had told him about the peregrine research team.

"They're up around Crescent Lake. Six or eight people in the group," said Paul. "Every year they have somebody up there. Guess it's a good place for falcons. Why you interested?"

"Just doing some research," Ross had answered smoothly.

Paul shrugged. "You always did like flying them birds."

At first Ross had considered trying a different, less protected location, but after thinking the situation over carefully, he had decided that the research team had already done the work of identifying several falcon nests. He could decide which one was the most vulnerable and make his move. It was foul luck that someone else seemed to have the same idea, he thought as he strode away from the cabin.

A thousand times he had considered going to the authorities about Robin's abduction, and a thousand times he'd decided against it. He knew the endless red tape and the frustrating pace at which anything was accomplished by the government. Prince Amund had already warned him that he was not a patient man. With Robin's life in danger, Ross couldn't afford to trust the slow, cumbersome mills of international law enforcement agencies.

Maybe there was still time to get the bird away from the man who had trapped it. Ross hurried down to the lake, furtively slipping through a band of trees that stretched nearly to the water. The rain had stopped, but a low haze drifted off the water. When he came to the mound of rocks where he had stood before, he looked below. The boat was still there, but it was empty. The man he had been watching was nowhere in sight.

For a long moment, Ross waited at the edge of the trees, listening for footsteps or any sound that would alert him to someone else's presence. In the high branches of a ponderosa pine a Steller's jay flapped his wings, sending a soft trickle of water through needled branches. Sunlight made a pristine brightness on glistening aspen leaves quivering on tiny stems all around him.

Ross moved forward out of the shadows, reassured by the pervading stillness around him, but he had taken no more than a couple of steps when a man lurched into view from behind a bank of rocks. He wore a rain parka that put his face in deep shadow.

He raised a rifle and fired.

A bullet clipped the bark of a tree inches above Ross's head, causing him to dive for the ground. Frantically he wiggled on his belly to reach some kind of cover. The underbrush of scrub oak was thin and low, offering little protection. Bullets bit all around him, striking rock and kicking up dirt.

With a lunge, Ross dived behind a decaying log. Crouching on his knees, he waited. His muscles were tense and poised for action. His ears strained to hear any sound of approaching footsteps. Silence. Nothing. After what seemed like an eternity, he heard the sound of creaking timbers and the swish of water.

Cautiously Ross raised his head. He saw the boat, and caught an indistinct glimpse of the man who was rowing the boat across to the other side. From the direction he was taking, Ross judged that he was making for the other side of the lake. Ross knew that from there a steep climb through thick stands of conifer trees was the only way to reach a logging road cut into the mountainside above the lake. Ross would bet that's where the man was heading.

The smuggler must have some kind of transportation waiting there, Ross guessed, although he hadn't seen any sign of another vehicle when he had parked his rental four-wheel drive in the shelter of some trees on that road. Hiking out of the area was not impossible, but time-consuming. The gunman could have come on horseback, Ross speculated, but he doubted very much that any smuggler would choose that means of escape.

Ross stared across the lake as the boat disappeared into a floating mist hovering on the surface of the water. Once the smuggler arrived at the other side of the lake, it would be impossible to track him. There was no way Ross could hike around the lake and intercept him. He'd be long gone before Ross could get there. What foul luck to have the gunman slip away so easily, he thought with fresh anger. The unexpected complication of another falcon hunter had put his own success in jeopardy.

Ross turned away from the lake. Shafts of bright sunlight pierced lingering gray clouds, and a quickening wind came off the lake, ruffling its surface with small whitecaps. A scent of pine teased Ross's nostrils as he walked over to the place where overhanging rocks offered some protection against the wind and rain.

He saw the man's footprints in the wet dirt. The gunman must have been waiting here for the storm to pass, Ross reasoned, remembering how the man had stepped out into the open and then started firing. Luckily his aim had been wild, but it had effectively kept Ross at bay until he'd made his escape.

Leaving the rocks, Ross followed muddy tracks down to the place where the boat had been pulled up on the edge of the lake. He stooped down and peered at the ground. Footprints—and what was this?

Tiny tufts of white feathers were embedded in the mud, obvious signs that the bird had been loaded into the boat. The smuggler had the falcon, all right, he thought grimly. The woman's story was true. It must have happened just as she said.

Anger and frustration made Ross kick at a pebble and send it sailing into the water. His plan to work unobserved had just been shot as high as a Fourth-of-July rocket.

What to do now? His eyebrows knit as he thought about the young woman who was like a wildcat protecting her young. She'd not be easily persuaded that he was innocent of the bird-snatching.

Would the smuggler be back? Was there more than one person involved or only a solitary bird snatcher? If an organized gang was working in this area, the competition for birds might make it impossible to lift two for himself, thought Ross. Once more the pressure of time descended on him. He felt his chest tighten with anxiety. What should he do? Leave and try to find another location? Or stay and pray he could avoid being caught in the danger that the other smuggler left behind?

As Ross struggled to reach a decision, the prince's time limit was like a shrieking locomotive racing wildly to overtake him. One false step, one delaying action, one unforeseen complication—and disaster would run him over.

He couldn't afford any mistakes.

He couldn't get caught in someone else's nefarious activities.

Above all, he couldn't bring the eyes of the law upon himself.

In short, he must somehow find a way to weather this unexpected disaster and quickly find the means to secure the ransom that would free his son. All of his life Ross had prided himself on his integrity and loyalty to his country, and only the love for his son could place him in such a desperate situation outside the law.

Ross walked back to the spot where he had been crouching when the girl flew at him. His canvas bag was still where he had dropped it. He cursed the circumstances that had convinced her he was the one who had trapped the falcon. He had definitely been at the wrong place at the wrong time. He couldn't blame her for attacking him, believing he was the one who had trapped her falcon.

He picked up the bag and started up the slope toward the cabin. He had to convince her of his innocence. Not an easy task. When she glared at him, a fierce, condemning glint in her eyes was hot enough to shrivel him to ashes. She had been angry enough to try to get the bird back by attacking him—a man who physically dwarfed her petite stature. She had fought him with a fierce courage. Brave and foolish and determined—that's what worried him. He'd never be able to accomplish his goal unless he could convince her that he had not taken her falcon.

The scratch on the side of his cheek still oozed blood. She was a fighter. A begrudging admiration mingled with his irritation as he reached the cabin door. He would have to handle the woman very carefully. He didn't want to hurt her, but he couldn't have her getting in the way. Not now. Not until he had the falcons that would save his son's life.

Chapter Three

Leaning against the wall, close to the door, Corey saw the doorknob move. Up came the wood! A prayer was on her lips as he stepped through the opening, and she brought the club down with all the force she could muster.

"Wh—?" Ross saw the movement out of the corner of his eyes and lurched to one side. Instinctively his arm came up and deflected the blow meant for his head. The chunk of wood only grazed his shoulder. He dropped the canvas bag and reached for her.

"No!" Corey tried to get away from him, but he quickly grabbed her.

"What are you trying to do?" He held her firmly against the wall, holding down her arms. "That club could have split my head open. Take it easy." He sensed her panic and his tone softened. "I'm not going to hurt you."

She didn't believe him. He towered over her, and she realized how foolish she had been to physically assault him. "Let me go."

"I will if you promise to quit attacking me with rocks and clubs. Can't we talk this thing out before you reduce me to a mass of cuts and bruises?" He smiled wryly. "You're a one-woman demolition team if I ever saw one. I'll drop my hands if you promise not to fly at me like a wildcat. Promise?"

She nodded. At the moment, it seemed the expedient thing to do.

He dropped his hands. Still guarded and watchful, he moved back a step.

She firmed her chin and looked directly at him. "Did you get the falcon?"

"No."

Her eyes slid to the canvas bag he had dropped. She knew the bird was inside. "Please, let me have it," she asked in a reasonable tone.

"This? All right." He picked up the bulging bag and handed it to her. "Take it."

Her eyes widened with surprise. He had given up the falcon without protest. She searched his face, but his expression was basically unreadable. Gray-blue eyes steadily returned her questioning gaze. He stood in front of her, taut and wary, as if poised to repel any more of her desperate assaults.

"Well?" he prodded as she stared at him. "I've given you the bag. Now what?"

A horrid truth shot through her. The bird was already dead. He knew that it was too late to save it. With sickening certainty, she fumbled nervously with the straps of the bag. Her mouth was void of moisture as she threw the flap back, reached inside and was prepared to feel the still-warm body of her tiercel. For a moment her fingers faltered, and then they touched the cold surfaces of boxes and tinned cans. Her eyes widened in astonishment. "Food!"

"Supplies I brought from my Bronco just before you leaped out of the rain at me."

"I don't believe you. Where's the tiercel?" She threw down the bag at his feet as if it were a gauntlet. Her fists were clenched, and her fiery eyes blazed into his. She took a step toward him. "What happened to the peregrine? I know you had him in that bag. I came down the hill just af-

ter you had taken him out of the net. There wasn't any time
for you to get rid of it.''

"You have it all figured out, haven't you?" His smile was
lightly mocking.

Her chin came up to show him she was not the least
afraid. "What have you done with the falcon? You must
have taken him out of the bag and hidden him somewhere." New rage swelled up. Her beautiful falcon—
trapped so callously! "How could you treat a beautiful bird
like that? Don't you know peregrine falcons are an endangered species—protected by the law?"

"I know." He picked up the bag, walked over to the table and began unloading the foodstuff. For a moment there
was only silence between them. When he had finished, he
surprised her by asking in a perfectly normal tone, "You
have a name?"

She'd have to play along with him. It was the only way.
She hoped her voice wouldn't betray the trembling that
fluttered under her rib cage. "Corey McCalley."

"I didn't take your peregrine, Corey," he said evenly.

Her first impulse was to challenge the statement, but she
could tell from the iron jut of his jaw that she wouldn't gain
anything by lashing out at him. Keeping him pleasant might
allow her to get at the truth and give her a chance to figure
out what she ought to do next. Maybe it was not too late to
save the tiercel.

She walked over to the cot and sat down on the edge. Her
knees still felt unreliable. "And you are—?"

"Ross Sinclair." He drew out his wallet, and flipped an
identification pocket open.

She saw an official-looking card bearing the lettering,
United States Fish and Wildlife Service, and the printed
name, Ross D. Sinclair. There was also a color photo, but it
was hard to tell if the mud-covered visage in front of her was
the same person. She thought she saw the same hard-

chiseled bone structure in the photograph, but she couldn't be sure with his face smeared with a coat of dirt. The eyes seemed a softer blue and not the dark wintry-gray ones he leveled on her, and the hair didn't look right, but, of course, now it was plastered down with rain and mud. "You're with the government?" she choked incredulously. A spurt of relief went sluicing through her. "You're a wildlife ranger?"

"That's right."

"But I don't understand. Why didn't you say so right away?"

"You didn't give me much of a chance, Tiger," he answered smoothly. "You kept me pretty busy defending myself."

He smiled at her, but the depth of his eyes denied his casual response. A wariness leaped out from him, as if tension was ingrained in every muscle and sinew. He was on guard. The knowledge came to her on some level beyond rational thought, and she wasn't quite ready to handle it. "I don't understand. What were you doing acting in such a suspicious way?"

"I was watching a man below the rocks, wondering who he was and what he was doing."

"The thief? You saw the man who trapped the tiercel?"

"Possibly. And between the two of us we let him get away," he said wryly.

Corey tried to digest this new information. Could it have happened that way? He could have been watching someone. She remembered the way he had been peering over the rocks when she first saw him through the rain.

As Ross stacked the canned goods, he watched her out of the corner of his eye as she weighed his words. Smart, he thought. No someone who would be easily fooled. He'd have to watch his step. She'd leap upon any inconsistencies. She was staring at him as if taking his measure inside and out. Wet clothes clung to her slender body, and he was aware of firm breasts and soft, rounded hips. Her deliciously feminine body sent an unexpected quiver of response through him, and the memory of pressing his body upon hers while they wrestled by the lake added to a sudden awareness of physical attraction. Such thoughts were dangerous, he schooled himself.

He gave her a persuasive smile. "I assure you, Corey, that I never touched your falcon. I'm as sorry as you are that the thief got away." He couldn't tell if she believed him or not. She was clever enough to pretend a blind acceptance of his story, while getting ready to pin him to the wall with his lies.

Corey gave him an enigmatic smile. "I guess I really fouled things up, didn't I? But how was I to know? You certainly acted suspicious to me." She sensed he was relieved that she had decided to believe him. "And why did you take away my boots?"

"So you wouldn't go running out there and get yourself in real trouble."

"Maybe I could have helped."

"And maybe you would have stopped a bullet." He told her about the gunman. He sat down on an old wooden chair as if he'd made a decision. "I apologize for being so rough with you. The whole situation had me uptight. And you didn't introduce yourself very gently." He touched the clotted blood on his cheek.

Now that her heartbeat had settled into a normal rhythm, she was able to return his smile. "I'm sorry." She began to view his rugged masculinity in a more favorable light as she assessed his bold features and arctic-blue eyes. "I guess I overreacted."

"That's understandable," he said generously. "I gather you've never been an aerie warden before?" He smiled at her.

"No." She knew he was trying to mend fences with her. Why was he so conciliatory if she was the one who had made the mistake?

"Do you enjoy what you're doing?"

"I did until today."

"I'm sorry about the tiercel. Have you been watching the nest for long?"

"No, only a few weeks." She decided to follow his lead in the conversation and see where it went. "Minna and I...Minna Gibbons, she's my colleague, we have a tent pitched at the base of a cliff just beyond the lake. We take turns observing and it was my shift until afternoon. I watched the tiercel leave the aerie." New anger coated Corey's words as she recounted what had happened. "The tiercel flew up on the high plateau, and I expected him to return in a few minutes to the nest with his prey—then I heard his frantic cry."

"And you climbed up the sheer side of the cliff to get to him?"

"Yes."

"Brave lady."

She saw a glint of approval in his eyes. She'd always been one to trust her instincts. Suddenly a weight slipped from her shoulders. He was not her adversary. The circumstances were weird, but she felt a quivering of exciting anticipation that had something to do with this stranger who had plummeted into her life with a flying tackle. She laughed with a sudden relief. "I didn't think I had any choice. The only way to get to the bird was up."

"You said earlier that you'd seen someone hiding near the trap."

"Well, I didn't exactly see him. Just caught a glimpse of someone rising up behind me. After he hit me on the head, I must have lost consciousness for a few minutes. When I came to, I hiked down to the lake and saw you."

"And the rest is painful history." He grinned. "I can see how you jumped to the wrong conclusion."

"What were you doing, crouching behind a rock like that? And with a canvas bag."

"I'd just come back from the logging road on the far side of the lake. It's as close as I can get to this cabin with my four-wheeler, so I've been carting the rest of my supplies on foot, a load at a time. The storm was about to hit, so I was hurrying back to the cabin. Then, I saw someone at the lake's edge."

"The smuggler?"

"Could be. The next thing I know, I'm engaged in a mud-wrestling contest with a fiery, kicking assailant. At first I thought you were a boy, short blond hair and all. But when I flattened you out on the bank of the lake, I knew better." His grin was frankly sensuous. "No boy ever felt that soft, in so many places."

"Your vicious tackle was really overkill," she answered tartly, not wanting to admit that under different circumstances her reaction to his flattering smile might have been different.

"Not if I didn't want to lose you in that downpour. Besides, I didn't know who you were or why you were attacking me. You were as fast and as slippery as a gazelle."

"I was furious that I'd lost my falcon and had gotten a bump on the head for my rescue efforts." She gingerly touched her hand to a rising bump that radiated jagged pain.

"Let me see your head." He sat beside her on the cot and gingerly eased away the matted hair.

She stiffened against his touch. "Ouch."

"Sorry. No skin broken. Just a hard swelling. Too bad, we could use some ice."

"No refrigerator in these deluxe accommodations?" she chided with good humor.

He grinned. "Not at the moment. But we could wait until winter, when there's snow up to the windowsills."

Her eyes rounded. "You're surely not going to live here in the winter?"

"No, I'll be a long way from here by then."

Corey watched his eyes become visibly hard and brittle. Tension was back in his shoulders. His expression did not invite any more questions. An undercurrent of some emotion she couldn't identify was at odds with his pretense of a relaxed manner. This was a complex man with layers of hidden facets, some of them dangerous, no doubt. Her relaxed feeling slipped away. "But I still don't understand," she prodded. "Why are you here?"

"We got a tip that a peregrine-smuggling operation had moved into Colorado," he said readily, as if the explanation had been prepared and laid right at hand. "So here I am."

"And now they have my tiercel!" Anger leaped through her again.

"So it would seem. I was about to jump the guy when I heard you come up behind."

"I guess I blew it, all the way around. But how did the thief know where my pair of falcons were nesting?"

"Sadly enough, there's usually an informant within the research team. Someone in the program who passes along the locations of the nests."

"No, I don't believe it. No one in our team is an informer."

"Money will loosen most tongues. Even a dedicated ornithologist weakens when he sees thousands of dollars flashing before his eyes."

"You're wrong. I know you are." Corey had a basic trust in people.

He shrugged. "Tell me about the people on your team. I was intending to make contacts as soon as I got settled in,"

he lied. "I didn't know one of the group was going to come
calling so unexpectedly." He frowned. "Are you sure you
weren't on your way to meet the man in the boat?"

"You think that I'm the informer?" she asked, appalled.

"Easy, Tiger. You can see how it's possible to interpret a
situation in several different ways. I only have your word for
what happened. But I believe you." He chuckled. She
looked ready to fly at him again. He wondered what it
would be like to gentle her. She'd be a handful—a delightful handful. He cleared his mind of such tempting speculations. "Now tell me about the others."

Corey took a deep breath. "All right. I don't know the
team very well, but they all seem nice and very professional. My tent mate is a graduate student from Texas.
Minna Gibbons. She's pleasant, easygoing and seems open
enough about everything."

"Who's in charge?" Ross asked as casually as he could.

"Professor Richard White. You must have heard of him.
He's earned a national reputation as an expert on raptors.
Very respected. One of the few professional biologists in the
country who has a practical background in falconry."

"Yes, of course," he lied. "How many in the team?"

"Let's see...six. Chester Carlson is the professor's young
assistant. Chester spent the last two summers in a research
program in Greenland. He's a funny little guy who bops
around at the professor's heels." She laughed. "He wears a
pair of binoculars around his neck that are almost as big as
he is." As she talked, Ross was evaluating his chances of
learning from Corey and the others where he might readily
lift a pair of falcons already identified by the project. "Who
else?"

"There's an older man, Jake Tewsbury, in his fifties."
Corey smiled wryly. "Jake's a veteran falconer and doesn't
like women taking part in the program. He's paired off with
Bill Collins, a friend of mine. I can vouch for Bill. He's as

honest as the day is long and loves falconry. We grew up together in New Mexico and we shared our first pair of prairie hawks. Caught them one summer and trained them to hunt on the sunbaked desert. He's the one who really talked me into being an aerie warden for the summer."

"And he can vouch for you, I suspect."

"Do I need someone to vouch for me?" she demanded.

"You could have been trying to divert my attention while your accomplice escaped with the bird."

"How dare you?" Her eyes flashed like sparks from a flint.

"I'm just returning the same kind of accusations that you directed at me."

"It's not the same thing at all."

"Isn't it? I'm trying to show you that circumstances are not always what they seem. Maybe you're not the person you say you are at all."

"And maybe you aren't, either," she snapped. "Right now, you look like a reject from a mud-wrestling contest."

"Thanks, so do you."

Her indignation ended in laughter. She instinctively touched a hand to her face and hair. Her damp hair was waving on her forehead, and even though she had a cut called a "short-and-sassy wedge," she knew her fair hair was flying all over the place. No wonder he was laughing. "I look awful."

"No." His soft gaze swept her face. "Quite the contrary." Her tousled hair made a nice frame for her face, and nothing was needed to heighten the natural beauty of her azure-blue eyes, slim nose and nicely bowed lips. He felt a tug of desire just looking her.

She lowered her eyes, trying to defuse the charged moment that had leaped between them as their eyes caught. "Where are my boots?"

"Tossed in the bushes, I'm afraid."

She stood up and would have fallen flat on her face if his reflexes hadn't been swift enough to have her in his arms before her buckling knees let her hit the floor.

Gently he eased her back on the cot. His tender touch confused her. And her reaction to his nearness sparked a quiver of alarm. She saw a softness in his eyes that was alien to his former crusty manner. His voice was threaded with an unexpected softness. "Take it easy."

She looked away from his face, wondering why she was reacting so peculiarly to his concern. It must be the bump on the head, she reasoned.

"Are you all right?" he questioned, keeping a hand on her shoulder.

"A little dizzy, but I've got to get back. Minna will be worried—and I have to tell her what happened. Those smugglers might come after the other bird."

"I doubt it. They'll probably move on to another nest."

"How could anyone sink that low! To put a whole species in danger. If I ever get the chance, I'll bring the thieves to justice." Her eyes blazed angrily.

"Yes, I believe you would." He gave her a measured look. "I don't doubt for a minute that anything would keep you from carrying out your responsibilities."

"What are you going to do about the situation? You're going to look into it, aren't you?"

"Yes. You can be sure of that." His eyes narrowed for a fraction of a second. Then he smiled. "Well, now, how about a cup of coffee before you start back?"

"And a couple of aspirin?" Corey added hopefully.

"You're in luck." He brought her a small first aid box and a tin cup of water. "I'll have the coffee made in a minute. I banked the fire in the stove before I left."

She gratefully swallowed the aspirin. A few minutes later, she sipped a mug of hot, strong coffee while she watched Ross wash his face and pour water over his head. Thatches of dark hair stood out on his head after a brisk towel-drying. Now that his skin was clean, a deep bronze tan highlighted his gray-blue eyes.. His cheekbones and forehead were well molded, balancing a straight but bold nose. She searched his features, trying to remember the bone structure in the photo.

"Well, what do you think? Do I look better without a mud pack?"

She was embarrassed by her pointed scrutiny. Why should she still be suspicious of him? He was being the perfect host.

"Would you like to wash up?" he asked. "I'll bring you some water and soap. It would make you look ... and feel better," he added hastily.

"Not very flattering, but I accept."

While he watched, she splashed water over her own face and blond hair. She gingerly patted around the throbbing bump. When wet, her naturally curly hair waved thick and springy.

He grinned as she handed him back the basin.

She didn't know why a sudden heat flared in her face under his scrutiny. It was ridiculous how important it was to her that he thought her attractive.

"Feel better?"

"Thank you," she said briskly, to hide her reaction to his approving gaze. "Now, I have to go. Minna will be worried."

"What about your friend Bill? Where's he?" Ross hoped the question seemed natural enough. He was trying to get a picture of where all the people were carrying out their monitoring duties.

"At a different location with Jake. Farther west. We see him often because he brings the supplies." She smiled, thinking about Bill's good-natured, freckled face. His visits were the bright spot in any day.

"From your expression, I'd guess he's more than just a friend."

"No." She set down the mug of coffee. "His father and mine were in law school together. Our families have always been close. But I haven't seen much of him of late. Not since we moved to Washington, D.C." She added casually, "My father's Patrick McCalley."

"The noted lawyer? The same Patrick McCalley who has just been appointed as a presidential counselor?"

She nodded.

"Whee," he whistled. "You move in pretty rarified circles. Your father's got quite a reputation. I've seen his picture in the newspapers a half-dozen times." His look was speculative. "I can't help but wonder what his daughter is doing spending her time watching nesting falcons."

"I graduated and passed the bar exam this spring, and I needed time to decide whether or not I want to become a partner in my father's law firm, or strike out on my own. My father had a big bash planned, ready to celebrate my joining him right after graduation. but I backpedaled away from the decision."

"You're not ready to make a commitment?"

"Right. That's why I decided to spend the summer away from people and pressures."

"Sounds like a good idea."

"How about you? Are you dedicated to the Forest Service?"

"No. I haven't decided what I want to do with the rest of my life. I'll be making some changes...." His voice trailed off.

"Do you have a family?" She only meant it to be a casual question. She was not prepared for the sudden flare in his eyes and the hardening of his jaw.

"I have a son. My wife died in childbirth three years ago. We weren't prepared for it. Everything seemed wonderful and exciting. Somehow a deadly infection set in, and she was gone before medical help could save her." He got up abruptly and walked over to the fireplace.

"And your son?"

He was silent for a moment, and then he said, "He's a joy. A bright, wonderful, three-year-old. I love him very much. Robin's my whole life."

Corey saw his expression harden as if he had retreated behind the barrier of his own thoughts. She wanted to say she was sorry that he had lost his wife, but his manner did not invite an expression of condolence. A moment ago he had been a pleasant companion, now he was a stranger. She didn't know what emotion raged within him, but she was suddenly afraid of it. She felt a renewed urge to get away from him. She stood up and was grateful that all her dizziness had passed.

To her surprise, he brought her boots and socks without argument.

"I'll walk back with you."

"No, I'm fine now."

"Sure?"

She nodded. For a moment they just looked at each other, waiting for the silence to be broken by the other one. Finally Ross said, "I'm sorry we met under such a misunderstanding, Corey." The regret in his voice seemed sincere.

"I'm sorry about the rock—and everything."

"Can't blame you for jumping to the wrong conclusion." He touched his shoulder. "You pack a mean wallop. I bet you were the best fighter on the block."

She smiled. "I could hold my own. Well, I'd better get back and talk everything over with Minna. She's not going to believe half of this."

"I can hardly believe it myself," he said wryly.

Her clear eyes were questioning. "I guess I'll see you around?"

"Yes, of course," he answered readily with a smile.

"Goodbye, then."

He opened the door for her, and she felt his intense gaze upon her as she left the cabin and made her way down the hill. Had she been a fool to confide in him the way she had? Talking about herself and her family? In spite of herself, she had been strangely drawn to him. And yet, there was something about him that disturbed her. She couldn't quite identify what it was in his manner that made her feel he was guarded in every word he spoke. Maybe he was just the cautious type. She was surprised at the feeling of wanting to know him better.

When she reached the lake, she turned away from it and headed in the opposite direction. Walking along a small creek at the base of the cliffs was the easiest and fastest route back to the tent. She was grateful that her equilibrium was back to normal, and her thoughts flew ahead as she walked. She'd have to carry some water from the stream and heat it for a bath. It would take several gallons to get rid of all the mud and grime.

The storm had passed quickly like most mountain storms. The day was fresh and lovely, but Corey's spirits refused to rise from the despondency she felt over the loss of the tiercel. She had been gone several hours, and she wondered if the female falcon was still on her nest—or had someone trapped her, too? Fresh anxiety hastened her steps.

When she reached the cliff where the nest was located, she went straight to the blind to assure herself that the female falcon was still there.

Peering through the telescope, Corey saw with relief that the falcon was still sitting on her eggs. Thank heavens! Corey watched for a few minutes as the bird preened herself. Everything seemed normal. Apparently the female had not been frightened enough by Corey's earlier presence to flee her nest. The falcon stroked herself with her beak, ruffled her feathers and seemed content. A half-eaten carcass of a crow from an earlier hunt lay nearby, so Corey guessed that she had been eating it, waiting for the tiercel to return with fresh food. How long would the female wait? When would she abandon her nest and hunt for food? Corey knew that if the falcon left the nest for more than twenty or thirty minutes, the eggs would cool off and never hatch. "Stay there, old girl," Corey breathed, not knowing if the bird would accept food the way chicks did when they were kept in a nesting box. Corey clambered from the blind and hiked down the slope to the tent. Her mind whirled with unanswered questions. What should she do now? The situation was beyond her experience. She had better get word to Professor White, who would know what they might do to save the eggs if the falcon abandoned them. Had Minna come back from fishing?

"Minna?" she called as she approached the tent. No answer.

She ducked under the canvas flap. "What—"

Corey saw the tip of an army boot too late. She tripped and sprawled forward on the tent floor. The next instant her arms were pinned at her side, and her head and arms were rolled up in a small rug Minna had insisted they put on the wooden floor.

She fought and she tried to scream, but choked from lack of air.

A suffocating sensation sent all air back down her throat. In a few seconds, she was as securely confined as the tiercel had been in the mist net.

Chapter Four

Corey frantically rolled from side to side in the small space between the two cots. Dust filled her nostrils. Air evaded her. She was wrapped up in the rug like a trussed fowl. She held her head at a painful angle to breathe air coming through the small opening in the rolled-up rug. The sense of claustrophobia was acute. And terrifying! She'd always hated to have her face covered. The thick carpet pressed against her nostrils and filled them with dust. She worked her arms, struggling to get them free, and after a terrifying eternity, the cloth began to loosen. Finally she eased one arm out and then the other. Pushing and shoving, she managed to throw off the binding rug. She sat on the dirt floor, gasping for breath.

Anger mingled with fright. The assault had been swift and unexpected. The intruder had tripped her as she came in the tent. A man? Yes, she was sure of it. She remembered the fleeting glimpse of army boots. But, who? What did he want? Had the smuggler come back for the other bird? Maybe he had ducked out of sight in her tent so she wouldn't see him. Or had he been waiting for her? This thought brought a new cold prickling on her neck. Why would someone want to frighten her?

Corey sat there without moving, tense, staring at the closed flap of the tent. Even though it had seemed like an eternity, she knew that she had been trussed up in the rug for only a few minutes. Her ears strained to hear any movement outside. Nothing. She got to her feet, ready to defend herself as best she could from the return of the intruder.

Maybe he was outside waiting.

Furtively she eased back the flap of the tent. Peering cautiously in every direction, Corey satisfied herself that no one was near the tent. The moment she stepped out, her heart lurched to a stop. A man was striding toward her.

He waved. "Corey!"

Bill. Thank heavens! She took a few steps toward him and then stopped short. Her eyes fell upon his feet as he shortened the distance between them.

"Army boots," she gasped loudly enough for him to hear.

He stopped and looked down at them. "What's wrong?" His freckled face was puzzled.

"You're wearing army boots!"

"What's wrong with that? Don't you remember Professor White took all the guys in the team to that army surplus store? We bought a bunch of stuff that day. Tents, hiking gear and army boots all around. For gosh sakes, Corey, what on earth's the matter with you?"

Her thoughts spun in a mad whirl. Bill, Jake, Chester and Professor White—all had army boots. Had one of them been in her tent?

"You look like you've seen a ghost," he said.

She moistened her dry lips. "No, not a ghost."

"Then what's the matter. You're as white as a lily."

"Did you see anybody else near here?"

His forehead furrowed. "I saw Minna fishing down by the creek. She told me to tell you that she'll be back in time for her watch."

"But you didn't see anybody else? A few minutes ago? Anywhere around here?"

"Nope. What's going on?"

She glanced down at his army boots. Some warning voice cautioned her not to tell him about the intruder. Not until she was sure it hadn't been him pretending not to have been in her tent when she arrived.

"Why aren't you up at the blind, Corey? What's happened?"

"The tiercel's gone."

"Gone? What do you mean gone?"

"Snatched."

She told him how the tiercel had been trapped in a mist net and what had happened at the lake when she had mistaken a wildlife ranger for the thief.

Bill whistled. "You always were one for dashing into a swarm of hornets without a thought! You could have put your own life in danger, Corey. What if he had been the thief?"

"I wanted to stop him if I could."

"I can't believe it. Smugglers working this area?" He shook his head in disbelief.

"It's true. Somebody deliberately snatched one of our birds, and he got away in a boat."

"This guy, this ranger you mistook for the thief, he's on the up-and-up?"

"I don't know," Corey said honestly. "He seems to be what he claims. I could tell that he was angry because I had interfered. His name is Ross Sinclair. He showed me some identification, but—"

"But what?"

Corey shrugged. How could she explain her uneasiness about him? She was certain that he had held his emotions under tight control, and his expression had been unreadable. She had sensed an invisible wall that he maintained between them, and yet there had been moments when she had felt strangely drawn to him. The lingering pain in his eyes when he talked about his wife and son had touched her.

She sensed a wariness that defied identification. "He gives me a funny feeling," she admitted.

"Well, we'd better get the sheriff in on this. I'll tell the professor tonight what's happened and see what he thinks we ought to do. Are you sure you two gals will be all right till we get back in the morning?"

Corey nodded.

"Why are you looking at me like that?"

"No reason," she lied. Ross Sinclair had said there was probably an informer in the group. Someone who told the smugglers where the aeries were. Could it be Bill? He could have been here earlier, checking to see if his accomplice got the bird. He could have been in her tent, wrapped her up the rug and then pretended to have just arrived.

"What's the matter, Corey? You're not sick, are you?"

She shook her head. "I guess I'm hungry. How about some grub before you start back?"

AFTER COREY'S DEPARTURE, Ross weighed the dangers of staying where he was against the time he would lose trying to find another location. By the end of the week, he had to be on his way back to Prince Amund with a mating pair of falcons. He knew that Prince Amund always followed through on a threat. The time limit had not been an idle threat. Every tick of Ross's watch reminded him of precious time lost. The thought of his son in such cruel hands brought a stab to his heart.

Ross put his head in his hands as he sat at the scarred old table. He hated going outside the law. It was against every fiber in his being. "Daddy!" The memory of Robin's anguished cry echoing through Prince Amund's chambers had made any legal judgments inconsequential. He knew the government. It would not be blackmailed. Many unfortunate hostages confined in living hell were testimony to that position. No, he had to rescue his son himself. What if they had taken Robin's nurse away from him, leaving the boy alone and forsaken? Maybe his little boy was ill again? Ross firmly pushed away such torturous thoughts. A muscle flickered in his jaw as he set his mind firmly upon the problem at hand. He had a job to do, and he must keep his mind unfettered by anxiety. How could he turn the present situation to his advantage?

It had taken two weeks to get himself into a position of access to the aeries around Crescent Lake. He feared that searching out new nesting places in another area would eat up all the days he had left. The complication of other falcon snatchers made his own task more perilous if he stayed. But the birds he needed were close by. Several pairs of them according to what Corey had said. Even though it was dangerous to expose himself to the research team, at the moment it seemed the fastest way to rob a nest. At all costs, he must keep attention on the smugglers and off himself. Now that the research team knew of his existence, he would have to effectively play his role as a wildlife ranger while selecting the best pair of falcons to lift. If he could win Corey McCalley's confidence, he could get the information that he needed from her and be gone before she realized he had duped her.

That wouldn't be easy, he reminded himself, remembering the penetrating scrutiny of those lovely blue eyes. The fact that he was sexually attracted to her was an insight he didn't dare to pursue. He'd have to watch his step. She was dangerously sharp and perceptive. And ready to strike out with clawed nails. It was difficult to know how much of his story she had accepted and how much she held in reserve. He wasn't certain she had been completely taken in by the old identification card. It had been authentic back in the 1970s when he'd been a wildlife ranger for a couple of years before college. After he'd received an engineering degree, he had decided to go overseas as a consultant in the building of irrigation systems. The photograph was of a much younger Ross Sinclair, and any careful scrutiny would reveal that the date had been doctored. Still, the card provided an identity that should last long enough for him to get the falcons and return for Robin.

He got out his maps and pored over them. From what Corey had said, he was able to draw a ring around a broad area where the research team was monitoring birds. He knew the names of the wardens and a little bit about each one. He had to find the nest that had the weakest protection. Somehow he had to get himself into a position to lift a pair of birds—and fast. Only nine days left. His forehead beaded in a sweat. Part of that time had to be spent getting the falcons out of the country. He spent several hours mapping out a plan for investigating each of the aeries until he found the one most vulnerable. And it would all have to be done quickly!

That night he dreamed about Corey McCalley and her blond loveliness. He was in swift water, struggling to keep from drowning, and she was on the bank, laughing at him. Not prophetic, he sincerely hoped when he awoke in the midst of the nightmare.

As soon as it was light the next morning, he dressed and headed in the direction that Corey had said she and Minna Gibbons were camped. When he was some distance away, he saw a small yellow tent at the foot of a steep cliff. The two girls were standing outside it, peering up into the sky.

"There she goes!" cried a slender redheaded girl pointing upward.

Ross tipped back his head and saw a bird high in the air. "What's happening?" he asked as he joined them.

"It's the female," answered Corey. "She's left the nest."

They all watched the falcon soar in a wide beautiful sweep, her wings beating the air. The first band of light bathed the ledge's rim, and after a night of solitary waiting, she had taken to the skies. The female falcon's voice was deeper than the tiercel's and her "kaa...kaa...kaa" echoed in the deep crevices of the cliffs. The bird flew higher and higher until it became a dark speck in the sky.

"She's gone," Corey said with a catch in her throat. "She'll never incubate those eggs now."

"Tough luck," said Minna.

"I wish I could get my hands on the man who destroyed everything," Corey snapped, her eyes flashing angrily.

"Wait a minute. She's coming back!" Ross said, joining the girls and pointing upward.

Holding their collective breaths, they watched as the speck became larger and larger.

"Here she comes!" Minna clapped her hands excitedly.

"Good girl," breathed Corey.

In a steep dive, the falcon came back to the cliff. She braked her feathers to light gracefully on her ledge beside the nest.

"Guess she was just trying to get a glimpse of her wayward mate." Corey laughed. "She sent out her call, and now she'll probably wait to see if he'll show up with her breakfast."

"Which reminds me," said Ross, smiling. "I haven't had any. How about it? Would you ladies offer a starving man some of that bacon and coffee I could smell a mile away?"

"Why, sure," said Minna, grinning at him. "You must be the ranger Corey was telling us about. Shame on you, Corey. Your description was totally misleading. Didn't do him justice at all. I think you were trying to keep this guy all to yourself."

"Minna," Corey said in a protesting tone.

"I'm afraid we didn't meet under the best of circumstances," Ross said smoothly. "Both of us came out a little worse for the wear. How's the bump on your head, Corey?"

"Fine." For a moment their eyes held. She was aware of a strange breathlessness, and yet she knew her heartbeat had suddenly quickened. "You're in luck," she said, trying to deny the magnetic attraction that this stranger held for her. "Minna's the cook this morning."

They served him a plate of hash brown potatoes, crisp bacon and mug of coffee. The three of them sat around the fire, eating and talking. Ross made every effort to be as sociable and disarming as possible. Minna was openly friendly, almost flirtatious at times. From time to time, Corey darted questioning looks at him, but on the whole seemed ready to accept his company. Maybe he was making progress. He needed her off his back before he could move.

He had them laughing at a story about a family of skunks that had invaded his tent when he was in the field. He had just finished his second mug of coffee when Bill Collins arrived.

"Hi, Bill. Join us for breakfast," Corey said.

Bill's eyes landed on Ross. His expression was so hostile when Corey made the introductions that Ross decided he'd better find a way to win this guy over before he caused trouble.

"Glad to meet you, Bill." Ross gave him a warm smile that the man did not return. "Corey tells me you two are old falconers. I used to fly chicken hawks myself."

Bill didn't follow through with an amiable response. He gave Ross a curt nod and then turned to the women.

"Professor White and Chester will be along shortly," he said. "I told them what happened. The professor says we've got to get those eggs. Put in these two dummy eggs to replace the four she had in the nest." He held out two brown speckled eggs made of plastic. "She can't count, so the change in number won't bother her. If she's conscientious about incubating them, and is still here when the fledglings are ready to return, we'll give her back her family. You have a date on when she laid the eggs, don't you?"

Both Minna and Corey nodded.

"I'll help," Ross said. "Between the two us, we ought to be able to get the job done quickly enough."

Bill hesitated.

"Why not accept another volunteer when you have the chance?" Minna urged, intercepting Bill's glare. "I'd say the sooner you get the eggs, the better."

"I'd really like to help," Ross insisted. He was relieved when Bill nodded. If he could ingratiate himself with this sandy-haired young man, he might head off any further suspicions.

"Okay. We'll have to come at the nest from above," said Bill. "No way to reach it unless we do.

Watching the men scale the cliff, Corey realized what a foolhardy thing she had done by climbing without a rope for protection. One slip on crumbling rock could have sent her vaulting into the air to crash on the rocky talus below. Seeing their danger, she was more nervous than she had been.

The climbers had just reached the top when the falcon suddenly flushed out of the aerie. The bird launched upward, showing her light undercoat and the striped feathers on her legs, and then she disappeared over the same ledge where Corey had had her last glimpse of the mate.

"Has she gone?" asked Minna, peering through her binoculars.

"I can't see her anymore. Maybe she's gone to hunt on the bluff."

The words brought a new sickening to Corey's stomach. Whoever had taken the tiercel might be after his mate, also. Even if they had scared the smuggler off, another trap could have been set. Corey wished she had gone up with the men.

It was pure hell just to sit and wait, staring at an empty ledge and watching the second hand of her watch creep around.

She jumped when she heard voices and realized Minna was waving to two men coming up the draw behind the tent. She saw Professor White's thick, muscular form, followed by a smaller man who squinted through his thick glasses as he bobbed along with his binoculars swinging from side to side. Chester was having a hard time keeping up.

The professor took long strides, while shocks of bushy white hair streamed out from under the his dirty Stetson hat. His eyes were narrowed under bristly thick eyebrows as he searched the ledge above. "What's happening here?" he boomed as he reached Corey and Minna. His face was florid and sweaty.

The two men had to have been walking at a fast clip, Corey thought as she answered, "The falcon left her nest about thirty minutes ago. It doesn't look as if she's going to be back anytime soon. Bill decided to go after the eggs. Mr. Sinclair offered to help."

He frowned. "Sinclair? Is that the guy Bill told me about? From the Wildlife Service?"

Corey nodded.

"What's he doing here? Those government guys can't even shuffle paper without causing some kind of disaster. Why isn't he out hunting the smugglers who made off with my bird?"

Chester echoed the professor's disgust. "He'll botch up everything. Look, he's going after the eggs. Not Bill."

The professor swore and started up the incline toward the blind. Chester scrambled up the rocky talus beside him, nodding his head at the professor's loud tirade centering on unflattering remarks about the "damn government."

Corey's eyes were fixed on a dark figure etched against ruddy volcanic walls. If the rope was sawed by those sharp rocks as he slipped downward . . . ? She lowered her binoculars for a moment against sudden fear.

"He'll bungle it! Go back, you blasted fool!" shouted the professor.

"Go back. Go back." Chester echoed, waving his arms.

If Ross heard them, he gave no sign of it. Corey raised her binoculars, and they bit into her flesh as she watched Ross's feet touch the narrow ledge where the nest lay.

Ross was schooling himself not to make any quick moves. He was well aware of the narrow crumbling ledge that could give way at any moment under his feet. Cautiously he inched along the shelf until he was beside the nest. Bending his knees, he eased down into a hunched position. He reached into the nest, carefully took out the eggs and put them into the cushioned box that had been secured to his belt.

Corey watched his every move through her field glasses. If he held the eggs too tightly...if they broke in his hand...if he lost his balance . . . ! A dozen ifs raced through her mind as Ross tied his rope onto the container and gave a light jerk to signal Bill to pull it up. She knew that any slight crack in the eggshell could kill the developing embryo, which was now almost two weeks along.

Bill must be sweating, Corey thought, as she saw his figure poised on the lip of precipice, slowly pulling the precious cargo upward. When the box bounced against a sharp edge, she and Minna gasped as one. A second later the box reached the top.

"Bill's got it," Minna breathed.

When Ross had climbed back to the top of the cliff again, Corey lowered her glasses. The whole procedure had taken no more than fifteen minutes, but the falcon had been off her nest almost an hour. Maybe cooling of the eggs had already started beyond reversal. The drama might be an empty gesture already doomed to failure, she thought with a sense of defeat.

At that moment they heard the low cry of the falcon. She swooped down in a gliding circle and then braked smoothly to a stop on the ledge where Ross had just been. There was a gray bird in her beak. She dropped it near the nest and then sat down on her dummy eggs.

Both Bill and Ross were grinning when they came down to the blind. Corey could see the professor talking and gesturing as Bill placed the eggs in the container he had prepared. When they got back to the tent, they were in a deep discussion about the best way to get the eggs to the laboratory in Boulder.

"You say your friend in Lake City has a charter airplane service to his resort?" the professor asked Ross.

"Yes, sir. One flight, late afternoon from Lake City to Denver."

"Good. We can arrange for someone from the laboratory to pick up the eggs in Denver and take them to the laboratory in Boulder. You can take them to the Lake City airport for us, Mr. Sinclair."

"What?" stammered Ross. The situation had gotten out of hand. He had volunteered to help, in order to ingratiate himself with Bill, not to play errand boy to Professor White. He didn't have time to run around delivering eggs to the Lake City airport.

"I'm afraid I couldn't," he said pleasantly.

"Why not?" The professor peered at him from under his bushy eyebrows. "You've got to go to town and tell the sheriff about the bird-snatching, don't you? Seems to me that's part of your job, Mr. Sinclair. Or doesn't the government give a fig that there are some varmints out there stealing our birds?"

Ross felt everyone's eyes on him. If he refused, the suspicions he had sought to waylay would spring up faster than weeds. Corey's eyes deepened with speculation. Bill frowned at him, his former hostility back. Chester's birdlike eyes peered through his spectacles at Ross as if he were something under microscopic examination.

"Well, Mr. Sinclair?" the professor prodded. "Are you going to take these eggs to Lake City or not?

Chapter Five

Desperation coiled in the middle of Ross's stomach. He felt sweat breaking out in the palms of his hands. He didn't have time to go chasing off to Lake City. He had to get himself in a position to put his hands on the falcons he desperately needed. His thoughts swirled. Playing errand boy would cost him at least one valuable day. It would be tomorrow afternoon before he could get back, but what choice did he have? To refuse to take the eggs and notify the sheriff would center a lot of questions upon him and a scrutiny he couldn't afford. He was inviting disaster either way he went.

"You have transportation, don't you?" the professor asked in response to Ross's hesitation.

"Yes. A Bronco, parked across the lake."

"Good." The professor turned abruptly to Corey as if the matter had been settled. "I want you to go with Mr. Sinclair, Corey. We don't want any bureaucratic foul-ups. You call the laboratory from the airport and make sure someone meets that plane. Also, alert the sheriff that someone's making off with our birds. Ask him for extra men to patrol the area. Bill can stay here with Minna while Chester and I search out another pair to make up for the loss of this one."

"Sound like a good plan," said Minna, grinning at Bill.

Chester gave his approving nod and shoved his glasses up again, but Bill frowned. "What about my own pair of falcons?"

"Jake can handle the other sighting alone, Bill," said the professor. "He's an old-timer at this. Better you stay here and help Minna out." He turned to Ross. "You should be back tomorrow, late afternoon, I imagine."

Ross nodded. He couldn't think of a way to refuse to go. If he didn't play his role, someone's suspicions could put him under surveillance and end his chances to snatch a pair of falcons. By tomorrow afternoon, he had better have the information he needed from Corey McCalley so that he could put a plan into immediate action. "We'd better get started. We have a long hike and ride ahead of us."

"When does the charter flight leave from Lake City?" asked Corey.

"Four o'clock. If we push hard we can make it. We'll stay the night at the lodge and be back sometime tomorrow about dusk. Just take a change of clothes. We'll travel light."

She nodded, went into the tent, dumped out the muddy clothes from her knapsack and packed some fresh ones. Minna followed her. "Don't say I never did you a favor," she whispered.

"Did *who* a favor?" Corey countered. "Don't kid me. You were thinking of me all the way, weren't you? Grinning like a Cheshire cat 'cause Bill's going to stay here with you."

"You don't mind, do you?"

"Not at all. He's fair game."

"Good." Minna looked pleased. "I'd really like the chance to get to know him better. He seems like a nice guy. And you don't find many nice guys around anymore. Don't hurry back. We'll understand if it takes an extra day or night!"

"We'll make sure the eggs get on the plane this afternoon and have a reception committee when they arrive in Denver an hour later. It's only thirty minutes to Boulder and the laboratory incubator that will keep them warm enough to hatch. I don't see any problem. I'll be back on the job tomorrow," Corey assured her.

"Hey, you wanted to go, didn't you?"

Corey wanted to deny the stirring of excitement within her. The challenge of delivering the eggs appealed to her sense of adventure, and the thought of being with Ross Sinclair was not all that unpleasant, which was pure idiocy, considering the circumstances. Looking forward to a nice hot shower and a change of menu wasn't all that bad, either.

"Well, it's a dirty job—but somebody's got to do it," she granted with a grin.

"Not to mention the company you'll be keeping. He's some guy. Did you see the way he handled himself on that cliff? Graceful as a mountain lion. On second thought, you stay and I'll go."

Corey laughed. "No dice."

"Would you buy some things for me in Lake City? Here's a scribbled list and some money." Minna looked apologetic. "I never seem to remember everything I need. Too used to running to the supermarket at all hours. Hope you don't mind?

"Don't mind at all." She gave Minna a hug before she ducked out under the flap of the tent to where Ross was waiting.

Professor White drew Corey aside and gave her a card. "Call this number and arrange for someone from the lab to pick up the eggs as soon as they arrive. I don't want to trust them to anyone else." His bushy eyebrows matted over his craggy nose as his glance went to Ross standing a few feet away. "You do the calling. Watch that fellow. There's something about his manner I don't like."

Corey's latent suspicions came swirling back like a school of fish descending on a hunk of bait. "What do you mean?"

"Just make certain the eggs are put on the plane and that someone from the lab is notified to take them off at the other end," he repeated. "We don't want them to end up in some collector's cache or sold on the black market. Watch him, Corey. He may be in cahoots with someone. They got the tiercel yesterday, and it might well be that they're after the eggs, too."

"You don't think that he's responsible?"

"I don't know. Somebody is trying to turn our project into a nice little nest egg for himself."

Corey's eyes fell to his army boots, as they walked back to rejoin the others. Could the professor be putting up a smoke screen to hide his own culpability? Someone had rolled her up in a rug because he didn't want to be identified. She was almost certain they were after the remaining female. The professor might be the one to watch. Was he leaving Bill's nest vulnerable so that Bill's pair could be taken next? For one moment, she hesitated. Maybe she should refuse to go. But how could she? Professor White was in charge of the project, she had to obey his orders.

"Take care," Bill said, and lightly brushed a kiss on her cheek.

She had to laugh, he looked so paternal. "I can take care of myself, Bill." Her eyes twinkled. "'Tis a warning you'll be needing yourself." She winked at Minna and then turned to follow Ross.

As he moved ahead of her, Corey was treated to strong and muscular legs tightly molded by jeans. He was an outdoors man, that was clear. He took a trail away from the lake where the old cabin stood, and once they left the water's edge, they began climbing.

She stopped to take a pebble from her walking shoe. He immediately turned around and came back. She felt guilty, seeing his concerned expression. "Did you twist your ankle?"

"No, just a pebble in my shoe."

"Do you need a rest? I thought we'd keep going until we reached the Bronco." He tried to keep his voice neutral. It wouldn't do to let her know how much pressure he felt.

"I'm used to running three miles before breakfast, but the altitude is higher here," she assured him. "I'm doing fine. Not tired yet."

"Good. We should make the best time we can."

"Then let's quit talking and go."

He smiled. "Right."

They struck out again. Corey hoped he knew where he was going, for she couldn't see anything as they wove through an infinity of trees. Deadfall crunched as dry needles, withered leaves and pine cones cushioned their feet. Once he stopped abruptly. He swung around and put a finger up to his lips.

Her heart stopped. The silence was deadly. Who was it? Had they come upon someone hiding in this tunnel of trees?

He motioned her forward. A doe and her fawn grazed peacefully until they leaped away as their nostrils caught the human scent. Ross smiled at Corey, and the impact of his warm eyes and curved lips was startling. The guarded rigidity in his muscles softened. So this is what he looked like when he peered out from behind that rigid composure of his, she thought with a kind of wonderment. This was the Ross Sinclair she would like to know. She only had a glimpse of that side of him before he turned away. "Come on, we can't dally or we'll never get there on time," he told her.

"Set the pace. I'll keep up," she answered just as briskly. The brief moment of intimacy was gone.

The climb up from the lake took them through stands of quaking aspen, over tumbled heaps of rocks, around clusters of spruce and pine. Corey spied wild columbines that grew in shady crevices near moss-covered rocks and logs. Tiny ferns made green carpets that were dotted with fallen pinecones under tall lodgepole pines.

An old logging road had been cut into the side of the mountain, and they were both breathing heavily in the high oxygen-thin air when they reached the place where Ross had parked his rented Bronco.

"Here it is." He unlocked the doors. They secured the small hamper in the back seat and put their backpacks around the hamper to protect the brown dappled eggs nestling in an electric warmer.

Before Corey got in, she looked around for a moment. Her intense expression made him pause with his hands on the steering wheel. "What are you thinking, Tiger?"

"The smuggler must have used this road. None of the maps show any other access into the wilderness area. If we keep our eyes open, we may be able to see some tracks," said Corey. "Because of the rain, any vehicle would have left an imprint yesterday."

"True." He didn't like the way her quick mind put things together. For the moment her attention was centered on the smuggler, but how soon would it shift to him? Would he be able to keep his pretense in place?

Corey peered out the window, glancing from side to side. About fifty yards down the road, she pointed. "There."

Ross braked to a stop. She was perceptive, all right. A rutted track led into a heavy stand of spruce.

"The imprints look pretty new," she said.

"Wide enough to be a four-wheeler," he granted. So the man in the boat had been heading for the road, all right.

"I guess the sheriff will be able to make some tire prints."

Ross nodded. "I'll tell him about them," Ross lied. They wouldn't be going anywhere near a sheriff if he could help it.

"Where's your friend's guest ranch?"

"Near Lake City. This road meets Highway 149, which goes north to Gunnison and south to Lake City. I doubt that the smuggler would go south unless..." His voice trailed off.

"Unless what?" she demanded impatiently. It irritated her the way his thoughts would go off without including her.

"Unless they decided to fly the bird out. Maybe my friend Paul Hines will know something. He keeps his hand in about everything that goes on around here."

"Could he be mixed up in something illegal like this?"

"No, of course not," he snapped.

She searched his profile. His response had been too emphatic, as if the possibility was one he didn't want to contemplate. She saw his jaw tighten. Did he suspect his friend of having something to do with the smugglers? She'd have to be on her guard when she met this Paul. Even though she had not seen her attacker, he had seen her, and maybe there would be some intuitive feeling that lay in her subconscious that would cue recognition when she met this Paul Hines. Yes, she'd have to be alert. Not trust anyone. Not even Ross Sinclair. The professor's warning lay fresh in her mind.

Under different circumstances, Corey might have enjoyed the ride and the excitement of being pitched about on a narrow rutted road where the hillside fell away thousands of feet on one side. Unfortunately, her heavy thoughts and the fear of fragile eggs being scrambled in the back took all the joy out of it.

"Can't you slow down?"

"Not if we want to reach the airport in time."

"It would be better to delay an extra day than arrive with scrambled eggs, wouldn't it?"

He didn't have an extra day, Ross thought. The pressure of time running out descended upon him again, bringing that tight feeling to the pit of his stomach. He silently swore at the bizarre circumstances that had delayed him like this. He had to deliver the eggs and return to the lake tomorrow. The time line Prince Amund had set was getting precariously shorter and shorter. He'd been a fool to walk into this situation where he had to play a role or be found out for the impostor that he was. Somehow he must turn this unforeseen delay to his advantage. If Corey accepted him, he could use her to locate the most vulnerable pair of falcons. Then he could lift them and be gone before she knew what happened.

Corey watched the deepening lines in his cheeks and wondered what were his thoughts. She knew he would turn aside any questions, but she had always been one to delve below the surface. Graduating at the top of her law class had been in part due to her insatiable need to ferret out details that would disprove her opponent's case. There was a whiff of mystery about the tightly controlled Ross Sinclair that intrigued her.

"Where's your home?" she asked in a conversational tone. "Are you a native Coloradoan?"

"Nope. I was born in a small town in Nebraska. My parents were wheat farmers. Both gone now. Nice little town. Good place to grow up."

"But you don't live there and work in Colorado?" she pressed the point.

"No."

"You must have a place in Lake City."

Ross shook his head, thinking quickly. "No, Gunnison. It's a bigger town, about fifty miles north. I work out of the office there," he lied smoothly.

"And what about your son? He stays in Gunnison while you're gone?"

Ross nodded.

"Who takes care of him?"

"He has a nanny. What about you, Corey, where's your home?" Ross asked as if there were nothing more to be said about his personal background.

"Before my father went to Washington, we lived in Philadelphia," she said, knowing that he had deftly turned the conversation away from himself. She knew she wasn't going to get any more information from him. For a few minutes she chatted about her girlhood home in New Mexico before her father moved the family East. The road was so bumpy that carrying on any kind of conversation was a challenge.

The heavy rain of yesterday had left pools of water lying in every low spot, and as the Bronco plowed through them, mud sprayed up as high as the windows. Serpentine curves kept the wheels spinning dangerously near the edge of sheer precipices. Even though she tried to keep her eyes averted, several times her wide-eyed stare fixed on the vaulting drop-off of thousands of feet.

Ross gave all his attention to the driving. Corey clutched the shoulder strap of the seat belt. Every time they climbed to the top of one hill, another rose before them. Then another and another. At last they came to a road that had been widened a couple of feet on each side of the car. Ross grinned at her. "You can take a breath now. We're over the rough part."

She gave a sheepish laugh. "That obvious, huh?"

"The greenish color of your face is a dead giveaway."

He gunned the motor, and the next bump sent her nearly to the ceiling. She closed her eyes and took a half-dozen deep breaths in succession. For the first time she wondered if he truly wanted to save the eggs. Was the mad rush, oblivious to life and limb, some kind of elaborate pretense? Had he brought her along just to confirm how valiantly he had tried to get the eggs to the plane, broken or otherwise? Professor White hadn't given him much choice.

Rocks spun out from under the wheels, and a cloud of dust rose from the now-dry road. Apparently yesterday's downpour had not reached this area, Ross thought.

As they descended between jagged clefts in the mountain, Corey noticed that the terrain had changed from thick conifers and aspen to low Gambel oaks growing in the midst of three-leafed sumac and stalks of pinedrops. A brassy sun beat in the car windows. Her head began to throb, and she wished she had swallowed a couple more aspirin. Her aching head didn't encourage her to pry into Ross's thoughts. She had just closed her eyes and leaned her head back when there was a loud explosion and the Bronco shuddered in wild jerks.

Ross swore as he brought the vehicle to a stop. Without looking at her, he swung open his door and was around the back of the Bronco in an instant. She got out and followed.

"Blast it all." Lines deepened in his forehead as he viewed the flat tire.

"How's the spare?" Corey asked practically.

"All right, I think."

"Don't you know?"

"Yes, of course," he said hastily.

She glanced at her watch. Three o'clock. Less than an hour left. Thank heavens, he was moving fast. He already had the car jacked up and was loosening the lugs on the wheel.

"Can I help?"

"No, I'll have it changed in a minute. We're not far from the highway."

He finished the job, threw the spare into the back, and they started down the dirt road again. Thirty minutes later they intersected Highway 149, which curved and followed the Gunnison River in its meandering channel.

"Now, we can make some time," Ross said with a sigh of relief. Tires screeched as he took the curves. "The airport isn't far now."

About five miles out of Lake City, he suddenly careened off the highway and onto a gravel road that led to a narrow bridge spanning the river. A wide expanse lay on the other side, and Corey could see several buildings and beyond them, a runway.

She dared a quick look at her watch. A minute after four! She couldn't see any plane loading on the runway in front of the small building. Had it already left? Were they too late?

Ross was tight-lipped as the car screeched to a stop near a door marked Office. He leaped out and raced toward the building.

"I'll bring the hamper," Corey said, following him.

A girl of not more than fifteen looked up, startled at their entrance.

"I have a package that has to go on the four-o'clock flight," Ross said in a loud voice that vibrated through the small office.

Her jaws worked with an audible chomp on some gum. "Yeah, well, you're too late. Smythie's just taxiing out now." She gave a languid wave out the window.

"Stop him! Get him on the radio. Tell him to come back!" Ross ordered.

The girl took an extra couple chews on her gum before she shrugged. "Won't do no good."

"Try! Now!" Ross's expression was fierce as he leaned toward her.

The girl blinked and sat down at the radio. With a nervous glance at Ross, she contacted the pilot. "Smythie, somebody's here with a package to go. Seems kind of het up." She listened and nodded. "Okay."

She looked up at Ross and gave another chomp on her gum.

"Well?" Ross demanded while Corey held her breath.

"Guess he's going to come back for it."

"Thank heavens," Corey breathed. Her knees felt extremely weak.

"Good." Ross's expression eased into a pleasant smile.

"Whatcha got in there?" asked the girl.

"Eggs."

Corey opened the hamper's flap and gently eased aside some of the wrappings. The eggs were as warm and cozy as if they rested on a down of feathers.

"Ugly, aren't they?" said the girl, looking over her shoulder.

"No, they're beautiful . . . just beautiful."

Ross took her arm, and, laughing with relief, they carried the hamper out to the plane as it taxied back. When the plane was airborne, they both breathed a sigh of relief.

Corey's luminous eyes met Ross's. "Thanks for saving them. I know they're going to hatch four beautiful birds."

"Does that make us parents or something?" he teased.

"Or something." She laughed.

"I'm glad we made it." He felt good about the exchange—four birds for two. The exchange eased his conscience a little. At least the pair he was going to steal would be replaced by the newly hatched chicks. The trip had cost him precious time, and a dire urgency settled upon him once more.

"Now, I have to make that call." Corey said.

They went back into the small building to a pay phone. Corey drew out the paper Professor White had given her. She dialed the university number in Boulder, Colorado. She explained the situation to a proper authority, and he promised to have someone meet the plane and take the eggs to the lab.

"Well, that's done," she said, hanging up and giving a sigh of relief.

"Guess we'd better be on our way." Ross smiled warmly at Corey as they slipped into the Bronco. "I'd like to know more about this research program to save Colorado falcons. How many nests did you say were in this area?"

Happiness had brought a glow to her face. Her nose was shiny, her hair mussed. A soft wave had drifted onto her forehead, and the yellow strands glistened like spun gold. An undefinable emotion caught in his throat.

They sat a moment looking at each other. He almost bent his head and kissed her. The realization that they were on the brink of crossing an important bridge stopped him. He turned away and started the engine. "I'm ready for a hot bath and some good food. How about you?"

She saw that his mask was back in place.

Chapter Six

"Shouldn't we notify the sheriff, first?" Corey asked.

Ross's mind raced ahead, searching for a way to handle the explosive situation. He couldn't have the sheriff looking at his doctored identification card or checking with the wildlife division personnel department. Somehow he had to avoid calling attention to himself. "We can do that from the lodge," he answered smoothly. "Save us an extra drive since the lodge is just down the road from here and the town is about ten miles beyond that."

"Lead on. I've had enough excitement for one day," Corey said with a buoyant smile.

They drove a short distance down the highway until they came to a wide spread along the Gunnison River.

The Cristobal Lodge was a sprawling two-storied building set in the middle a wide meadow. Surrounding buildings included well-kept stables and corrals. Sleek riding horses dotted green pastures, and some cattle grazed under tall trees along the river where white-foamed water rushed over large rocks and sprayed mossy banks.

Ross parked in front of a long flight of wooden stairs leading up to the veranda skirting the lodge. They entered front lobby that was furnished like a large sitting room with overstuffed chairs and couches.

"Why don't you stay here and I'll see if I can find Paul or Helga," Ross said.

"All right."

He strode away, leaving Corey gazing at a magnificent grizzly bear that had been mounted in a lifelike stance at one end of the room. The grizzly was standing on his hind legs with teeth bared and claws poised as if threatening the hunter who had killed him.

"Kind of makes you want to skedaddle up the first tree, doesn't it?" someone asked with a chuckle in her voice.

Corey turned around.

A plump woman with graying carrot-dyed hair gave Corey a ready smile. Her ample frame filled out one of the easy chairs placed in front of a huge stone fireplace. She was dressed in jeans, cowboy boots and a western plaid shirt. Freckles spilled across her face.

Corey smiled. "Was my yellow streak showing?"

"Just a wee bit, but then that grizzly's more than double your size. Sit down. Take a load of your feet." The woman nodded toward a deep, soft sofa opposite her chair. A wide smile creased her round face. She was obviously wanting company, Corey thought.

"Thanks, I think I will." Corey gave a sigh of satisfaction as she settled back in the easy chair. "This beats a camp stool any day."

"My sentiments exactly. I leave the outdoor stuff to my menfolks. You just checking in?" she asked in open curiosity. Her eyes sparkled with interest as they centered on Corey.

"For overnight. Tomorrow it's back to a canvas tent and canned beans."

"Then you'd better enjoy yourself at the lodge," the friendly woman said. "My name's Trudy Cochran—from Oklahoma."

"Corey McCalley—from back East."

"Glad to meet you, Corey. My sons and I come to Colorado every year," offered Trudi, her round face perpetually creased with a smile. "Our first time at Lake City, though. When my husband was alive we used to spend our summers at Colorado Springs. You on vacation, too?"

Corey shook her head. She didn't want to get into any discussions about endangered falcons, so she just said, "No, I'm working on a university project."

"Oh, a student," she said, jumping to the wrong conclusion. "I think it's wonderful they offer classes out in the open these days instead of in a stuffy classroom. My boys spent one whole summer in Greenland and got a semester's credit for it."

Trudi had a deep laugh, shining blue eyes and the kind of open friendliness that put aside all formalities. Corey was laughing at a story about a bear cub who raided Trudi's tent one summer, when the woman looked over Corey's shoulder and waved.

"There you are, Delvin. Come here, honey, and meet someone." She beamed as the young man walked over to her chair. "Here's one of my sons," she told Corey proudly. "Delvin, say hello to Corey McCalley."

"Hi," said a slender young man with sun-bleached highlights in his wavy blond hair. His smile was as friendly as his mother's and he sat down on the arm of her chair. He wore tailored western pants, hand-tooled leather boots and a white western shirt that Corey suspected was pure silk.

"We've just been chatting away, resting ourselves," said Trudi.

Delvin sent Corey an apologetic grin. "You'll have to excuse Ma. She never met a stranger in her life."

"Aw, go on with you." Trudi laughed. "People are just plain nice. And I couldn't ignore this pretty new face. Corey's a student," she told Delvin.

Corey opened her mouth to explain, but Trudi didn't give her a chance as she passed along information in nonstop fashion. "I told her about your summer in Greenland. By the way, where's your brother?" she demanded with a frown. Corey suspected she kept a tight rein on her sons.

"Upstairs. D.J. will be down in a minute, Ma."

"My boys are twins," Trudi said proudly. "The spittin' image of each other. Handsome as their late pa, too."

Delvin smiled at Corey. "You're staying at the lodge?"

"Only overnight."

"That's too bad. Maybe you'll change your mind," he said hopefully. "It's a good dude ranch. All kinds of things to do. Horseback riding. Fishing. Eating and dancing. A great place for having fun. I'd be happy to show you around." His manner was openly flirtatious. He had a smile that was infectious.

Corey smiled back. It was nice having such a handsome fellow give her a flattering smile, but she wasn't interested. "Sorry. I'm just an overnight guest."

"Oh, you're with someone?" Delvin asked in a disappointed tone.

"Just business. Nothing personal." At that moment, Ross appeared in the doorway of a small office. She stood up. "It was nice meeting both of you."

Trudi nodded. "Sure 'nough. Maybe we'll see you and your friend at dinner?"

"Maybe..."

"There's a bluegrass band in the lounge tonight," Delvin said quickly. "Real nice."

"I'll probably turn in early," she said smoothly.

Delvin gave her another smile. "Well, if you change your mind, I'll be around."

When Corey joined Ross at the bottom of the stairs, a deep frown creased his forehead. "Making new friends?"

"No. Just some friendly people from Oklahoma."

"The way that guy was coming on to you, I thought you might be in need of my protection."

"Protection!" Her eyes flashed. "I can *protect* myself very well, thank you."

"All right. All right. No argument." His expression softened with a grin. "I know better—my shoulder is still sore from your last assault." Then he sobered. "None of my business. If you're taken with the guy—"

"I'm *not* taken with the guy. But I don't like anyone throwing a protective shield around me."

He raised a mocking eyebrow. "Is that what I was trying to do?"

"Yes."

"Maybe you're right. Come on, we've got rooms on the second floor. You can meet Helga later. You'll probably want to shower and rest." He unexpectedly slipped his arm through hers.

What an infuriating, unpredictable person he was, she thought as they climbed the stairs. His moods were like quicksilver, and she never knew whether to laugh or put up her guard.

Ross was asking himself about his reaction to seeing a guy make a pass at Corey. Heaven knows, her vivacious charm would attract anyone with warm blood in his veins. Why he felt like shoving the guy's white teeth down his throat, he wasn't quite sure. But she was right. He had no proprietary rights on her. And never would have, he thought with a deep sense of loss.

He stopped in front of a door near the head of the stairs and handed her a key. "This is your room.... I'm in the one across the hall. Have yourself a rest and I'll see you later for dinner."

He acted like someone who wanted her out of the way for a while. "What are you going to be doing while I rest?"

"I'm going to track down the pilot who flew the charter flight to Denver yesterday. Apparently today's pilot, Smythie, alternates with this guy. He might know if anyone tried to take out a trapped peregrine yesterday."

"Sounds like a good idea," she agreed. "Maybe we ought to tell the sheriff first." In her own mind she was debating whether she should go with Ross. Professor White had told her to keep her eye on him.

"I'll do that while I'm out. You enjoy a hot shower and I'll see you at dinner."

"Maybe I should go along?" she insisted.

"Why? Now who's being protective?"

Under his direct gaze, she felt foolish. "All right. I'll see you at dinner."

"It's a date," he said with a teasing twinkle in his eyes. "I may even bring flowers."

She laughed and closed the door.

Ross let out a breath of relief as he bounded back down the stairs and out to his Bronco. He had decided his best protection lay in finding out as much as he could about the other smuggler. It would be disastrous for him to be caught up in somebody else's illicit activities. The more he knew about the situation, the easier it would be to keep everyone's attention focused elsewhere while he removed his own birds.

Upstairs, Corey walked over to the window and watched the Bronco leave. A sudden tightening in her stomach took her by surprise as she watched him drive away. Something was wrong. She knew it. She sensed a discrepancy on some intuitive level. Like an illusive name that refused to come to mind when she struggled to recall it, the answer evaded her. She went back over everything that had happened since yesterday—her climb up the cliff, finding the bird in the net and almost seeing the one who hit her on the head. She was certain she had caught up with the smuggler when she saw

Ross hiding behind those rocks. Her encounter with the wildlife ranger had been bizarre. When he had arrived this morning to help rescue the eggs, she had been surprised and a little uneasy. Somewhere she had missed an important clue or detail. Something was out of place. What was it?

She sighed and turned away from the window. Her room was spacious and clean, furnished with maple furniture that was simple but attractive. Bright floral curtains picked up colors of brown, beige and yellow in the carpeting. Towels in the bathroom were soft and sweet smelling. Eagerly she stripped and stepped into the shower stall. Scented soap, small bottles of shampoo and conditioner awaited her pleasure.

As she washed her hair and rubbed her skin pink with the scented soap, her thoughts lingered on Ross Sinclair. He created feelings in her that were not as clear-cut as she would have liked. There were times when his eyes met hers that she could have sworn she was physically attracted to him—and he to her. That was foolishness, of course. She hardly knew him, and the situation certainly wasn't conducive to anything romantic. But what did she really know about him when it came down to the bottom line? And why did she hesitate to take him at face value? What was it about him that kept her so on her guard?

She was still asking the same questions when she lay down to rest. The clean, soft bed soon lulled her into a quiet content, and she slept for a couple of hours. Refreshed when she awoke, she put on tan slacks and a soft summer blouse in a brown-and-yellow paisley print. Quickly she ran a comb through her hair. It was cut short in a fashionable wedge style with feathered bangs that lay softly around her face. With feminine satisfaction, she decided that the blouse harmonized with her golden-yellow hair, and impulsively she slipped on a tiny pair of gold earrings.

When she let herself out of her room, she crossed the hall and knocked on Ross's door. No answer. Either he wasn't back yet or he was waiting for her downstairs. A sense of uneasiness assaulted her again. I should have gone with him, she thought.

As Corey walked down the hall, she met a young man at the top of the stairs. He didn't smile at her even though she recognized him as Delvin Cochran. Politely he let her go down the steps in front of him without a greeting, and then she realized that he must be Delvin's twin. D.J. looked like his brother, but his choice of clothes was entirely different. He wore rather faded blue jeans and a cotton checkered shirt that had seen several washings. His boots were overrun and scarred. Nothing of the rich young playboy about him. Corey had the feeling she might like him better than his brother.

At the bottom of the stairs, a matronly woman with blondish braids around her head greeted Corey with a smile and held out her hand. "You're Ross's friend, aren't you? I'm Helga Hines. Is your room all right, Miss McCalley?" Her German accent was heavy.

"Perfect. I had a wonderful shower and nap."

"So nice to have you with us. You're one of the research team, Ross tells me. Professor White stays here all the time. His wife is German, too, like me. We've known them for a long time. He and Paul—" She broke off, as if her tongue were running away with her. "Well, they do business together."

"What kind of business?" Corey realized her question was much too swift. The unexpected link between Helga's husband and Professor White was suspect, considering that a nefarious connection probably existed with someone in the research team.

Helga's expression showed her reluctance to answer Corey's direct question. She gave an embarrassed laugh. "I talk too much, eh?'' Her hands moved nervously on the sides of her full peasant skirt. "Dinner will be served in about a half hour. A drink in the lounge, perhaps?"

"Have you seen Ross?" Corey asked.

Helga shook her head. "Not since he signed for the rooms. Excuse me, please?" She scurried away, leaving Corey staring after her.

As Corey walked toward a door marked Watering Hole Tavern, her mind whirled with the new information—Professor White and Paul Hines, business associates? She remembered Ross's reaction in the car when she had suggested his friend might be involved in the smuggling. Ross's attitude toward his friend had indicated that he wasn't quite sure about Paul Hines.

As Corey hesitated in the doorway of the small lounge, Trudi waved a chubby arm at her. "Come have a drink with me and D.J."

There were about a dozen other people in the lounge, and they looked up to see who Trudi's cheery voice was welcoming. A little curious to make the acquaintance of the twin sitting beside Trudi, Corey nodded and made her way to their table.

"Land's sake, don't you look pretty now? Fresh as a golden brown-eyed daisy blooming in a meadow. Corey, this here's my other son, Delbert James, We call him D.J."

He politely rose and acknowledged the introduction, holding out a chair for Corey. But despite his quick manners, he seemed ill at ease and ready to let his mother dominate the conversation. Unlike his twin, D.J. kept his eyes on his beer and made no attempt to be friendly or to enter the conversation. The glances he sent Corey were shy and quick, completely lacking in the flirtatious air of his twin brother.

"Delvin ran off to Lake City," his mother said. "Taking a date to the French restaurant they have there. What'll you have to drink, Corey? Gin and tonic okay? Good. D.J., go get us one from the bar. It's kind of self-service around here. Helga and Paul don't have a lot of people waiting on you hand and foot, and that's what I like. Darn if I like someone at my elbow all the time. Well, what do you think?'' she asked when D.J. was at the bar getting their drinks. Trudi beamed with open pride. ''Aren't my twins every girl's dream?''

Corey had to laugh. ''You have very nice and very attractive sons.''

Trudi nodded in agreement. ''D.J. loves horses, just like his dear departed father.'' Trudi started a story about the number of horses they used to have on their ranch before her husband's death. D.J. returned with the drinks and sipped his without taking part in the conversation.

When Ross appeared in the doorway, Corey saw that he had changed to russet slacks and a sweater flecked with cinnamon-and-orange tones. For a moment her heart did a peculiar twist like a wild gyroscope. A sensible voice silently mocked her reaction. She waved. He smiled in recognition and moved purposefully through the tiny lounge to their table.

Corey made the introductions, and Trudi greeted him like an old friend and insisted that he sit down for a drink, but he deftly refused the invitation. ''Thanks, but they've just opened the dining room and I'm ready for a sizzling beefsteak. Maybe later,'' he promised with a smooth smile.

Trudi looked disappointed as he very deftly spirited Corey away.

''Every time I turn my back, I find you with another guy,'' he teased. ''They keep coming out of the woodwork. I hope you didn't mind our quick exit.''

''No, I like Trudi, but her friendly chatter wears me out. And D.J. is one of those boring silent types. I was glad of an escape.''

''Will wonders never cease? You prefer *my* company?''

"Under the circumstances, yes," she countered, trying to match his lightness. She wanted to ask him if he'd found out anything. Should she repeat what Helga had said about Professor White being in business with her husband? She hesitated. Paul Hines was a close friend of Ross Sinclair. He wouldn't take kindly to any suspicions sent in that direction. A horrible thought leaped at her—was it possible that Ross, Paul and Professor White were in business together? All three of them could be engaged in smuggling falcons out of the area. The professor could be the inside man, and warning her to watch Ross could have been a smoke screen.

Corey removed her arm from Ross's guiding hand, and he looked down at her with a puzzled expression. He felt her withdrawal. She seemed to have suddenly put some kind of barrier between them as they walked to a small table for two at the far end of the long, narrow dining room.

"What's the matter?"

"Nothing," she answered curtly. Why had she let him go off on his own without her? She wouldn't make that mistake again.

A buffet had been set out with several meat entrées, vegetables, a nice salad bar, and homemade cakes and pies. The aroma of beef roasted in an outdoor iron smoker was mouth watering. Corey set aside for the moment thoughts of anything else but appeasing her growling stomach. She filled her plate almost to overflowing and even took a dessert back to the table, as if the blueberry pie might all disappear while she ate her meal.

A waitress in western garb kept their coffee cups filled but did not intrude upon their conversation. After weeks of cooking outdoors and eating off unbreakable plates, it was pure luxury to sit at a table covered with a blue checkered tablecloth and eat off blue-rimmed stoneware. She had almost forgotten what a cloth napkin felt like.

Ross was in a good mood. He must have found out something from the pilot, she thought. But would he tell her? Suddenly she was angry with him and herself. Why pussyfoot around with him? Her training as a lawyer might stand her in good stead now. She laid down her fork and looked at him over the rim of her coffee cup.

"Did you find the pilot?" she asked casually.

"I was wondering how long it was going to take before you started giving me the third degree." The corners of his mouth quirked in an amused fashion. "You're really quite transparent, you know. I think you'd make a terrible corporation lawyer."

"Thank you."

"I meant it as a compliment. You have an open honesty that's a lovely quality. I would hate to see the practice of law ruin it."

"Are you saying all lawyers are dishonest?" she flared.

"I'm saying that you probably wouldn't be a successful big-business lawyer unless you lost some of your sensitivity and vulnerability. What's your mother like?" he asked suddenly. "You've talked about your father some but not your mother. Does she like it that you're a lawyer?"

"My mother's main concern is that I make the right kind of marriage, and that means money and prestige." She looked at her engagement-ring finger, and for a moment a lovely pronged diamond flashed in a mental image.

He followed her gaze. "Oh, oh. I sense some romantic involvement gone astray."

She was able to smile easily. "Yes. I was engaged for about six months. But we both decided it was a mistake. Matthew is a Philadelphia attorney who's about to launch himself on a political career, and he needs the right kind of wife to support his ambitions. He's a great guy, but I don't like that scene. I've seen enough of the pressures and fan-

fare that goes with public office. I don't want that kind of
life.''

''And what kind of life do you want?''

Her eyes met his. ''That's one of things I'm taking the
summer to find out.''

Neither of them moved. The moment stretched.

She cleared her throat. ''Tell me what you found out.''

''You're very direct.''

''Very. Tell me.''

''All right, Counselor, Smythie was very helpful. My
hunch was right. I'm convinced the tiercel was taken out on
that charter flight yesterday. Most of the passengers were
vacationers, but Smythie said a bearded young man wearing a stocking cap bought a ticket at the last minute and was
carrying a case big enough to hold a small bird when he
boarded the plane.''

''There could be dozens of people like that carrying bags
and boxes on planes. Purely circumstantial evidence,'' she
countered, not without a smile.

''I know, but I think that was our man.''

''What makes you so sure?''

Ross reached into his pocket and took out a small piece
of paper. ''This is the name the man gave for the passenger
list.''

Corey read it twice. She looked up at him. ''You're kid-
ding!''

''No, I'm not. I think our smuggler has a sense of humor. He's rubbing our noses in it just for fun. That's the
name he gave. Honest!''

Corey read it again. ''Mr. P. Tiercelli.'' Her eyes locked
with Ross's. Peregrine Tiercel!

Chapter Seven

The arrogant confidence of the man sent a chill up her spine. Tiercelli! He had left the message for anyone who might be looking for him. A childish challenge—but one reeking with the promise of danger to anyone who tried to stop him. If only they had been here yesterday, before he left Lake City, but now he had a twenty-four-hour lead on them. He could already be pocketing his share of the money for delivery of the falcon.

"He'll have his tracks completely covered by now," Ross said, as if voicing her thoughts.

"Do you think he'll be back?"

"I don't know. If he's a loner..." Ross let his voice trail off without conviction.

"But you don't think he is."

"No, I don't. I'm betting somebody on the inside is giving them information about the location of aeries that Professor White is using in his study."

"I agree with you," she said. "It isn't likely that a smuggling operation was set up for only one bird. You notified the sheriff, didn't you?"

"Stopped by his office after I'd talked to Smythie," lied Ross. "I told him everything we knew. He said he'd look into it." He hadn't gone near the sheriff's office. At the moment, he didn't want to be noticed by anyone in authority.

"Since the falcons will be migrating as soon as their young can hunt for themselves, the smugglers can't wait very long between snatches," she said. She still couldn't believe that there was an informant in the research team. Who could it be? Bill? Minna? Professor White? Chester? Jake? "I wonder who's feeding them information."

Ross shrugged. "I don't know. But that's the way a gang like this works. Someone scouts the area, just like a burglar casing a location for a robbery. An inside man is the perfect cover, because a member of the research team would know where every site was and which one was the most vulnerable."

Corey's ire came up instantly. "And because Minna and I are female, they picked us for the first job."

"Probably." Then he smiled. "But they didn't know what a rock-wielding, wood-slugger you are." He touched his tender shoulder where a huge bruise marked the spot she had hit him with the piece of wood.

"I wish it had been Mr. Tiercelli's head! The arrogance of the man makes me livid. And he got away. Now there's nothing we can do. The falcon's gone."

"Our Mr. Tiercelli may not be as clever as he thinks. Lake City is a small place and someone may remember him, now that we have a description. I'll alert Paul and Helga. If he shows his face again, someone will notice him."

"I know." She brightened. "Trudi!"

Ross looked puzzled. "What abut Trudi?"

Corey laughed. "I sincerely doubt that anyone could come within a five-mile radius of the lodge without her knowing all about him."

"I guess it wouldn't do any harm to ask her."

"Maybe Delvin and D.J. will know something. They seem to get around a lot. After dinner I'll have a drink with them and find out."

Ross frowned. He didn't want Corey playing up to either of them just to get information. He'd seen the way Delvin had flirted with her. "I'll talk to them," he said stiffly. "You don't need to wrestle wolves on top of everything else."

She laughed at him. "I'm only after information. Besides, I can handle myself. I told you that. You're being protective of me again, aren't you?" she challenged, expecting him to smile in return. He didn't.

"You're on your own," he said shortly.

"Good. Now that we have that settled, I think—" She stopped when she saw Ross smiling at someone coming up behind her chair.

"Paul!" Ross was on his feet. "Where have you been hiding out?" He shook hands with a lanky, lean-faced man wearing faded jeans and a work shirt as if they were a wrinkled part of him.

"Just back from an overnight pack trip. Getting too old for sleeping on the ground." The man grinned and rubbed his chin with one hand.

No doubt about it, Paul would be at home in a corral or barn, Corey thought, and wondered why her reaction to him wasn't more positive. Was it her preconceived notion that he might be a part of the smuggling activity? Or was it something deeper? The man's hazel eyes were narrowed in a habitual squint, as if the sun were constantly in his eyes, and Corey felt uncomfortable under their scrutiny.

"This is Corey McCalley," Ross said following Paul's questioning gaze.

"Nice to meet you, Corey."

"Likewise," she said.

"Helga was telling me you're with the university outfit."

"Yes. I'm one of the aerie wardens."

"Sounds pretty boring to me. Sitting and watching birds all day."

"It has its exciting moments," she said dryly.

"Sit down, Paul. We need to talk with you."

Paul motioned to the waitress to bring him some coffee and sat down in a chair next to Corey's. "I haven't seen much of Ross. Showed up out of the blue, a couple of weeks ago. Now here he is back again, with a pretty lady in tow. Always had a good eye, I'll say that for him. And it's about time somebody put a lasso on him again."

"We're just friends," she said rather primly.

"Well, now, any friend of Ross's is a friend of mine," Paul said smoothly. "I have to warn you, though. This guy's about as trustworthy as a fox in a henhouse. 'Specially when it comes to women." He laughed. "Ain't that right, Ross?"

Ross just grinned patiently. "Lies, all lies. You're the one who played Romeo to every poor lass who came around."

They teased each other for a few minutes, and on the surface, it seemed like good-natured male banter, but Corey thought she sensed some nettles in the verbal barbs. Ross's expression was unreadable, as always. He was smiling and laughing, but the depths of his eyes were guarded and solemn. She was aware of the tight control he had on his emotions. The knowledge brought a warning—don't be taken in by his outward charm. She mustn't allow her feelings to get in the way of maintaining a detached perspective about him.

"Well, now," Paul said, "What can we do to make your stay at the Cristobal more enjoyable?"

"Actually, old buddy, we'd like some information," Ross replied. "We're interested in a young fellow with a full sandy beard who might have been staying at the lodge the last few days and left yesterday. Wearing a green stocking cap, a bulky sweater and hiking boots."

Paul squinted even more, as if trying to remember such a fellow. "Hmm, can't recall anybody that fits that description. Young fellows aren't wearing as many beards as they used to back in the sixties. Even keeping their hair cut these days. Nope, can't recall any young bearded guy around the place. Course, I don't see everyone who stays here at the lodge. Just the ones who show up at the barn for horses. Probably Helga could tell you though. What's up?''

While Ross told him about the falcon-snatching and Corey's part in the drama, she watched Paul's face. Maybe he already knows—the thought flitted unbidden through her mind. For a suspicious moment, she wondered if he'd really been on a pack trip, or had he been helping someone get away with her falcon.

"Well, I'll be darned," Paul rubbed his chin in his habitual fashion. "You've got yourself a mystery, all right. Guess peregrine falcons bring a nice bit of money to the right party."

"I think it's detestable!" Corey snapped. "How could anyone sink low enough to do such a thing? It puts a whole species in danger of being lost forever. I'll bring the full force of the law down on the culprits if I get a chance."

Paul raised an eyebrow and smiled at her. "Well, now I'd hate to get crosswise with you. You sound pretty hard-nosed about this."

Corey bristled. "I believe in upholding the law. I have no sympathy for anyone who deliberately flaunts it."

Ross was silent.

Paul rubbed his chin. "I can't rightly say I've seen anything suspicious going on around Lake City. Pretty quiet place. You say you saw the smuggler, Corey?"

"No," Ross answered before she could. "Corey heard the tiercel's distress cry and was foolhardy enough to climb up a sheer cliff to try and rescue it. You should have seen the climb she made, and without a rope, too."

She picked up a begrudging admiration in the censure. It was amazing how the slightest whiff of approval from him sent her spirits winging. She didn't know why it was important that he thought well of her. Or maybe she did.

"Some guy took several shots at me when he was leaving in a boat," Ross said. "I saw bird feathers in the mud, and I'm sure he must have had the falcon."

"So you're after the yahoo who stole the bird, and you think this bearded fellow had something to do with it?" Nothing in Paul's face indicated he knew anything about the incident. It was hard to look into his narrowed eyes and read any expression there.

Ross showed him the slip of paper. "Smythie, the pilot, says this is the name he gave."

"Well, I'll be jiggered! I've heard of burglars leaving their calling cards, but this takes all. Mr. P. Tiercelli." He laughed dryly. "A calling card if I ever saw one."

"He thinks he's clever, but he may just trip on his own cuteness," said Ross grimly. "Especially if we can find someone who will give us some information about him and discover what his real name is."

"Sure wish I could help. I'll have a word with Helga as soon as she has a minute. She's always busier than a hound dog with cockleburs. We've had a full lodge since Memorial Day weekend. And there are a lot of other motels and cabins in the area, especially around San Cristobal lake." He shook his head. "Take a lot of time to check all of them out."

"I know," agreed Ross, "but we might get lucky if he comes wandering back."

"Well, I'll keep my eyes open. Guess I'd best be checking on some of the guests. Glad to see you again, Ross." As Paul got up, he said to Corey, "Watch out for this guy. He's smooth. Ross could steal your eyeteeth while you're smiling at him." She knew he was teasing, but somehow the mirth didn't reach his smile.

What was going on between those two? As Paul walked away, the question must have been in her eyes, for Ross said quickly, "He's just reminding me that I took a gal away from him once. We spent a winter in Alaska together. He was working on the pipeline, too. Anyway, there was this gal and—"

"You stole her from him?"

"Not really, but Paul thinks I did. Actually she was playing us both against a brawny lumberjack whose attention she was trying to get. Paul never misses a chance to rub it in."

He laughed, but Corey had the impression there was more to the story than that.

"I want to be on the road as early as possible in the morning," Ross said, trying to appear relaxed when every minute, like a waiting serpent, time passing breathed down his neck. He couldn't afford to use up any more of the precious few remaining days. It was imperative that Corey provide him with the information he needed, so that by tomorrow night he could have zeroed in on the best pair of falcons to be lifted. "Say about five o'clock?"

"That's too early," she said flatly. "I have to go into town and pick up a few things for myself and Minna."

No! There isn't time! He covered the unspoken protest with a teasing smile. "Don't tell me you're one of those women who have shopping as a hobby."

"No, I hate shopping."

"Good."

"This list isn't long. Shouldn't take more than a few minutes. Anyway, don't you have to report to someone about this whole thing? Isn't that part of your job?"

Her eyes were guileless, but he felt a squirming in the middle of his stomach. He was reminded how adroit she was in her thinking. He had better watch his step, or his impersonation could blow up in his face any minute. He gave her

a boyish grin. "Did you have to remind me? I hate paperwork, and once I step into the office, that's what will be
facing me." He sighed. "Well, I guess there's no help for it
if we go into town. I'll check into the office while you do
your shopping."

At that moment, they heard the sound of an electric guitar coming from the lounge. Other guests began to leave the
dining room and head in the direction of the lounge.

"Shall we find Trudi and talk with her?" suggested
Corey.

"Unless you'd rather take a walk in the moonlight with
me?" He like the sound of the offer even though he knew it
would never happen. She wouldn't be sidetracked.

"I feel like dancing."

"With me?"

"If the twins aren't around," she teased.

Ross signed the dinner check and ignored Corey's protest that they should go dutch. She gave in gracefully. Although she liked paying her own way, there were times when
the old-fashioned gallantry was enjoyable.

A trio of musicians filled the small room with vibrating
music. The dance floor was postage-size. There were only
two other couples dancing and only a few scattered guests
at the small tables. The Cochrans were not in the tavern.

"They'll probably be along," Corey said as they sat down
at a small round table and ordered two Black Russians.
When Ross asked her if she'd like to dance, she said,
"Sure."

He was a smooth dancer, not showy or artistic. At first,
his physical nearness invaded her senses, and she felt like
someone about to take the first dip in a roller coaster ride.
She stiffened against it. She didn't realize that he, too, was
holding himself defensively away from her, until the tension went out of his body. He lowered his head, and his
cheek pressed warmly against her soft hair. Their bodies

swayed in harmony with the music and each other. She tried to interpret the charge between them as something building in her imagination, but she could not deny the heat of her body nor the way his lips almost touched her forehead. When the music ended, he kept his arm around her waist as he led her back to their table.

"I'll get us another drink."

While he waited at the bar, he swore silently at himself. What a fool he'd been to take her in his arms. His body had reacted with instant desire. It seemed that she was attracted to him, too. It was there in her eyes. Everything about Corey spoke of honesty and integrity, and the knowledge choked him. He was ready to manipulate her and sacrifice her the instant she threatened his goal. And she was no dummy. That business about his reporting to the local office was sharp. He couldn't afford the time, but he saw no way out of refusing to go into town. His forehead beaded with sweat. Robin . . . Robin. Anxiety over his son brought a new wave of urgency. He had to get the falcons and be on his way back to Amund. He couldn't afford any slipups. Trying to use Corey as his informant was like fooling with a land mine. He needed to keep his wits about him, or she'd trip him up for good. As he walked back to their table, he knew that he was going to have to move and move quickly. Tomorrow he'd pretend to check in at the office, and then he'd head back to the lake with Corey. Very quickly he'd have to decide then which pair of falcons he'd go after.

Trudi's cheery voice greeted them above the bouncy tune, "Mammas, Don't Let Your Babies Grow up to Be Cowboys." Her son D.J. was at her elbow. "Hello, there," she said, smiling broadly. "We drove to the Powderhorn Resort for dinner. Great place."

While D.J. got their drinks, Trudi talked about the wonderful trout dinner they'd had. Before long, she and Ross were deep in a discussion of the best bait to use when fishing for stream trout as opposed to lake fish. As he talked, Corey pictured Ross gracefully tossing his line out into a roaring stream, and a glow on his face as he reeled in a silver rainbow. He threw back his head and laughed deeply with Trudi when she told them a story about the time Delvin landed a trout with such force that it caused him to topple the boat with all of them in it. Something inside Corey tightened. She saw how deftly he was manipulating them. At the moment, Ross acted as if there were nothing more on his mind than enjoying the Cochrans' company. When he had hooked them with a few amusing tales of his own, he reeled them in.

Very casually Ross asked, "I don't suppose you happened to notice a bearded young man around here a couple of days ago? Sandy beard, likes to wear a knitted stocking cap?"

Corey gave her attention to her drink, casually stirring the mocha liquid, but she was really holding her breath and waiting for Trudi's answer.

"Young man with a beard," she mused. "Was he staying here at the lodge?"

"I don't know." Ross answered.

"What his name?"

"I don't know that, either. How about you, D.J?" he asked the quiet twin. "See anybody around who looked like that?"

"Nope, but I don't mix very much. Delvin's the one you should ask. He just got back from his dinner date."

"Go, hurry him up, D.J. Tell Delvin to come join the party."

Her son hesitated, looking at Corey as if he realized his chance had come to make her notice him. Ross saw the covetous look D.J. gave Corey, and he stiffened. The quiet twin was taken with her, and for a moment, Ross thought D.J. wasn't going to go after his brother.

"Go on, son," said his mother impatiently.

D.J. looked away from Corey and quietly left their table.

Corey asked Trudi about the other lodges in the area. She gave them a quick rundown on places and people, but nothing she said helped them. Corey and Ross exchanged disappointed glances. Obviously no help would be forthcoming from Trudi. In a few minutes Delvin joined them, wearing white slacks and an open-neck shirt with a gold medallion shining on his bronzed neck.

"Hello, hello," he said, slipping into D.J.'s empty chair. "Glad to see you again, Corey."

"Where's D.J.?" asked his mother.

"He'll be along in a minute." His eyes slid around the room and came back to rest on Corey. "I told you this place rocks at night. Would you like to dance?" His white smile bathed her with its warmth. "If your date doesn't mind," he added.

"I don't mind," Ross said readily.

A little too readily, Corey thought as they made their way to the dance floor. She had been amused at his protective attitude, but that seemed to have disappeared now. He seemed to be saying, have a good time—and find out what we need to know.

Delvin was a polished dancer. The bluegrass band was quite good, she thought, as Delvin deftly twirled her around the floor. She should have been enjoying herself, but she was glad when the music stopped. Delvin's hands had a way of slipping all over her, lowering on her back just slightly more than was necessary, touching a breast as he swung her close or away from him. When the music stopped, Delvin kept his arm around her waist. "I'm glad you decided to join us," he said in a suggestive voice.

She made herself remain passive in his embrace when she wanted to tell him to keep his wandering hands to himself. She smiled at him. "Paul and Helga really provide for their

guests, don't they? I was wondering, did you happen to see
a fellow around here a couple of days ago? Has a sandy
beard and wears a green knit cap?''

"Sounds nauseating." Delvin laughed, his beautiful white
teeth showing. "Don't tell me you hang out with a weird
character like that?"

"No. I'd just like to talk with him."

"Well, the grubby look went out with the sixties. Haven't
seen anybody around who looks like a leftover hippie. I'm
sure I would have remembered him. Another dance?"

Corey drew away from him. She'd found out what she
wanted to know. "No, thanks."

As they walked back to the table, Delvin kept his hand on
her arm, making light trails on her skin.

She could tell from Ross's smirk that he had taken it all
in. "Kind of like dancing with an octopus, wasn't it?" he
whispered.

She glared at him and didn't answer.

"How about it, Corey?" Delvin said as he sat close to her
on the other side. "Have you decided to stay over and let me
take you boating on the lake and horseback riding in the
hills?"

"Sounds like fun, but I have to get back to work."

"You could change your mind..."

"I won't."

The loud music vibrated in her head, and a headache
lurked at the base of her neck. She was glad when Ross
suggested they leave after a second round of drinks. Delvin
protested that the evening was young.

Trudi smiled. "Nice meeting you folks."

"Happy vacation," Corey said.

Ross took her arm and guided her ahead of him through
the lounge. "How about a breath of fresh air?" he asked.

Corey nodded. That's what she needed to stall the beginning of a headache.

They went out a side door onto a wide porch that ran the length of the building. Passing up summer furniture, they walked to a corner of the building and leaned against the railing, looking out at the Gunnison River twisting like a silver streamer in the moonlight. A clean fresh scent of pine needles mingled with smoke from an outdoor cooker.

"Well," he asked anxiously. "Did you get anything out of Delvin?"

"Nothing."

"Blast it all. Well, I guess we'll have to depend upon Paul to keep his eyes open."

"And the sheriff," Corey added. "You told him what Smythie said, didn't you?"

"Of course," Ross lied again. He prayed he could keep Corey away from the authorities when they went into town in the morning. If she said anything to the wrong person, they could be detained for questioning. What would he do then? What if— *Stop it! Don't anticipate a crisis. Keep to the plan.* Ingratiate himself with Corey. Get information he needed from her. "Nice night," he said casually. "Stars bright and clear."

"Lovely setting," she mused, looking up at nearby cliffs that hemmed in the ranch. At night huge slabs of rock looked soft against the night sky.

He nodded. "Paul and Helga have worked hard, but the resort hasn't been a real financial success. I guess they had to bring in more investors this last year. I think your Professor White is one of them."

"Oh, that's what Helga meant," said Corey in relief. "She told me that he and Paul were in business together. I thought, I mean I wondered, if Professor White might be the informant and Paul the smuggler."

Ross didn't answer for a moment, and she glanced up at his profile. The muscles in his cheek flickered.

"Did I hit a bit of a nerve?"

"I don't know. People change. Sometimes a need can make a man put aside his integrity."

"Something like money?" she scoffed.

"Personally, I don't care about money," he said. "Never have. Some people organize their whole lives around financial success, but that's never been important to me. I want you to know that. You believe me, don't you?"

Why was he looking at her so intently and talking so earnestly about money? She didn't understand the message that lay beneath his words. Shadows stirred in the depths of his eyes. And she saw a deep hurt—the kind that would make any woman want to do everything she could to ease it.

"I believe you," she said quietly. "I wasn't accusing you of anything."

"Corey, I don't know if Paul is guilty or not. But whatever happens..." His voice trailed off.

"What's going to happen?" She touched his sleeve. "What's going to happen, Ross?" she repeated. Her eyes searched his face. His expression softened as he looked down at her. The blue in his eyes deepened.

"Now? This minute?" His fingers traced the smooth curve of her cheek. He smiled. "I'm going to kiss you." When his mouth touched hers, warm and soft, she realized that she had been waiting for him to do just that.

She'd been kissed before, but this was the first time she actually knew what the old cliché "swept off her feet" meant. She was soaring when Ross drew away and steadied her with hands on her shoulders.

"I don't want to hurt you, Tiger," he said softly, letting his fingers feel the sweet softness of her arms.

"Ross, what are you trying to tell me?"

For a moment his jaw worked as if searching for words, and then he only sighed.

"Are you married?" she asked with a catch in her throat.

He laughed at that and his expression eased. "No, I'm not married."

"You wouldn't lie to me?"

"About being married, no."

"But you might lie about something else?" she countered swiftly.

"No, of course not. I wouldn't dare." He kissed the tip of her nose. "You'd find me out…and trip me up, wouldn't you?" His tone was light and facetious.

"I'd try."

"Is that a warning?" he quipped.

"Do you need one?" Her azure-blue eyes were questioning.

"No, of course not. Come on, let's go in." He smiled, hiding a sense of rising danger, knowing full well that they were skirting treacherous shoals. "We'll have a hard day tomorrow."

When they reached her room, he unlocked her door and handed her the key. "Good night. Sleep well."

After that intimate moment on the porch, his distant manner washed over her like a sudden plunge into an ice-cold creek. "I had the feeling you were about to telling me something, Ross. What is it?"

"Nothing except you're a very special woman, Corey. I want you to know that."

He was warning her again. But of what, she didn't know.

Chapter Eight

In his room, Ross stared out into the darkness. Nights were the worst. The bedtime ritual with Robin had always been a poignant ending to the day's activities. Nana went home to her own family, so the little boy was all his until the next morning. Every night was the same—a story, a kiss, a prayer and sleepy cuddling, some delaying maneuvers on Robin's part, and finally a soft, "Night...Night" when he tucked him into bed. Often Ross would remain in the small room to watch him fall asleep. His son was beautiful; tousled fair hair, long curling eyelashes that lay on pink cheeks, a bowed mouth soft and relaxed, and his little chest moving in the rhythmic breathing of sleep. Love would swell like a warm spring inside of him, and he thanked the Lord for the miraculous gift.

How he missed hearing that bright, chattering little voice, feeling his little hand slip into his and watching those blue eyes widen and twinkle with wonderment. A groan issued form his chest. Worry and loneliness overwhelmed him. How had it happened? He was caught in a diabolical nightmare. Had there been warning signs? Had he ignored them? He cursed himself for being so trusting. He had taken Robin to the palace many times to play with the prince's numerous children while he and the prince talked falconry. What a fool he'd been! He had heightened Prince Amund's appetite with his talk of North American peregrine falcons and put his son's life and that of Nana in danger. Robin's nurse was a motherly Arabian woman who was fiercely protective, but what could she do under the circumstances? Ross feared that her life would also be in jeopardy if he failed to return with the falcons. Prince Amund would not hesitate to silence the woman.

Ross threw himself onto the bed and thought about Corey. His loneliness and despair had sought a moment's solace on the porch with her when he had taken her into his arms and kissed her. For a dangerous moment he had been tempted to tell her the truth. Thank God, he had resisted the impulse. He had seen evidence of her integrity and knew that her anger at the disappearance of the tiercel was real and deep. It was stupid to think that she would willingly step aside and let him abduct a pair of peregrines with her blessing. She had faith in the law. Her father was a presidential advisor. Undoubtedly she would insist that he contact the authorities to get his son back. He didn't trust the wheels of government to handle the ransom demands with any expediency, and time was what he didn't have. He cursed the position Professor White had put him in, making it impossible to refuse the errand of bringing the eggs to the airport. Ross prayed they would hatch safely and make up for the pair he was going to take out of the country. Tomorrow he had to get back to the area and put into action a plan for lifting a pair of falcons.

Ross stared unseeing at the ceiling. If he told Corey and she agreed to help him, what then? What if he was caught and she was involved as his accomplice? Her life would be ruined—and he would be the cause of it. No, he couldn't tell her. She had to be kept out of it for his sake and hers. He had no choice but to lie and to manipulate her as the situation warranted.

THE NEXT MORNING, Ross was already in the dining room when Corey came down. "Good morning," he greeted her with a smile.

"Am I late?"

"No, not at all. I couldn't sleep so I came down early. I'm on my third cup of coffee."

Corey ordered one of her favorite breakfasts, biscuits and sausage gravy. As she sipped a fragrant cup of coffee, she leveled a steady gaze at him. Dark shadows under his eyes accented his bold cheekbones. What was the matter with him? He hadn't slept, she could tell that. "You look awful."

"Thanks. I needed that." He grinned at her. "Just not used to such luxurious accommodations, I guess. The bed was too clean and soft. Before I found the cabin and its rickety cot, I was sleeping on the ground in a sleeping bag. Guess I missed all the lumps and squeaks."

She wasn't fooled. She knew him well enough by now to know that he was trying to make light of something eating inside him. "This smuggling business really has you upset, hasn't it?"

He blinked at the bluntness of her question. He kept his eyes on his cup. *If you only knew!*

"Well, I think we're making progress," she said with an optimistic smile. "We know that a man calling himself P. Tiercelli probably took the bird out by plane. We have a description of him so the police can check on his arrival in Denver and maybe track him from there. I'm sure the sheriff will want to come up to the sighting and check for clues. I'm surprised he doesn't want to talk with me—after all, I was there from the beginning."

"I'm afraid a stolen bird isn't high on his priority list," said Ross smoothly. "Some cowboy got drunk the other night and shot a fellow he was playing poker with. The gunman fled up into one of the ravines, and the sheriff and

his deputy have their hands full right now looking for him.''
Ross hoped Corey didn't know about the incident that had
happened five years earlier. It was the best lie he could
manage out of thin air. He should have expected that she
would be wondering why there wasn't some investigation
going on.

"Sound like the wild, woolly West, all right. Guns. Poker.
The whole scenario. I bet Lake City has a great history.''

He silently let out his breath. So far, so good. It was imperative that he keep the sheriff out of the situation until he
made his own escape. "Have some more coffee." He picked
up a pot and filled her cup.

Corey chewed a piece of delicious sausage and wondered
why Ross was so nervous. The tension in his muscles made
his smile tight and his laughter thin. Had he found out
something about the smuggler that he wasn't telling her?
Could his friend Paul be an accomplice and Ross know all
about it? She took a sip of coffee and then said casually,
"Of course, someone else could have snatched the falcon
and turned it over to Mr. Tiercelli for transport.''

Ross nodded. She wasn't going to let it go, he thought
with rising impatience. What he didn't need in this dire situation was someone like Corey turning over every piece of
evidence and questioning it.

She wiped her mouth with her napkin, then smiled. "I
wondered if your friend Paul saw anyone on his pack trip.''

Ross surprised her by laughing. "You're not very subtle,
Counselor. Why don't you just ask me if I think Paul lifted
the falcon?''

"Do you think Paul lifted the falcon?''

"No.''

"He could have. He said he was away on a one-day pack
trip.''

"He didn't do it.''

"You wouldn't lie to me, would you, Ross?''

The question was like a dart thrown dead center at his heart. "Lie to you?" He managed another laugh. "Why would I do that?"

"I don't know," she said thoughtfully. "I don't know."

LAKE CITY WAS a delightful mining town left over from the early mining days. Corey was instantly enchanted by the tiny Victorian houses with their gaily painted gingerbread trim and window boxes.

"I can't believe it's real," she said, used to the bustling cities of the East. A tiny main street called Silver Avenue was void of traffic. No stoplights, and only a few slow-ambling people wandered along the narrow sidewalks. Most of the buildings were false-fronted like those of any western movie and looked as if they had been built about the time the first stage clattered out of town in a cloud of dust.

"Not much here now," Ross agreed. "Great vacation spot, though. Good fishing and hunting."

"Oh, there's the Fish and Wildlife Service office," she said, catching sight of a small brick building snuggling against one that housed the Black Crooke Theatre. Billboards advertising a coming melodrama decorated the outside walls.

"Yes, I guess I'd better report in," Ross answered. "Tell them about our conceited Mr. Tiercelli. I'll park the car in the next block so you can do some shopping."

"Oh, I'll come with you."

"No need. I'll get the paperwork done faster without you." Ross stopped the Bronco in front of a small drugstore painted a bluebird blue. He left Corey to make some purchases while he crossed the street and headed for the office of the U.S. Fish and Wildlife Service.

Corey hadn't planned on calling her folks, but a public telephone booth inside the drugstore worked on her conscience. Calling collect, she gave the operator the number, and soon her mother's carefully modulated voice was on the line. "Corinne, what a surprise! Where on earth are you? Back in town?"

"No, Mother, I'm in Lake City, a little town in western Colorado. Just came in for some supplies."

"My goodness, I never know where you're going to be next." She gave the deep sigh that Corey knew so well. It encompassed disappointment, disapproval and a hint of the martyr. "I don't know what in the world made you run off like that. Spending the summer looking after some vile birds."

"They're not vile birds, Mother." They had been over this many times before. Her mother represented a narrow sect of the population who saw raptor birds as meriting extinction from the face of the earth.

"They're killers. They attack pretty little birds and eat them!"

"They hunt their food, Mother, as all natural species do."

"Well, I think it's revolting and utterly disgusting."

"Really, when was the last time you ate chicken, or turkey, or even Cornish hen?"

"That's different, and you know it. I've said it many times before, Corinne. I think it would be a better place to live if we got rid of all the vultures and hawks and—"

"And half of the human race," Corey finished. Her mother would never understand that when one species disappeared from the face of the earth, the carefully balanced existence of all life forms was threatened. "I don't want to talk about it, Mother. I just called to let you know I was okay, in case you were wondering."

"Now don't use that tone with me, Corinne. We're all waiting for you to come to your senses. Matthew was just here yesterday, asking about you. He really was upset about the broken engagement."

"Now, Mother, don't pull that hearts-and-flowers stuff on me. You know very well that Matthew was as relieved over the split as I. We're still friends, but we aren't suited to spend our lives together."

"He's such a nice boy."

Corey laughed. "Mother, you make him sound like a date to the prom."

"Matthew is going to be an important politician. You wait and see." Her tone added that Corey would be sorry she let him go.

"I wish him well, but that kind of life isn't for me. I've seen too much of it already, watching you and Dad cope with all those pressures."

"I don't understand you at all, Corinne. Aren't you proud of your father—advisor to the president of the United States?"

"Of course I am," Corey said impatiently.

"Then why are you hesitating to take your place as a partner in his law firm?"

"I'm not sure that becoming a corporate lawyer is for me. Maybe I want to practice some other kind of law."

"And what kind would that be?"

Corey could imagine her mother's nose twitching. "I don't know, but that's why I'm taking this summer break," she said firmly. "It's my decision to make. Not yours. Not father's. Mine."

Her mother sighed. "You always were headstrong, Corinne. I remember how all the other little girls would go to ballet classes and you would traipse all over vacant lots with Bill Collins, catching horned toads and other vile creatures. I suppose I shouldn't be surprised that you prefer living in a tent to a Washington town house."

"You'd be surprised how lovely the landscape is—and not a gardener in sight."

"We all want you to be happy, honey."

"I am happy." Strangely enough it was true. She didn't know the reason why she felt so alive and excited. Or maybe she did. "I have to go now, Mother. Give Dad my love."

"I will, darling. Take care of yourself."

"I'll call again as soon as I'm in town, but I don't know when that'll be. Don't worry about me." Corey hung up, feeling a little guilty about the fact that she hadn't told her mother about her encounter with a bird snatcher. If her father had been home, she would have told him.

She left the drugstore with her purchases and walked a block to a small shop where she bought a sweatshirt that Minna had on the list.

As she passed the small building housing the Wildlife Service Office, she glanced in the windows. She couldn't see Ross. On impulse she went in.

She asked the woman behind the counter if Mr. Sinclair was still with the ranger.

"Oh, sorry. Mr. Emory isn't in today. He's out in the field until late this afternoon."

"But," Corey stammered. Then her eyes narrowed. "Did a man come in here about thirty minutes ago asking for him? Ross Sinclair?"

"Nope, you're the only one who's been in all morning." She smiled at Corey, "Not what you call a bustling office with only one ranger."

Corey's mouth went dry.

"What's the matter? Is something wrong?"

"I . . . I don't know."

"Are you a visitor in Lake City?"

"Not really. I'm with a research team observing peregrines near Crescent Lake. Yesterday one of them was stolen from the aerie I was watching. I thought that Ross Sinclair was in here telling the ranger about it. But if he didn't even come in . . ."

"I told you. No one's been in today."

She heard herself explaining in an even, neutral voice. "Ross Sinclair showed me an identification card and I'm wondering if it was valid—and if he is really assigned to this area. Perhaps you can help me." She didn't want to hear such suspicions coming from her own lips, but suddenly her doubts had a volition of their own. Even as she spoke them, the questions echoed in her ears, taunting her and bringing a quick stab of pain as she voiced them. Before she realized it, some rational, analytical part of her brain took over. "Do you have a list of the wildlife rangers working in the state?"

"No, but I suppose I could get one from the office in Denver. They'd have one. Would you like me to check it out?"

Corey almost said no. Like someone about to step into a dark room, she mentally took a step back. How could she accept the fact that Ross might have deceived her from the beginning? She straightened her slim shoulders. "Yes, I would."

"And your name?"

"Corinne McCalley."

"Address?"

She gave her parents' address in Washington, D.C.

The woman's eyes widened. "Any relation to Patrick McCalley, the president's new legal advisor? I saw his picture in the paper this morning."

Corey nodded. "Yes, he's my father."

"Oh, my!"

Corey wished the woman wouldn't look so impressed. Now she regretted telling the secretary anything. Who knows what she would do with the inquiry now that she knew who had made it. Corey realized that she should have made up some story instead of telling the secretary about the peregrines and her suspicions about Ross. Well, it was too late now.

"I'll look into this right away," the smiling woman promised. "We don't know everyone who is on special detail."

"Thanks."

Corey left the office and walked back to the corner with her thoughts whirling madly. One thing was certain—Ross had lied to her. He hadn't reported to the office at all!

She crossed the street and was walking toward the drugstore when she heard the spitting of gravel from a side street and turned to see the Bronco emerge glistening wet from a car wash. Ross braked the car with a grin, "Sorry if I kept you waiting."

She avoided looking directly at him as she got in.

"What's the matter? Did you think I'd gone off without you? We needed gas and I ran the car through a car wash while you were shopping. Ready to go?"

She nodded.

"We'll stop at the lodge, pick up our stuff, check out and be on our way." He sent a quick glance at his watch. His forehead knit, and she saw a muscle flicker in his cheek.

Corey wanted to confront him with the fact that he had not gone into the Wildlife Service office, but she held back. He had lied to her once and he would only do it again. She would wait until she got a report back from Denver.

"What's the matter? You've got that counselor's frown again. Am I in for some cross-examination?"

"No," she said, but she kept her eyes away from his face as they left Lake City and followed the Gunnison River north to the lodge.

They returned just in time to check out. When they paid the bill, Ross protested at Corey's insistence that she pay her share. "Dinner is one thing," she said. "My lodgings are another." He knew from the fire flashing in her eyes that he had better acquiesce gracefully. This was one independent lady.

"Get your things and I'll meet you in the lobby."

She nodded and hurried up to her room to pack her overnight bag. Ross Sinclair was a smooth one, she thought angrily. Never an indication that he had not reported to the office. She didn't understand him at all. Why would he pretend to be a ranger when he wasn't? What was he doing in this area? The answers she got did not please her.

When she came back down, Ross was not in the lobby, but Helga was in the office. The German woman gave Corey a friendly smile. "Nice to meet you. You are welcome anytime. By yourself—or with Ross." It was obvious Helga was curious about her relationship with Ross, but she was too much a lady to pose any questions. The truth was that Corey wouldn't have had an answer if Helga had voiced her curiosity. At the moment, Corey didn't know whether he was friend or enemy.

"The room was lovely," Corey said. "The food excellent."

"Come again, anytime."

"Do you know where Ross is?"

"He went down to the stables to say goodbye to Paul."

"I'll wait for him in the Bronco."

Corey left the lodge and threw her things into the four-wheel-drive parked at the side of the building. She started to get in. A glimpse of a large red building through the trees at the bottom of a slight hill stopped her. The stables. Curious about any conversation taking place between Paul and Ross, she decided to follow the path that led through a thick stand of aspen and conifer trees to the stables.

She was startled when a young pup bounded up from a cool spot under a ponderosa pine where he'd been sleeping and almost tripped her as he threaded her legs and jumped up on her.

"Hello, there!" Laughingly she stooped down and scratched his ears. He licked her hand, twisted his tail enthusiastically and twirled in a circle. Corey disengaged herself from his exuberance by picking up a stick and tossing it down the path. She made her escape as he tumbled after it.

When she reached a clearing in front of the stables, she saw Ross. He and Paul were talking by a Jeep Renegade, which was covered with clay mud as high as the windshield. It looked exactly like Ross's Bronco had until this morning when he ran it through a car wash.

Corey hesitated a moment in the shadow of the trees, her ears straining to hear the conversation between the two men. Ross was smiling, and Paul's lanky frame was leaning against one of the fenders as they chatted. It was foolish to let the sight of a muddy vehicle affect her the way it did, but questions lurched upward like wild grass thrown in fertile soil. Could this have been the vehicle that had brought the bird and his captor down the muddy road day before yesterday? She knew there were dozens of roads around here where a car could get covered with mud like that. And yet, Ross and Paul were old friends. Accomplices? She felt her stomach take a sickening plunge at the thought. Ross had deceived her. She knew that. Why?

Doubts and suspicions made her turn away and retreat back up the path. The puppy was still cavorting in playful fashion under the trees. He looked up at her and then barked as he tugged at something in the low underbrush. Corey would have walked right by the spot where he was digging if a soft fluttering like snowflakes hadn't arisen from where he was jerking and pulling. Snow? Absurd thought. No, not snow. "Wh—?" Then recognition was like vibrating blows on an anvil inside her head.

With a cry, Corey pushed through the bushes and looked down at the place where the dog was digging with his clumsy little paws. The puppy took his buried treasure in his mouth and shook it, sending feathers fluttering into the air.

She blinked and felt the earth lurch under her as she touched one hand against a tree trunk for support. Shock sent dizzy vibrations surging through her.

An empty hole had been left in the dark, rich earth where the puppy had dug up an empty mist net. It was shredded to pieces and filled with telltale white, blue-black and motley-gray feathers.

Chapter Nine

Corey heard Ross laughing with Paul. The sound was like a trigger going off in her head. She turned, took a few steps down the path back to the barn, and then she stopped. No, she was too shaken by her discovery to think clearly. Better give herself a chance to get on top of her emotions and decide what must be done. Let Ross think she was as much in the dark as always. She needed time to put all the facts together. The buried net put the smuggling ring right on these premises. The bearded man in a knitted cap had been here all right. Or maybe there had never been a Mr. P. Tiercelli! Ross could have created the name. She felt a twisting nausea in the pit of her stomach. Maybe he hadn't gone to see the pilot at all. The description might be a clever red herring to keep anyone from looking too closely at someone connected with the lodge. The big production about saving the eggs had been a way to win her confidence, to manipulate her and lull her suspicions. Even that tender moment on the porch last night could have been contrived. How easily she had been duped.

With her jaw clenched, Corey hurried back to the Bronco. Her mind raced with the new discovery. Someone had trapped the falcon and brought it here. The picture of Ross and Paul laughing together beside the mud-covered four-wheel drive taunted her. Were they gloating over their successful operation? The muddy imprints on the logging road could very well match Paul's vehicle. Undoubtedly Ross had known that Paul's Jeep Renegade was parked there all the time.

Corey got into the Bronco and slammed the door. It riled her to think how stupid she'd been. She'd watched him cleverly play up to Trudi to get the information that he wanted. Ignoring subtle cues, she had allowed herself to be blinded by Ross's charm and had let down the barriers against the physical attraction he held for her. She enjoyed being with him, and his touch could send her on a Ferris wheel ride. She was furious that she'd been such a push-over.

"There you are!" Ross's breezy voice was a mockery to her churning emotions as he slid in behind the wheel. "Sorry to keep you waiting. Had to shoot the breeze with Paul a minute." He started the Bronco and drove at a fast speed down the highway. "Well, now, let's see what good time we can make getting to the lake. I bet you're ready to get back to your job."

She had to admire his approach. So casual. So deceiving. As always, his thoughts were hidden from her. A familiar tenseness was evident in tiny lines around his eyes. She knew how clever he could be. From the beginning, he had played her like a fish on his line. She knew now that he lied glibly when expedient. Even when he was being most pleasant, he never let the deep, dark waters of his thoughts run freely on the surface. He was an enigma, a stranger, and as dangerous as he was attractive.

He shot her a quick glance. "What's the matter? Something happen I don't know about?"

"I'm sure you know everything that's going on," she answered crisply, her eyes biting into his.

He raised an eyebrow. "What does that mean?"

"You tell me."

"Are we playing twenty questions or something?" he said, half teasing, but his eyes delved searchingly into hers.

"No." An accusation sprang to her lips, but she trapped it before the words were out. What good would it do to confront him? He would just lie to her. Or do something worse. There was a hard core to his personality that she didn't understand. She had never seen him really relaxed. He was tense even when he pretended to be casual. She didn't understand the dark intensity that showed in his eyes and in the tightness of his lips. He was like an animal poised for attack or flight. Was he afraid that she might have discovered something to connect him with the smuggling? To challenge him might put her own life in jeopardy. She turned away and stared out the window without answering.

"Are you afraid the eggs didn't get there? We could have called the lab this morning and checked. Would that have put your mind more at ease?"

"I'm not worried about the eggs. I suppose I could have called at the same time I made my call home."

"You called home?" He raised an eyebrow. "How did it go?"

She decided she'd take a leaf from his book and be as sociable and pleasant as he pretended to be. "Like always," she said lightly. "My mother did her usual 'why don't you straighten up and fly right' routine."

"I bet you've always been a challenge to your mother." He grinned.

"Why do you say that?"

"Just a wild guess."

"It's true. We've had a contest of wills from the very beginning. She's a darling and should have had a meek, conforming daughter instead of a renegade. I guess I take after my father. Stubborn and determined. Not easily dissuaded when we make up our minds."

He sobered. "Yes, I had surmised as much. I suspect you're a formidable adversary in the courtroom or any-place else."

"Is that how you see me?" she queried quickly. "As an adversary?"

"Why do you ask?" he parried.

"You haven't been honest with me, have you, Ross?"

"About what?"

She knew she shouldn't challenge him. Her vow to keep her mouth shut was slipping away. "Lots of things."

He sent her a quick look. "I don't know what you're talking about, Corey. What's bothering you?"

"Oh, just a few loose ends. A few deliberate lies." She was certain now that Ross hadn't been to talk with the sheriff any more than he had gone to the Wildlife Service office. How easily he had manipulated her, persuading her to stay at the lodge while he supposedly took care of everything. That story about a hunt for the cowboy demanding the sheriff's attention was undoubtedly pure fabrication. "When did the sheriff say he'd start investigating the theft?" she asked pointedly.

"He didn't say. A day or two, I guess."

She had to give him credit. He was smooth. Corey looked out the window in an unseeing stare. Her thoughts were brambles. She knew that she must divorce her feelings from the situation. She must stick to the facts as she knew them. Three years at Harvard Law School had taught her that. She was certain that her tiercel had once been in the mist net dug up by the dog, probably brought to the lodge in the muddy Renegade Jeep and then transported to the charter plane for a flight to Denver. And she was beginning to put faces to the culprits.

Several times Ross sent her inquiring looks. An uneasi-ness stirred within him. He didn't like that parade of expressions flitting across her face. She was worrying something through. He had too much respect for her intelligence to ignore her deep concentration. Once, he directed her attention to the silver stream of a waterfall and an abandoned mine. She made superficial responses and then lapsed back into a heavy silence.

When they reached the end of the logging road and got out of the Bronco, she said crisply, "I want to take another look at those tracks."

He raised an eyebrow. "All right."

She didn't know much about tires, but the impressions in the ground seemed to match the broad ones on Paul's Jeep. The dirt was the same color as the mud that had covered his four-wheel drive. It could have been Paul's vehicle that had been parked here.

Corey walked a little way into the underbrush. "Footprints." She pointed to the ground. "Two sets or one?"

"One, I think," he answered, stooping down to look closer. "The imprints all seem to be the same size. Whoever it was could have walked back and forth, making the two sets of tracks."

"Do you think a pair of army boots could have made them?"

He looked at her quizzically. "I haven't any idea. Why'd you ask that?"

"When I got back to my tent the other day, someone was hiding there. He tripped me when I came in and rolled me up in a rug. I glimpsed army boots." She watched for his reaction.

"Do you have any idea who it was?"

"No. But every man in the research team bought a pair from an army surplus store. It could be one of them—or somebody else." She looked at him pointedly.

With a hint of a smile, he threw out his hands in a gesture of innocence. "I swear to you I've never owned a pair of army boots in my life."

She doubted that Ross had followed her from the cabin to hide in her tent, but at the moment her thoughts were in such a mire, she was ready to concede anything was possible.

"We'd better start hiking. The day's slipping away fast." He gave an anxious glance at the sun already well on its descent toward the western horizon.

"Did you tell the sheriff about these tracks?" she asked.

"Sure."

Why didn't she believe him?

They left the logging road and started their hike down the rugged mountainside to the lake. Every step demanded concentration. Loose rocks, craggy cliffs, dense bands of trees and heavy undergrowth made hiking down the steep slope a challenge.

As she followed Ross, Corey was glad to have an emotional release in strenuous exercise. Once more he set a grueling pace. She wondered what hidden furies drove him. His vigorous features caught shards of light coming through needled tracery, highlighting ebony tones in his dark hair. On every level, her mental struggles to put him in the framework of a villain failed miserably. She couldn't forget the tender touch of his fingertips as he traced her cheek. His kiss—so soft, so loving, so caring. How could he be guilty of all the things that added up to his deliberate deceit? And yet, she knew he'd been lying to her.

Ross was well aware of Corey's scrutiny, and he was bewildered by it. What had happened? From the time she climbed into the car at Lake City, she had been acting like a cat with its hackles up. Had she talked with someone? Or phoned the authorities? He knew she had been on the telephone. Something had put her on guard. What had she learned to put the dark shadow of suspicion in her eyes? His attempts to be sociable had met with cool rejection. Unless her attitude changed, she would never give him the information he needed.

When they reached the lake's edge, he made a decision and stopped abruptly. He turned around and put a hand on her arm. "All right, Corey, let's have it."

"What do you mean?" she parried, off balance because of the suddenness of his demand. "Why are we stopping?"

"Because you have something to tell me, don't you?"

"No."

"You're lying. Your eyes give you away, you know. There's something bothering you more than just a chat with your mother."

If there had been room between the rocks, she would have brushed by him. "I have nothing to say to you."

The tight grip he put on her arm made her wince. How could she have thought him gentle? His whole body was poised on the edge of anger. "What do you have to tell me, Corey?"

"Nothing. Nothing at all. But I intend to tell Professor White and Bill a few things when we get back."

"I don't want to hurt you, Corey, but I have to know. Something happened at the lodge. Suspicion flames in your eyes every time you look at me. What is it? Tell me."

"Why should I?"

"Because I don't have time to play games," he said in a deadly tone. "If you've discovered something, I have to know. Now!"

She felt a desperation behind the plea, and she stiffened against the appeal. She knew she should keep quiet about the net until she told someone else about it. As a kind of compromise she said, "You lied to me. You never intended to stop at the ranger's office. I went in and the girl said the ranger wasn't even there."

"That's why I didn't go in. I knew he was in the field," Ross said too quickly, and Corey knew she had been guilty of leading the witness. She had given him the explanation he needed. "I told you that I didn't want to get caught up in a bunch of paperwork. I'd be there yet filling out triplicate reports. You know how the government works. Everything is hamstrung with red tape and regulations." Bitterness laced the words. "Government bureaucracies move as slow as snails—if they move at all." He tried to lighten his tone with a laugh. "Anyway, there'll be time enough for reports later. I'm sorry if I upset you."

Should she tell him that she had requested an inquiry be made about him? She feared his reaction, so she set her jaw tightly.

"For God's sake, Corey, don't fight me on this." His hands were on her shoulders, gentle but firm. "When I got in the Bronco back at the lodge, I felt antagonism as strong as tear gas coming at me. What happened after we got back to the lodge this morning? What is it?"

She was frightened now. He was a stranger, his hard eyes of steel boring into hers. "Nothing."

He gave her a light shake and his fingers sank into her flesh. His face was just inches from hers, dark and tense. "Don't lie to me! Please, Corey. Don't lie to me."

Suddenly it was a relief to spit it out. "I walked down to the barn and I saw you standing with Paul beside that muddy Jeep. It looked just like the Bronco before we washed it this morning."

He nodded. "I thought the same thing and I asked Paul about it. He said it had been that way for over a week and he'd never gotten around to having it washed."

"And you believed him?"

Ross didn't answer right away. He dropped his hands from her shoulders. "I don't know. That girl I told you about in Alaska. Paul has never forgiven me for turning her in to the authorities for arranging under-the-table rebates on some materials. They never found out who her accomplice was."

"And it could have been Paul?"

"I was sure at the time that it was the girl's other boyfriend. But now, I don't know. Although, I can't believe Paul would have anything to do with an ugly business like the illicit sale of raptors."

"Then what was the mist nest doing on his place?" she asked with the swiftness of a prosecuting attorney.

"What net?" He looked genuinely astonished. "I don't know anything about a net."

Relief surged through her. Her instincts told her he was telling the truth. "The one filled with peregrine feathers and slashed so that a bird could be removed from it." She told him then about the puppy, the flying feathers and the half-buried mist net. "Just off the path to the barn."

"Why in heaven's name didn't you say something about it?" At her expression, he sighed. "Oh, I see. Guilty by association, is that it? You were convinced that I knew about the net being there."

"Yes, and I wondered if you really did go to see the pilot or if you just made up that description of the young bearded man and his knit cap."

"I see. Well, I'm surprised that you climbed back in the car with me at all. It does look rather incriminating, doesn't it? You think that Paul and I are in some kind of a nefarious partnership, is that it? I'm the inside man. I locate the nests and he comes and gets the birds?"

"Isn't that the way it works?" she countered. "You described the scam for me the first day. It adds up that way." She waited for him to chide her for jumping to such a conclusion, but he didn't. A plunging sensation flipped her stomach. No, it couldn't be true. "Ross?" There was a pleading edge to her tone. "You and Paul, you aren't partners?"

"I swear to you that if Paul is involved in any smuggling of falcons, I'm not aware of it. And I hope to God you're wrong. I'll admit finding the net there puts the action at the lodge, with or without his knowledge."

She had an absurd impulse to reach up and soothe the deep creases from his brow. Instead she said softly, "I'm sorry. I really didn't believe you had anything to do with it, not deep down. You aren't that kind of person. You knocked yourself out to get the eggs safely to the lab." She gave a little laugh. "I guess I let my imagination run away with me all right."

"Yes, I'm afraid you did. You believe me, don't you?"

"Yes." It was clear to her now. Ross didn't go into the ranger's office, because he knew Mr. Emory was in the field, Corey told herself. There was nothing sinister about it. And he must have talked to the sheriff, just as he said. For the moment, she would accept everything he had told her—but only for the moment. A waiting, cautions part of her mind stayed alert.

He saw the reservation in her eyes. He touched her cheek and then drew back. He swallowed and said hoarsely, "Come on. Let's get on the move. Time's awastin'."

As they walked around the broad part of the crescent-shaped lake, Ross tried to compute the new information. Paul could have lied about the muddy Jeep. It looked that way now, for sure. The mist net certainly put the smuggler on his property, and Paul always needed money. He could have been involved in that scam in Alaska. Paul had sworn his innocence and Ross had believed him. But now he couldn't be sure. He had been relying on their old friendship to help get the birds out if the pressure was on. Now he would have to keep out of the clutches of the research team, as well as a gang that might include Paul. Maybe there had been no Mr. Tiercelli at all. Smythie could have been lying.

t's the kind of thing Paul would have thought up as a joke on his old buddy.

And what was he going to do about Corey? She was fearless and shrewd, and that's what worried him. Finding the net had fueled her uneasiness about him. Maybe he had been able to defuse her suspicions and maybe he hadn't. If he alerted her friend Bill, his chances of quickly lifting one of their pairs would be greatly reduced. There was only one thing to do. He had to keep Corey lulled into an acceptance of his innocence until the deed was done. Playing on the wonderful excitement that sparked between them was about as low as he could get, but in his desperate situation, it seemed the only way to keep her from talking to someone. For the moment, she seemed to believe him, but she was no fool and time was running out. He'd have to get his falcons before the other snatchers were in position again. As always, thoughts of his son made everything else insignificant. He couldn't worry about anyone else but Robin.

And he couldn't waste any more time. He had to lift the falcons—and quickly!

Chapter Ten

About midafternoon, Ranger Clyde Emory returned to his office.

His secretary, Emma, greeted him with her eyes flashing. "Hi, I'm glad you're back."

"What's up?" It was easy to tell when there had been something different in the boring routine. He could read it on Emma's face. She loved anything out of the ordinary. She was a hard worker and a very social person, greeting anyone who came into the office with a cheery smile and calling them by name. Unfortunately, she was also one of the town's most generous contributors to the grapevine. The young ranger and his wife had learned to keep their private business from Emma's eager ears.

"We had a visitor this morning," she announced eagerly. "One of those university people studying peregrines in the Crescent Lake area."

"Yes?" Emory knew about the project and had supplied maps when the university requested them.

"A nice-looking girl. Big blue eyes and pretty curly hair."

"What did she want?" the ranger prodded, trying to halt Emma's point-by-point description.

"Well, she was real upset about somebody snatching a falcon that she was observing."

"What?"

Emma nodded. "Somebody made off with it. Can you imagine? Anyway, she was asking about a fellow calling himself Ross Sinclair. Seems he's been flashing a U.S. Wildlife identification card, and she wanted to know if it was for real. I told her I'd never heard of him."

"His name doesn't ring a bell," granted Clyde, "but this is my first summer around here. And I never know who all has been assigned duties in the area. He could be working for another division out of Denver."

"That's what I told her. Well, I decided to check it out, since I was talking to Denver anyway." Her eyes glittered with suppressed excitement. "Guess what? No Ross Sinclair on the current roster, in Colorado or anywhere. Looks like he's an impostor."

She had Clyde's attention now. "You're sure?"

"Positive. Denver's going to contact Washington and see if he's ever been connected with any government agency. He could be pretending to be with the department so he can get at peregrines. Remember last year, a gang worked the same kind of scam in Idaho. Some aerie warden was even killed." Her eyes rounded. "Do you think the same thing's going on around here this summer?"

"Are you sure the girl said someone snatched a falcon?"

"Her words almost exactly. She said that the day before yesterday, someone stole a peregrine she was observing. Then she asked about this Sinclair fellow. Seems he was supposed to have come into the office to tell you all about it, but I never saw hide nor hair of him!" She gave a bob of her head as punctuation. "Mighty suspicious if you ask me. Mighty suspicious."

"There might be a simple explanation," the ranger hedged. He had enough work to do now without getting involved in some illegal black market in falcons.

"I can't think of one," Emma said emphatically.

Emory leaned back in his chair. "Seems to me I heard the department was thinking about setting up a sting operation to catch some of these fellows. Maybe this is a part of it."

Emma remained unconvinced. "I think you should talk to the sheriff right away."

"He probably already knows about the snatching."

"Guess what the gal's name was? Corinne McCalley. I asked her if she was any relation to Patrick McCalley. You won't believe this! The president's new counselor is her father!"

He whistled.

"Mighty influential people, I'd say." Emma gave an emphatic bob of her head.

Emory sighed. He liked the quiet life in Lake City, and he didn't fancy some important politician breathing down his neck.

His secretary reacted to his lack of enthusiasm with more of her own. "Don't you see what a feather in our cap it would be if we could arrest somebody? Think of the publicity. A caper like this would put Lake City on the map!" Emma touched a hand to her hair as if she were thinking of the news photographers who would be crowding into the office, interviewing her and taking her picture.

"I guess we should confer with the sheriff," he conceded, and sighed. He knew that everyone else in the valley would know the particulars as soon as Emma got on the phone. "Sheriff Wooten will probably want to ask some questions, have a look around and check into this Sinclair fellow."

"That's what I thought," Emma agreed eagerly. "I have a feeling we might catch ourselves a smuggler."

ROSS AND COREY hiked around the lake to the cabin. Ross dumped his things inside and then insisted that he accompany her back to her tent.

"There's no need."

"I'd feel better about seeing you safely home," he said with a soft smile curving the corners of his mouth. "Part of my gentlemanly upbringing."

"All right," she conceded, wondering why she was glad she was going to have his company a little longer.

As they walked along the small stream, he pointed out some geological formations that told a story of the earth's upheaval centuries ago. She knew he was making a great effort to be amiable and entertaining. She wondered why.

When they caught sight of the high cliff where the familiar aerie was marked by white excrement, Corey's gaze searched for any sign of the remaining female falcon. It was too far to see the nest clearly. "I wonder if she's deserted her nest to forage for herself and has abandoned the dummy eggs?"

"I'm glad we have the real ones safely away."

She smiled at him. "So am I. At least, the whole thing hasn't been a complete disaster. Now that we've been warned, they won't get away with another bird. We'll be ready next time. I'd love to have the chance to wrap the thief up in his own net."

Ross kept an easy smile on his face. So far, Corey had avoided giving him any definite information about the locations of the other nests. She was too shrewd for him to ask any direct questions. All he knew was that there were two other nests somewhere within a five-mile radius. Sweat beaded on his forehead and a sense of urgency descended upon him. Time was running out. He calculated that he must be away with the birds in a couple of days at the latest in order to have enough time to get them out of the country.

"Minna?" Corey called when they were still yards away from the tent. "Bill?"

A figure emerged from the flap of the tent, a tall, gaunt man with rounded shoulders. He had his back to the western sky, so it was difficult to see anything but a dark silhouette until they almost reached the tent.

"Who's that?"

"I think it's Jake, the volunteer who's paired off with Bill. What's he doing here?" Her usually soft voice was strident.

Ross searched her face. "Don't you like him?"

Now that Ross had posed the question, Corey realized that she disliked Jake Tewsbury. She gave a guilty laugh. "Jake's a male chauvinist through and through. We exchanged heated words before we were even introduced. He let it be known from the beginning that he thought women wardens were excess baggage in a program like this. He's given Minna and me a wide berth. No doubt he thinks it's our fault the tiercel was taken."

"He might have been the one to set up this particular aerie for the snatching. What do you think?"

"I guess if I had to finger someone in the group, it would be Jake. He's been flying falcons all his life. In his fifties, I would guess, but he doesn't seem to hold with all this research and recording business. He and Bill seem to get along all right, but then Bill's easygoing with most everybody. I don't know what Jake's doing here."

"I guess we'll find out soon enough."

The lanky man had begun walking toward them and waved a long arm in greeting.

Corey responded and tried to control the nervous fluttering in her chest. "Hello, Jake," she said as soon as they were close enough. "I didn't expect to see you here. This is Ross Sinclair, from the U.S. Fish and Wildlife Service."

Ross held out his hand, "Glad to meet you, Jake."

Jake's deep-set eyes were unsmiling, and he barely touched Ross's hand. Animosity vibrated like a tuning fork from the man.

"Where are Minna and Bill?" Corey asked quickly.

"At my site. This aerie didn't need two people, not with the tiercel gone and the female likely to take off any time, so I switched with the two young folks and let them watch the other pair."

"Then the female's still on her nest?"

"Yep, but she's not much of a hunter. Takes her a long time to find a feed and bring it back. She'll never be able to handle a brood all by herself. It's a good thing you took them eggs when you did. You got them to the lab, I reckon."

"Yes," answered Corey. "But we won't know for ten days or so whether or not they are going to hatch. I need to talk to the professor."

"He'll be heading back this way in a couple of days. In the meantime, Professor White said you were to check out a new sighting at the far end of the lake. Someone reported a pair of birds nesting there but couldn't tell whether they were peregrines or hawks. If they're falcons, that would make three pairs in this area. Quite a find."

"Or a haul," Ross added, watching Jake's face closely. He needed someone else to take the suspicion off his own activities. Maybe Jake was the informer for Mr. P. Tiercelli.

The man's narrow face was all sharp angles as he glared back at Ross. "What do you mean by that?"

"Three pairs of falcons would make it worth somebody's while to set up a series of snatchings in the next few weeks, don't you agree?"

Jake turned and spat brown juice on some rocks, and Corey realized that he had a chaw of tobacco stuck in his cheek. "Well, now, I wouldn't be knowing about that, but then that's your business, isn't it? The damn government can't keep its nose out of anything.''

Ross only smiled back. "Yep, a bunch of snoops, that's us.''

Jake ignored Ross as he gave Corey instructions on where to look for the new sighting.

Ross listened, silently praying that it was a pair of peregrines and not hawks. If they were falcons, he had a chance to lift them before any kind of monitoring was set up. "I could check out the sighting," Ross offered casually, "and report back. No need for Corey to make that long hike. She'd been concerned about the remaining female falcon and what will happen to it."

"Don't you worry your head none about this nest," drawled Jake. "I'll watch the falcon until she leaves.''

Corey threw a quick glance up at the cliff. How could she be sure that the falcon was still there? Maybe the female had already been seized and made ready for the return of Mr. Tiercelli. Jake could have set up the whole thing and was lying about what she was supposed to do, getting them out of the way on some wild bird chase. He could have talked Bill and Minna into exchanging sites, leaving him unsupervised at this one. How did they know whether there had really been a sighting at the other end of the lake? It was only Jake's word.

"I'll just take a peek at my lady," said Corey.

"I tell you, she's fine!" Jake swore under his breath but loudly enough for Corey to hear.

She ignored him and hiked up the slope to the blind.

"Damn fool women!" muttered Jake.

Ross's mind was busy trying to decide what course of action he should take. Spending precious time checking out a new aerie was a calculated risk. If the sighting was false, he would have lost at least another twenty hours. If there *was* another nest, he could be on his way out of the area with the precious falcons without anyone the wiser. Except Corey—unless he could convince her not to go.

When she returned, she nodded to Jake. "She seems settled enough for now. Maybe she'll stick around until we bring the chicks back. I guess there's nothing more to be done."

"That's what I told you," he growled.

"So you did, Jake," she agreed generously. "I guess you'd better stay here while I check out the new sighting."

"Unless you want me to do it," Ross offered. "Jake could get back to his own aerie . . ."

"The professor told me to stay here." Jake squinted at Ross. "And he wants Corey to check on the new birds. He doesn't take kindly to outsiders sticking their noses into the project."

There wasn't anything Ross could do. Corey repacked her bag, and soon they were retracing their steps. They talked little on the hike back to the lake. Ross set a rigorous pace, wanting to reach the cabin before sundown. Finding a pair of falcons before anyone else had a chance to put them under surveillance was the break he had been praying for.

"We'll have to spend the night at the cabin and be on our way first thing in the morning," he said, his mind racing ahead. If they found a nest, he could have the birds in his possession tomorrow night. If not— He stopped that line of thought. He didn't want to think about a contingency plan. Not just yet.

"It's going to be quite a hike around to the far point of the lake," Corey agreed. "Just think, maybe we'll find another pair of falcons."

"Or a hawk's nest," he reminded her.

"I'm optimistic." She gave a determined lift of her chin.

He laughed back at her, realizing with a poignant tenderness how beautiful she was. Feelings that he fought to deny threatened to overwhelm him as he looked at her. Her vibrant, passionate spirit made her a rare woman, the kind any man would be proud to claim. He'd never been attracted to anyone on so many levels—physically, emotionally and intellectually. She was a rare find, but she wasn't for him. Circumstances dictated that he would probably never see her again after the next nightfall or two. If there were falcons, he would have to get her out of the way, snatch the birds as quickly as possible and then be off with his precious cargo. He wouldn't let himself think about all the things that could go wrong. For his son's sake, he must make certain he didn't fail.

Corey felt his withdrawal. Once more, a deep uneasiness flickered through her. Ross had not wanted her to come. His suggestion that he check out the sighting had been casual enough, but by now she was attuned to hidden forces within him. He didn't want her company. For personal reasons? Or because of some hidden motive? She didn't know, but she intended to find out.

By the time they reached the rocky path leading up to the cabin, twilight had begun to fall upon the mountain valley. High peaks sent purple, possessive shadows across the lake, whose surface was already void of color. Several times Corey stumbled against an unexpected rock or rise in the ground. Luckily Ross had a small flashlight, which made a wavering circle of light as they climbed upward. At last, he swung open the door of the cabin.

They found it just as they had left it. The chill of the unheated room added to a coldness that had been invading Corey as a nebulous sense of uneasiness mounted.

Ross quickly laid a fire in the stove, and Corey started one in the fireplace. Wearily she sat down in front of the hearth and stared passively into the dancing tongues of fire. Even her well-conditioned muscles protested the hours of hiking that had taken her from the logging road around one side of the lake, up the canyon to the tent, back to the lake again and up the hillside to the cabin. She couldn't quite believe she was here. Her thoughts were still back at the nesting site, and she entertained a feeling that she shouldn't be here at all, that somewhere she had missed the direction signs.

"I don't know about you, but I've had enough hiking for one day," Ross said in a compatible tone.

She nodded, vowing that she would not allow her emotions to be manipulated by his charm and nearness. Some mocking voice reminded her that she needed to be made of stiffer stuff than she had been before.

"Are you hungry?" he asked, unloading some of the provisions he had bought in Lake City. "We're having my son's favorite dinner. Robin thinks peanut butter sandwiches are second to none."

It was unusual for him to make any personal reference to his son. Corey grasped at it as a sign that he was emerging from behind his protective bulwark. "Tell me about him, your son," she invited as casually as she could.

His mouth eased into a soft line. "You'd like Robin. He's a precocious three-year-old. Sharp as a razor, my unbiased opinion, of course. He has curly blond hair, deep blue eyes and a dimple that charms everyone at first glance. And what a chatterer!" He chuckled. "Talks your ear off. And the questions he asks. Keeps his daddy on his toes."

"Who takes care of him?"

"A woman who was a dear friend to my wife before she died. She'd give her life for him." His eyes flickered almost imperceptibly, as if in pain.

"It must be hard on you being away from him," she probed. She knew she was touching some sensitive wound and she hated herself for being so callous, but a surprising need to know all about him drove her. If she found his Achilles' heel, maybe she could understand him.

"I don't have a choice."

"How long were you married?"

"Five years."

"What was she like?"

"Elaine? She was a very nice person, sweet, caring. I met her overseas. We were good friends before we got married. Both of us were lonely and wanted a family. Good enough reasons for marriage. It's been lonely since her death. She was good company."

"And you haven't wanted to marry again?"

"I don't want to get married just to get married. Do you?"

"No." He was clever the way he always tossed the ball back into her court.

Corey sat Indian-style on the cot and leaned her back against the rough wall. They enjoyed companionable silences while they ate, now and then talking about childhood memories and vacation trips when the food had been memorable. They discovered they both liked all kinds of ethnic dishes, loved books and movies that ended with an uplift and preferred early morning to any other time of day. Like two skates fearing soft ice, they skirted deep feelings and stayed with a surface companionship. They smiled and laughed and sometimes just looked at each other.

"Do you come from a large family?" she asked.

He shook his head. "An only child."

"Me, too. I always hated holidays when I was growing up," she admitted. "Shooting firecrackers all by yourself is no fun, nor seeing what Santa Claus brought when everyone else in the house is still sleeping."

"Elaine and I wanted more children." The hurt was back in his eyes. "Robin is the most precious thing in the world to me."

Why did the confession seem to torture him and make the cords in his neck tighten? The tension was back in his body.

"Well, it sounds like we have another hike ahead of us tomorrow. No sense in both of us going to check out the sighting, Corey. You can stay here in the cabin while I hike around the lake."

The comfortable spell was broken. There it was again! An attempt to get rid of her. "No, I'll go with you," she said stubbornly. "If we do find another aerie, I'll stay there until the professor and Chester come."

His jaw was set. Silently he sighed. *All right, my lovely Corey. We'll do this the hard way.*

Corey took her nightclothes and went out to the privy. When she returned in her pajamas and warm robe, she found him stretched out in front of the fire, his eyes closed. She couldn't tell from his breathing whether he was asleep or not. For a moment she watched the firelight flickering on his bronzed face, and she felt a lump forming in her throat. She had the absurd impulse to kneel down beside him, lay her head on his chest and feel the firm rise and fall of his breathing. The longing to be close to him surprised her. If he had turned and looked at her, she might have gone to him. But he didn't. She slipped into her sleeping bag lying on the cot and turned her back to the fire.

Burning wood snapped and settled in the grate. Outside, a tree branch scratched against the side of the weathered logs. A night bird made a melancholy call to the moon. Darkness wrapped around the cabin like a cocoon.

"Good night," he said. His gentle voice startled her.

"Night." She held her breath, waiting, but he didn't say anything more. The distance between them could have been the width of the lake. She didn't understand him at all. Had she fallen in love with him? She hadn't felt like this with Matthew, none of this emotional confusion nor an aching need to be held close and loved. Ross had only kissed her once, and yet she felt stirrings of desire that mocked his indifference.

Ross was aware of her steady breathing and her warm body just a few feet from him. He lay on his back, stared wide-eyed at the roof of the old cabin and longed to go to her, but he knew such a weakness would only bring more pain. His emotions must be kept detached and razor sharp. He couldn't allow any feelings for Corey to alter his actions, not when the life of his son was at stake. She would hate him soon enough when she found out how he had deceived her. Under different circumstances, he would have welcomed her companionship and a loving relationship. If only he had met her at some other time, when he could have given in to his feelings.

She turned over, facing him. Her eyes closed, she sighed deeply, on the edge of sleep. Firelight flickered on her sleeping face, burnishing her sensuous lips and laying thickly lashed shadows on her cheeks. With every fiber of his being, he wanted to love and protect her. Cold sweat beaded on his body. What could he do to save her the heartache she would feel at his betrayal? Nothing. She was strong in her convictions that the law should be upheld. She never would condone his actions. She must not know what he was planning. He couldn't chance failure—not now, with time running out.

He turned his back to her. If they located a pair of falcons tomorrow, he had no choice but to manipulate her with the heartless expediency that the situation demanded.

Chapter Eleven

"You're tired from yesterday," he said, smiling warmly. "Why don't you take it easy this morning while I take a hike up to the other end of the lake and see what I can find." He hoped the suggestion sounded casual, for he did not want to alert her to the pressure building in himself. *If* he moved fast enough, he could have the falcons in his possession and be on his way before Corey or Professor White realized what had happened.

"No, it's my job to check out this new sighting. Since I've been relieved of one responsibility, I'd better find another."

"But Jake said that the professor wasn't certain it was a peregrine that they saw. If it's only a hawk, there's no need for both of us to waste the time and energy hiking to the other end of the lake."

"I doubt that Chester or the professor is easily mistaken," she countered. "If they thought it was a peregrine they saw, it's worth a hike to find out." Her solemn wide eyes underlined her determination that he was *not* going without her.

For a moment, he wondered if she was on to him.

She smiled and said, "You can't get rid of my company that easy."

"Not that I'd want to. You look very pretty in the morning." It was an honest statement. Her hair made a soft cloud of blond curls around her face. Her eyes, bright with the color of lapis blue, were thickly fringed, and he knew that her eyelids would be warm and soft under a gentle kiss. For a moment he was tempted to draw her close and bury his mouth in the deep crevice of her throat and taste the sweet warmth of her body. If everything went well, in a few hours there would be nothing but a memory of her loveliness left to him. He would have destroyed everything else.

A silence stretched between them. Corey saw the parade of expressions across his face, caring, wanting, and felt her own desires leap in response to his hungering eyes. Why didn't he reach out to her? What held him back? Anger and frustration swept over her. She wanted to know the truth and yet was afraid of it. "I'm going," she said flatly, breaking eye contact.

"Well, we can come back for our stuff if we locate them."

"No," she countered evenly. "We'll take everything now. We won't want to leave the nest once we find it, will we? Not with Mr. Tiercelli flaunting his cleverness. If one of our team is an informant, the smugglers will soon hear about the new sighting and be after this new pair. We ought to be prepared. I don't intend to let another bird get away so easily. This time I'm going to be on my guard and ready."

"And how are you going to do that?"

"Any way I can."

He knew it was true. She would fight viciously to keep anyone from touching another bird under her watch. She had become his most dangerous foe, and he couldn't think of any way around it. *Corey... Corey.*

"Well, if you're determined," he said. "Let's get on with it." He steeled himself for what must be done.

A light haze lay low upon the lake, and dew sparkled on diamond-tipped needles and grasses. An outcrop of rock that had tumbled into one side of the lake gave the body of water its crescent shape. They had a choice of climbing along the rocky promontory or following the lake's edge, which was like the hollow side of a new moon.

Corey tipped back her head and eyed the steep buttress. They'd have a hard climb to the top, and maneuvering along the irregular edge of the cliff would be treacherous. "The lake's edge looks like the best route."

Ross agreed. They could make better time along the bottom, he reasoned, and then make the climb upward if they were lucky enough to spot an aerie on one of the high ledges.

Corey had insisted that they bring everything needed to set up a camp and an observation blind. Ross had not dared argue for fear that she would realize he had no intention of remaining long enough to set up a warden post. To lull her suspicions, he had to keep up pretenses until the falcons were within his grasp. His greatest fear was that the professor and Chester had really been mistaken or had deliberately arranged for him and Corey to be sent on this wild-goose, or in this case, a wild-falcon chase. If that was the case, he would have lost precious time and been outwitted by someone on the team who had already marked another aerie for snatching. Ross's mind shuttled back and forth, weighing this possibility with another.

They picked their way over tumbled rocks that rose out of the lake. Ross's thoughts were cut short by Corey's sudden squeal and the splash of water. He swung around and saw that she had lost her footing. Fortunately, at this point, water in a shallow eddy was just above her ankles.

"Taking a bath?" he teased as he held out his hand and pulled her back onto the bank.

"Brr, the water's as cold as melted icicles," she said, laughing.

"Are you all right?"

"Yes, fine." She looked sheepish. "I got off balance, that's all. Just got my shoes and pant legs a little wet. Do we have to hike as if the devil's furies are after us?"

"I'm sorry. I didn't realize that I was setting such a demanding pace. Are you sure you didn't hurt yourself?" Her sudden fall had instinctively brought a tremor of fright up into his chest, and he had been ready to leap into the lake after her.

"Yes, but I'd better change my socks. I have another pair in my backpack." She sat down on a rock, and Ross knelt down and pulled off her walking shoes. He stripped off her thick socks, which were dripping with lake water. "My gosh, your feet are ice-cold." He took one slender foot into his hands and rubbed it, trying to get some warmth back into it. "Is that better?"

She nodded, trying not to show how his touch was sending peculiar tremors through her. The reaction had nothing to do with the recent ice-cold footbath. In fact, she didn't feel cold at all as he tenderly massaged each foot. His touch ignited every sensory bud on her skin, and her breathing quickened with expectation. When he looked at her, his eyes were hooded. He started to say something and then checked himself. The barriers were still there, she thought, half-angry at herself for expecting him to suddenly change.

He reached down and picked up her shoes. "These are wet."

"I'll change to my walking boots later," she said, putting them on.

He nodded. "We'd better keep moving. You go in front."

She struck out ahead, setting the same kind of grueling pace. She was furious with herself for the kinds of feelings that mocked her usual indifference toward men. She couldn't help but wonder if she was doing the right thing, going with him to follow up on the new sighting. Should she be going in the opposite direction, trying to find Bill or

Minna or locate the professor and Chester? She shivered in the warmth of the rising sun and recognized the emotions for what they were, fear and disappointment. Some nameless presentiment rode on her shoulders.

Reflected sunlight on the lake put a silver sheen upon the water. Early-morning crispness made everything new and bright, but the day's beauty was lost on Ross. His eyes and ears were attuned to one thing as he scanned the sky and high cliffs. No sign of any birds except for a few jays and an energetic woodpecker that was stabbing away at a fallen log at the edge of the lake. He flew away with an indignant flap of wings when they disturbed his breakfast.

Corey started when the woodpecker darted over her head, and she realized how tense she was. Maybe the professor and Chester had not seen any peregrines at all. If one of them was the informer giving information to Mr. Tiercelli, this could be a way of keeping her and Ross out of the way until the next snatching was completed.

She glanced back at him. "Coming?" she taunted, seeing that he had dropped back a little.

"I'm still here," he assured her with a wry grin. They had been searching the cliffs carefully as they passed, but failed to see the telltale sign of a nest. "Time for a rest?"

"Not unless *you're* tired."

He grinned. "Lead on."

Up, down, over, they picked their way along the steep talus, sometimes sending loose stones rolling down into the lake. The farther around the lake they hiked, the deeper it became.

"Careful," he warned her. One careless step could mean disaster. No shallow eddies here, but water so deep that the bottom was lost in murky shadows. Even a good swimmer could be overcome by the bitter ice-cold water in a few seconds. Ross stayed close to her, ready to grab her.

"I'm not going to fall," she snapped when she saw how he was hovering close by. "Watch your own big feet."

He chuckled and dropped back a little. "All right, Tiger. Get your claws back in."

His protective air rankled her. And so did some other things. He hadn't wanted her to come. She knew that. Even though he had been casual about the whole thing, there had been an intensity about him that alerted her on some level of intuition. When he suggested that she stay behind, she entertained a sickening certainty that once he walked out of the cabin door, she would never see him again.

Suddenly she screamed, "Look!"

Ross saw the bird at the same time. A dark speck floated in the air at the far end of the lake. Both of them raised their binoculars.

"What is it?"

Ross swore. The bird had already swooped and disappeared. They searched the sky but were unable to find it again.

"What do think?" Corey asked, excitement bringing color into her tanned cheeks.

"I don't know. It was too far away to get any markings. It could have been a peregrine or a hawk or an eagle."

"Did you see where it went?" she asked.

"No, but it seemed to be heading for those cliffs, at the other end of the lake. It must be the same sighting that Chester and the professor had."

"We'll soon find out," she said eagerly.

"We'd better take frequent breaks so we can search the cliffs as we go. We might find the aerie closer than we expect."

With renewed energy, they increased their pace even though the rocky talus around the lake's edge became steeper and more dangerous. The excitement of having seen the suspect bird made them eager as they climbed higher, traversed rock ledges and made their way precariously along vaulting walls.

As they looked upward, the cliffs had the appearance of soft variegated cloth, but their texture was deceptive, thought Corey. The rocky terrain was sharp and craggy and treacherous. At one point high cliffs rose almost perpendicular from the lake's edge, and Corey and Ross had to turn sideways and press up against the sheer rock face as they made their way past that spot.

Repeatedly they stopped to search the terrain above, sometimes with only a narrow ledge for footing. Using their binoculars, they searched the high rock shelves. No sign of the white excrement with orangish lichen that usually marked an aerie.

Nothing. No falcon. No sign of a nest.

"We'd best stop for lunch," Ross said. The sun was overhead. The morning had gone. Fierce frustration, combined with his feeling that he was wasting precious time, caused a tightening in his empty stomach. He didn't have time to spend on an empty search. The bird they saw could have been anything. A hawk. An eagle. Anything but the falcon he desperately needed.

They dumped their gear onto a narrow stretch of smooth rocks that had fallen from the cliffs above. They ate in silence. Water lapped and sucked against the rocks. Wind rustled reeds and needles in a lazy summer song, and a warm sun bathed their faces.

Corey shaded her eyes with her hand as she looked across the lake and up at the sky. She blinked against the brightness of the scene and felt the stirring sensation of sun, wind and water. She turned to find Ross looking at her. The intensity of his gaze brought sudden breathlessness. Her heart felt tight in her chest, and her palms were suddenly sweaty. "What is it?" she said in a strained whisper.

"Corey," he began in an emotional, threaded tone.

He's going to tell me, she thought, suddenly frightened. Somehow she knew that there would be no going back, or on, if he confirmed her suspicions. There was so much about him that she didn't know, and she was afraid.

"Yes?" she breathed, unconsciously stiffening.

At that moment a rushing sound of wings came from a ledge almost directly above where they were sitting. High above, a blue-black peregrine launched himself into the air with short, brisk flaps of his wings. As he mounted upward, a white breast, malar stripes and yellow beak contrasted against the dark rock. In effortless movement, making leisurely turns and sweeps, he was a captivating study of grace and fluidity.

"It *is* a peregrine!" Ross breathed. "A male, I'll bet!" The tiercel was smaller and usually more agile than the female falcon. They watched in breathless silence as the bird went out over the lake and then made a fast dive into the rushes on the far side and rose with prey in his beak. In the next minute, he returned to the cliff, flying high above their heads. They heard his inviting "kaa, kaa."

"He's bringing home the bacon, as Minna says." Corey laughed.

"I wonder where the little lady is."

"There!" Corey pointed as a second falcon launched from a ledge. "She's going to meet him."

The flight of the two birds above them was poetry.

"Marvelous," Ross breathed.

In a captivating aerial ritual, the female rose to meet the tiercel. They circled each other, and in the last instant before they touched, the female falcon turned upside down and took the prey from the tiercel with her talons rather than her beak. Then the female dropped down to the aerie ledge and disappeared while the tiercel floated back over the lake. Corey had never seen that kind of food exchange before, and her chest was tight with delight.

"Beautiful," she breathed, her rounded blue eyes misty. The extinction of this magnificent creature was suddenly a personal loss. A few weeks ago, she would have laughed at such emotion, but now all that had changed. She was personally involved and committed to the preservation of this endangered species. No one would get their hands on this pair, not while she had any breath in her own body. "The nest must be set back from the ridge."

"Yes," Ross said.

She was so happy she didn't see his expression imperceptibly change to one of calculated hardness.

"I guess we'd better figure out how to get to it."

Chapter Twelve

"Do you think we can reach the nest?" Corey asked.

"Of course," he said briskly. I have to, he thought as he let his gaze travel up the nearly perpendicular cliff.

"We may have to come at it from above," she speculated. The nest was located at the highest point over the lake.

That would take time. Urgency rushed at Ross. The first spiral of relief at having located the falcon dissipated in a realization that the aerie might not be reached from below, nor from above, nor from any direction. Falcons and eagles often chose inaccessible sites for their nests. Observing birds from a distance with binoculars was one thing, but actually getting close enough to set a snare to trap them in their nest was another. He couldn't set a mist net out in the open as the other smuggler had done. His approach must be different, because he had to have two birds, male and female—and the only way to get them both was from the nest! He knew that locating a pair of falcons was only the first challenge. With Corey constantly at his side, the capture was going to be even more difficult. He hated to involve her in this. If only she wasn't so stubborn, things would go a lot easier—and safer.

"Do you think we should retrace our steps, maybe back to the cabin, and come at it from atop the ridge?" she asked.

"No," Ross said quickly. Too much time would be lost to go back and try a different route. He'd lose a whole day—a day he didn't have. The ransom deadline was getting closer with every passing hour.

"But there's no way to the top from here," Corey protested, frowning. "Not even if we had climbing gear." Why was he being so stubborn? The falcons weren't going anywhere. The access to the high ridge was less steep near the cabin, she thought.

He looked upward. From where they stood now, near the end of the lake, the cliffs overlooking the water were much higher and more treacherous. "Let's hike a little bit farther," Ross suggested. "See what we find around that next bunch of rocks."

Corey nodded, searching his face. Stress was written there. The lines around his eyes were deeper and his jaw was set. Illusive feelings stirred within her. She was both attracted and frightened by the intensity of deep emotions that seemed hidden under the surface of his outward composure. A few minutes ago, before they spied the falcon, he had seemed ready to come out from behind his mask. "What was it you were about to tell me?" she asked.

He looked at her questioning face and his expression softened. "Nothing important, Tiger."

"I don't believe you. What was it?"

"I was about to say something foolish, that's all. It'll wave. Right now, we have more important things to decide," he said, silently thankful that he hadn't given in to the urge to confide in her. In a moment of weakness, he could have blown his chances for lifting this new pair of falcons. Her joyful rapture as she watched the tiercel's flight mocked his foolishness. No, he'd be a fool to gamble that she would be willing to let him steal the peregrines. In any case, his feelings for her were too strong to make her an accessory in his infamous business. He must put everything else out of his mind now that they had located the aerie. He must snatch the falcons without Corey's knowledge or interference. But they had to find access to the nest.

They walked a short distance before they stopped and surveyed the high terrain again.

"The nest must be on that narrow scarp," Corey said, pointing upward to a steep overhang.

"I bet it's in the opening of that hollowed-out section in the wall of the cliff." He silently swore. "I don't think we could reach it from above even if we made it to the ridge over that spot."

"I don't think so, either. Looks like our only chance is from below."

"The ledge will be wide enough to walk on if we can reach it." He followed the ledge with his binoculars. "It seems to extend for some distance on both sides."

"If we could find a way up to it, we'd be in business," she agreed.

Real business, he thought as he studied the shelf in both directions. "Let's hike farther and see what develops. We can always work our way back if we have to." He prayed that the efforts to come this far had not been for naught.

As they climbed over rocks at the lake's edge, they kept their eyes on the clump of juniper that marked the aerie. It was almost lost from sight when they reached a deep rocky depression where layers of rock had split. In rainstorms, water rushed down this natural, steep culvert to reach the lake below. But at the moment it was dry. For several breathless moments, they both scrutinized it.

"What do you think?" Corey asked.

"I think we might be able to climb it, but I'm not sure that it would do us any good."

"Only one way to find out."

"Half of those rocks are loose, ready to fall." He turned and looked at the lake below, deep, dangerous and filled with jutting rocks. "If you fell—"

"I'm not going to fall," she answered shortly, annoyed that he assumed she would be the one to lose her footing. She glanced at her wet pant legs and was angry at herself that she had lost her balance once before that day. She'd make certain it didn't happen again.

"No use both of us risking neck and limb only to find out that we can't reach the ledge from here."

Her eyes narrowed. Was he trying to leave her behind again? "It looks promising to me," she argued.

"Try to be reasonable, Corey. You could wait here. If I make it to the ridge, I'll give a shout and you can follow," he coaxed.

She sensed there was something unspoken in his plan. "No, we'll both give it a try. You might need my help."

He tried to keep his expression placid as he thought, *she's going to stick to me like flypaper.* He shrugged. "Okay." He knew she was already resentful that he had tried to leave her behind in the cabin. "We'll have to climb on all fours. I'll go first. Test the rocks as we go." Once more he glanced downward to emphasize that a fall would send them crashing upon jagged rocks washed by the green-blue waters of the lake below. If something happened to her! He shoved the thought out of his mind. "Ready?"

She nodded. "Ready."

He saw that her face was flushed and her beautiful eyes wide with excitement. Suddenly her eagerness made him angry. He felt a deep sense of despair. How could he guarantee her safety? He needed to concentrate on the task ahead, not divert himself by concern for her well-being. "Please, stay here, Corey, and let me go. It may be a dead end before we reach the height we need."

"I'm going with you. All the way." Her velvet voice was firm and unyielding. It was a statement without compromise.

"You're the most infuriating, exasperating woman I ever met."

"Then we're a matched set. I've never met such a stubborn, pigheaded male." She grinned. "Now that we understand each other, let's go."

"Me first," he said, as if trying to stay an argument.

She made a mock bow. "Be my guest."

He felt his way upward, finding purchase for his hands and feet on the rugged incline. She was right behind him. Sometimes they dislodged loose rocks, and they could hear the stones tumbling down the slope to fall into the lake below. The sound was a chilling one, a warning that a falling human body could expect the same treatment. Ross kept looking over his shoulder to make certain she was safely behind.

Once, when they reached a ledge that jutted off toward the aerie, they followed it, only to discover they were still far below the scarp where the falcons were nested. Disappointed, they inched back to the draw and climbed farther up the treacherous cleft.

Neither of them dared look down. They stretched their necks to look upward, but they couldn't see how close they were getting to the ledge they sought.

"How you doing?" he asked when they paused to catch their breath. Her fair hair had drifted forward into curly bangs on her forehead, her cheeks were damp with perspiration. Gutsy! That was the name for her. Perched high on a treacherous piece of rock outcrop, she showed no sign of fear. She even laughed. "Fine."

"Are you secure?"

"Enough. But I don't think I'll stop and powder my nose."

"Your nose is lovely. All bright and shiny, like the rest of your face."

"Gee, thanks, you really know how to flatter a gal," she chided, blowing air at a dangling piece of hair in front of her eyes. She didn't dare loosen her hold on the rocks to brush it away. "How much farther?"

"Don't know," he said honestly as they began to climb again.

He feared that the rocky draw would run out at any moment. Urgency pounded in his veins. What if the aerie was inaccessible? A nervous sweat broke out on his brow that had nothing to do with physical exertion. Dear God, what if he had to start over at some other aerie with all the dangers that that would entail?

A few moments later, he swore. It was exactly as he had feared, the draw didn't go high enough.

"What's the matter?" she asked anxiously, trying to peer around him.

"No more chute." He looked upward. He could see where water had come out of the mountain and dropped to the crevice they had been following. Above the place where melted snow had spilled over the rocks, a sheer cliff like the walls of a fortress blocked off any chance to climb higher.

Ross couldn't see a way to mount the smooth, high boulders to get to the top. For a moment, he thought there was nothing to do but go back down the way they had come.

"I think we could maneuver to the left side," Corey said.

Ross turned his head and saw what she meant. A leap of excitement overrode his disappointment. Like a child's building blocks, the shelves of rocks were irregularly stacked. By mounting them carefully, they might be able to reach a flat promontory, which blended into a narrow drift of aspen and pine trees. They could walk along it, back toward the nest. With luck, they might be right in line with the ledge they sought. "Let's give it a try," he said eagerly.

"We'll climb up there and see if there's a way back down to the ledge where the nest is."

"Okay," she answered as if he had suggested a casual walk in the park. As they started moving again, she dared not look down or up. She kept her eyes on Ross's legs and feet and followed in the same pattern.

He eased out onto the first block of stone, moving slowly upward in a zigzag pattern. Each shelf was wide enough to stand on, but not continuous. Like steps built into the side of the cliff, the climb was easier than it had been coming up the draw. New hope spurted through him.

The sun was peering through white cottage-cheese clouds and beating hotly down on them. Steady exertion brought beads of sweat upon their brows, as they struggled upward step by careful step until they reached a place were they could pull themselves over the lip of the promontory.

"Hooray!" Corey gave a triumphant cry as she stood up and surveyed a narrow expanse covered with wild grass and straggly patches of juniper that had found a roothold in the rocky terrain. A short distance away, aspen saplings were fighting to maintain their ground from encroaching firs and pine.

"Now let's see if we are in the right place for accessing the aerie," Ross said eagerly. They walked along the edge, searching for the ledge with the clump of junipers that marked the location of the nest.

"There are the junipers." Corey laughed excitedly.

Even though they couldn't see the aerie, it would be easy to follow the ledge a short distance until they reached the spot where the falcons had their nest.

"Thank God," breathed Ross. "We'll camp here."

"And set up a blind on the ledge below," Corey said. She dumped the pack from her back and collapsed on the ground. "But let's rest first."

Now that the peregrines were nearly in his grasp, Ross was anxious to finish the nasty business. "Why don't you take it easy for a while? We can make camp later. I think I'll see if I can get a glimpse of our happy family." He waited for her to protest and was relieved when she just sat there and nodded.

"Okay." She watched him as he eased himself over the edge down to the ledge that ran around to the peregrines' nest. Then she lay back and gazed up at the heavens, her thoughts drifting and reforming like the nebulous clouds above. Every time she thought she read Ross Sinclair correctly, he broke the communication between them. Was it her, or would his attitude be the same toward any woman who tried to become a part of his life? Did he cling to his freedom like a wild falcon? Was he afraid of any kind of romantic commitment? He was the most fascinating and bewildering man she'd ever met. As Corey let her thoughts wander and stared overhead, fleecy clouds were hypnotic, and without realizing it, she began to relax. They had found the aerie. Professor White would be pleased. She and Minna would have a new pair to watch. Her thoughts drifted away and she dozed.

When she woke up, the sun was lowering behind the western peaks. "Ross," she called, sitting up. Where was he?

"Coming." His voice floated up from below. And then his dark hair appeared as he pulled himself up the lip of the cliff. He gave her a satisfied smile and threw himself down beside her. "Looking good. It's just as we thought," he said, his eyes glinting with satisfaction. "The nest is back under the overhanging rocks."

"And the female's sitting on eggs?"

"No. Both birds were preening at the edge, but there were broken shells around the nest."

"DDT! The eggs were too soft to hatch!" It was a familiar story. The birds absorbed the chemical into their bodies, which caused thin-shelled eggs to be laid. The pesticide had nearly wiped out the peregrine population. Even though DDT had been taken off the U.S. market, enforcement was weak and the birds were infected when they flew to southern territories in the winter. Maybe she should use her law degree to work toward new and better laws to protect endangered species. The idea was one that she put aside for further consideration. "The eggs broke when the birds sat on them."

"Yes, that's probably what happened," Ross said. "But most pairs will lay a second clutch." He couldn't believe his luck! If there had been eggs in the nest, catching the two birds together would have been difficult because only one would be on the nest at any time, but this way both birds were free to move as they wished. It was the best time for capturing both birds at once. He had watched them settling closely together and decided exactly where he could put the snare to get them both with one quick pull on the wire.

While Corey had been asleep, he had flushed the birds away long enough to suspend a collapsible snare over the spot where they had been sitting and then ran the release cord back to the place he had selected for the blind. If he could keep Corey that far away, she would never discover the trap he had laid. Early tomorrow morning, he would snare the birds and be on his way.

"We'll have to set up a blind so we can start recording," she said eagerly. "I remember how excited Minna and I were when we found four eggs one morning in the nest. We could hardly contain ourselves. Now I'll get to watch another pair and their chicks. I really felt cheated that day when you replaced the real eggs with dummy ones." She firmed her chin. "Nothing's going to happen to this pair."

Ross looked at her earnest beautiful face, and he regretted the pain he was about to inflict upon her. It was the last thing he would choose to do. Just being with her had brought a brightness into his life he had never known before. He had been lonely in a foreign country, thinking that his only happiness lay in watching his son grow. Even without Prince Amund's treachery, he had decided to return to the U.S. and raise his son in America. Now that option could be taken from him. If charges of smuggling were made against him, he could never come back to the States again. He jerked his thoughts away from this avenue of thinking.

"What's the matter?" she asked, watching the shadows on his face. "You don't think someone in the group will tell the smugglers about this new aerie, do you?"

"It's possible," Ross said honestly, knowing that he had to be a jump ahead of whoever had trapped the other falcon.

"They wouldn't dare."

He smiled at her fierce expression. "They'd think twice about it if they could see you ready for battle, Tiger." Then he quickly changed the subject. "My stomach says it's time for supper. That lunch we ate on the way is long gone. How about some grub?"

"What would you like?" she asked.

"I'll have red wine, a steak sandwich, French fries and hot apple pie," he said with mock solemnity.

"Coming right up."

He watched her lithe movements as she dug into their provisions. His chest tightened. For a moment he allowed himself the luxury of imagining her supple body curved next to his every night, her lips and eyes warm and teasing as her touch fired his desire. He had not wanted a woman to share his life after he'd lost his wife, but that was before he met Corey McCalley.

"Hey, this isn't what I ordered," he chided as she handed him cheese, ham, bread and an apple. "Where's the wine?"

She gave him a canteen. "Room service isn't all it should be."

"But the view can't be beat." He pulled her down beside him.

They ate in companionable silence. Ross filled his spirit with the panoramic scene, like a miser hoarding the memory. He sighed.

"What is it?" she asked in a soft husky voice. "You have that haunted look that fades the color from your eyes."

"Right now, sitting here, with the world at our feet, and your nearness filling my senses, I feel pain, joy and regret."

"Pain? Regret?"

"Happiness can be a torturous thing." Looking at her, he could feel the wanting, the desire, the need to take her in his arms and make love to her. If only she wouldn't look at him like that, with her azure eyes warm and inviting, her lips curved and soft. He should get to his feet right now and break the current that flowed between them. But soon he would be gone and she would know him for the thief he was, and the love in her eyes would change to disbelief and then to hate.

"Please, tell me what it is." She lifted her hand and stroked his cheek. "Down there by the lake, you were about to tell me something. What was it?"

He fought an overwhelming urge to confess. If she knew the whole story, would she compromise her own integrity and help him? She might. He knew that she was attracted to him, but he didn't know how deep her feelings went. But even should she decide to help him, if they were caught, her future would be ruined. Her career as a lawyer would be washed up. No, he couldn't chance it. He couldn't put that kind of burden on her. "I was just going to tell you what a great gal I think you are. And that I hope whatever choice you make about your career is the right one."

The polite good wishes were a mockery to any honesty between them. His mask was back in place. Obviously he had changed his mind about confiding in her. He was a stranger. Her heart lurched with sudden uneasiness. In a neutral tone she said, "I guess it's time to turn in for the night."

He nodded. "I'll get a fire going."

In silence she settled herself in her sleeping bag. Closing her eyes, she turned her back to him and the small fire.

Ross watched the fire for a few minutes, then he walked over to the edge of the cliff and looked across the lake. Night was coming fast as twilight seeped into the mountain valley. The smooth water on the lake reflected a prism of colors from the sky's fading evening tapestry. Even as he watched, the pastel pinks and soft peach tones faded into tones of dull gray. As his gaze swept across the shimmering lake, a movement caught his eye.

His heart lurched. Hastily he reached for the binoculars hanging around his neck and leveled the glasses at a black moving object.

A rowboat! Headed toward the other end of the lake where the cabin stood.

A nervous sweat beaded his brow. Who was it? Authorities or the other smugglers? It didn't matter. Whoever it was spelled danger. Thank God, night was falling fast. Come daylight, he would have to be up and gone,

His time had run out.

Chapter Thirteen

At the first gray light of dawn, Ross eased out of his sleeping bag. He had placed it far enough away from Corey and close enough to the shelf so he could move without disturbing her. He was fully dressed and ready to carry out his plan. All night, urgency had built within him. Other people were in the area, the authorities, smugglers or members of the research team. It really didn't matter. They all spelled danger. He had to act now, take the pair of birds coldly, efficiently and without concern for anything but success. Until he had the birds in his grasp, Corey must not know what he was going to do. He slipped on a dark blue windbreaker over his plaid shirt.

Dull light was easing away dark shadows of the night. The lake below was still obscure, and silhouettes of surrounding mountains were still black against the sky, but there was enough light to show him where to put his feet on the ledge as he eased over the side of the cliff. He was glad that he had everything in place. There had been a tense moment once when Corey decided to take a look at the nest. Fearful that she would see the snare he had set above the nest, he had successfully distracted her, hating himself for coldly manipulating her. If only he could get the birds and be gone before she realized his intent. He wasn't certain how he would deal with her if she challenged him. Nothing could get in his way now—not even a courageous, beautiful tiger who sent his pulse racing.

He moved stealthily along the ledge, cursing a loose rock that went spinning out from under his feet. His moving figure was only another shadow on the face of the cliff. The first pearly light was just touching the mountain peaks, but the valley was still in dark shadow. He knew that falcons didn't fly in the dark, but once daylight heralded morning, they often took to flight early. He had to have them in his snare before that happened. He stooped over and ran his finger along the ledge, searching for the wire that he had stretched back from the nest. One jerk on it and the wire cage would fall.

Where was the trigger wire? He was certain that he was in the right spot on the ledge. Precious moments were being wasted. The birds were moving, he could hear them rustling. The sky was getting brighter every second. A shaft of color broke over the mountains. Daylight! Then he saw the silver glint of the wire only a couple of feet in front of him. He moved quickly. Too quickly! He flushed the birds from their nest.

With a swish of wings they took off. Ross watched them helplessly as they shot higher and higher, floating in circles over his head. He had blown it! No telling how long it would be before they both came back to the nest again. Meanwhile, precious time would be lost—and he would have Corey to deal with. And no telling who else. A coil of anguish twisted his stomach as he made his way back to where they had camped.

Corey stirred. "Is it morning?" she murmured sleepily, hearing his movement. She burrowed farther into the down sleeping bag and peered at him over the edge of it.

"Just. Stay where you are. I'll get a fire going. Coffee coming up." He was surprised how normal his voice sounded when frantic thoughts raced in his head. He'd have to lift the birds as soon as they were both on the nest again. When would that be? And what would he do with Corey? He couldn't let her see the snare. She looked so damn lovable, all cuddled down in her sleeping bag. He wanted to take her in his arms and delight in the warmth of her supple body. He'd never wanted a woman so much. How could he be a traitor to her?—and yet he must. He turned away angrily.

In a few minutes, she was dressed in cords and a red turtlenecked pullover whose long sleeves felt good in the early-morning air. She laced up her hiking boots near the fire and let the poignant wood odor fill her nostrils. "Why are you up so early?" she asked Ross.

"Couldn't sleep."

She looked up at the cloudy sky. "I think it's going to rain," she said solemnly while her eyes twinkled at him. "We might have to spend the whole day in the pup tent."

She expected some flirtatious answer, but it didn't come. She had seen the flicker of desire in his eyes a moment before when he had looked down at her in the sleeping bag. And then the softness had been instantly snuffed out. He was holding himself in tight check. She asked herself why and didn't like the answer.

He looked up at the overcast sky. "I hope not." No smile curved his lips as he handed her a plate. "It's early yet, the fog will probably burn off."

She suddenly felt cold, and it didn't have anything to do with the chilly morning.

Ross squatted near the fire and drank his coffee. His thoughts were obviously miles away from her.

"What's the first order of business?" she asked in a neutral voice. "Setting up the blind?"

"Good idea," he said readily, as if he had just thought about it. "We'll need some supports for the canvas. Do you think you could scare up some?"

"Here?" She looked around the narrow precipice.

"No, up there. On the slope. See that stand of spindly aspen? Their flexible branches would make a good frame. Think you can handle a Boy Scout ax?"

"I've handled a few in my day."

"Boy Scouts?" he teased.

"Those, too." She felt her mood lighten. "How many supports will we need? I think Minna and I used six or seven to make ours."

"A half dozen ought to do it. I'll get the other things into position."

"We'll have to set up shifts, watching the peregrines. The way Minna and I did. Unless you like cozy quarters with two of us behind it?" she teased boldly, waiting to see how he would react.

"We'll see," he said evasively. "We'd better hurry in case it does rain." His tone was unmistakably urgent.

"The birds aren't going anywhere. No need to knock ourselves out."

"The sooner we work, the sooner we play. Isn't that the way it goes?" His smile was forced.

"I don't know how it works," she said, looking at the face of a stranger. Distant. Calculating. And tense. "What's the matter, Ross?"

"Nothing, I just—" he began.

He was going to lie to her again. "Never mind," she cut him off abruptly. They finished their breakfast in silence.

Streamers of pink and melon orange made fluffy white clouds look like colored whipped cream. Against this pastel confection, two dark spots circled over the lake.

Corey saw them. "The falcons?"

"Could be," he said laconically.

"They're out early. Looking for breakfast, no doubt."

"I guess they found it. Here they come." He couldn't keep joyful relief out of his voice as the birds dropped out of sight onto the ledge. They'd come back to the nest—both of them.

Corey watched Ross's expression change as he turned to her. The spontaneous joy that had been there a second before was gone, now his eyes were distant. "We'd better get that blind in place," he said. "You get the saplings and I'll begin making a frame that will fit on that ledge."

She studied him. "All right. Where's the hatchet?"

He handed it to her and she strode away from the fire.

"Be careful," he called after her. Something in his tone made her turn around.

"I'm always careful," she said with a jut of her chin. Why was he looking at her like that? Why had he put up a wall between them?

As if braced against her unspoken questions, he turned away and disappeared over the edge of the ledge.

Corey made her way upward toward the stand of aspen some distance from the promontory where they were camped. She had barely started hacking the saplings when she caught the heel of her boot in the crevice of some rocks. She yanked her foot to pull it out, and the heel came off.

She sat down and viewed the exposed nails. The boots were an old pair. She should have known better. She took the boot off and tried to hammer the heel back on with a rock. No luck! She'd have to go back and change into her walking shoes. She hoped they were dry now after yesterday's dunking.

She limped back down the slope to their camp. A rolling haze covered the waters of the lake and gave the cliffs a ghostly look in the early morning. Visibility extended only a few yards down the ravine. The sun was making a valiant effort to pierce the morning clouds. Her spirits were suddenly as dank and leaden as the weather around her.

She tossed the boot away and listened to it tumble down the face of the cliff. As she quickly changed shoes, she cocked her ear and listened for sounds that Ross was busy on the ledge.

The stillness was oppressive. It brought a deep uneasiness within her. What was he doing?

Corey stood up, waited a moment and then walked over to the edge and peered down. As far as she could see, there wasn't any sign of a blind going up. Maybe he had decided to put the blind closer to the nest, she thought. A tingling apprehension made her chest tighten. She wanted to trust him. She wanted to turn away and go back to her chores. Instead, she let herself down over the edge and walked quietly along the shelf toward the rocky scarp that they had identified as the aerie.

She stopped when she saw him.

Ross was squatting on his haunches, his eyes fixed on the preening birds just a few feet away. The falcons sat close together at the edge of the nest. She had never seen a pair nuzzling this close before. They were fine specimens, beautifully colored, with healthy feathers and trim, supple bodies.

She was wondering how to share this exquisite moment with Ross when it was shattered, finally and horribly! With a lightning jerk on a wire, he released a snare. It came down, covering the birds, trapping them inside.

Corey's cry was lost in the screech of the birds.

Not knowing she was there, Ross leaped forward and wrapped a black cloth around the wire snare, putting the peregrines in darkness and stillness. The exuberance in his face was unmistakable.

Mentally, emotionally and physically, Corey was stunned. He had trapped the falcons! The knowledge was a shock to her whole system. She couldn't think. She backed up silently, wanting to scream and fly at him with her fists, but she knew that she couldn't physically challenge him. In any scuffle, he could easily throw her off the cliff. The man who

was busily putting a cover over the wire snare was a dangerous stranger. She had been played for a fool all along. How
he had deceived her!

"What'll I do?" The answer came as anger spilled
through her, motivating her to action. She had to get help.
Stop him before he got away. It was a long way around the
lake to his Bronco parked on the logging road. Someone
would help her to stop him before he got that far with the
birds.

She started down the uneven rocks, descending carefully
from one to the next. He wasn't going to get away with it.
She'd show him she wasn't the fool he thought. Rage poured
adrenaline through her numbed body, and she reached the
treacherous water chute that they had climbed from the
bottom of the lake.

A refreshing wind off the water tore at her tangled hair
and cooled her flushed cheeks as she slowly made her way
down the steep mountainside. All the time, her mind raced
with questions. Why would he do it? He had said money
wasn't high on his priority list, and she believed him. His
clothes and personal possessions like watches and binoculars were modest. No, it wasn't money, at least not for himself. Was it the challenge of trapping, like a hunter who
didn't need food but was compelled to track the illusive elk
or deer each season? She couldn't believe that. Look at the
concern he'd shown for saving the eggs. None of it made
sense. None of it!

She reached the bottom and started along the edge of the
lake. As she climbed over the rocky talus, she mentally re-
viewed the nightmare scene again and again. The snare had
been ready. It was obvious that his plan to trap the peregrines had been deliberate and well prepared. He must have
put the snare in position earlier, maybe while she had slept
yesterday afternoon. The knowledge brought fresh pain.
Sending her off this morning to get saplings had given him

he time he needed to get into position. He had thought she would be away for some time getting the sapling branches. f the heel on her boot hadn't come off, she would have been n hour at least. Long enough for him to get the birds and eave. What had he planned to do with her? The possibili-ies were too torturous to consider.

It all was clear to her now. He'd never intended to stay at his new sighting. It had been a pretense. All the time they ad been together, he had only wanted one thing—the per-grines. He had tried to leave her at the cabin, but she had /anted to be with him and had insisted on coming. Hyster-cal laughter bubbled up. What a stupid fool she'd been!

She felt anger rising in hot waves. It was then that she eard the soft plop of oars in the water. The muffled sound eached her ears and alerted her that there was a boat on the ake. She couldn't see clearly because of the morning haze. he sun was still only a smudge in the sky, and gray mist was loating low on the waters. Brushing away feathered bangs, he stared at the rolling mist until she saw a dark shape noving through the gray whorls toward the place where she ad just descended from the cliff. A boat! She could not see learly enough to even determine if there was more than one erson in it. Who was it? Then the answer was like an ar-ow to the mark. His accomplice! Ross had arranged for omeone to pick up the falcons.

Instinctively she ducked down, finding a hiding place mong some rocks and shrubs at the water's edge. As she unched and waited, she heard the sound of footsteps com-ig along the lake's edge from the direction of the cabin. Vas someone coming to meet the boat? The figure was al-nost by her before she glimpsed a pair of army boots. Her reath quickened as she peered through the thicket. It ouldn't be! Recognition was bewildering. Chester. There as no mistaking his light, bobbing figure.

Was he going to meet the boat? And Ross? Chester dis
appeared around an outcrop of rocks hugging the lake
Corey slipped out of her hiding place. Was his errand in
nocent? She had to know.

Low misty clouds gave an eerie, wraithlike appearance to
the shoreline, blending rocks and cliffs and water into in
distinct shapes. It was easy to remain undetected as she fol
lowed him. Was he the informer? The one who had wrapped
her up in the rug that day?

She heard voices, the sound of the boat hitting the shore
and then Chester's high-pitched greeting.

One question was answered anyway. Chester had come to
meet the boat. Who was in it? Authorities? Had her inquir
ies at the forestry office alerted someone, and had Cheste
come to meet them? If not the law, who? She would have to
know before she revealed herself. If the sheriff or ranger had
come, she would lead them to Ross. They would stop him
from taking the trapped birds. From where she cowered near
the edge of the lake, the voices that floated to her were
muffled, and the floating mist made their forms shadow
and indistinct.

One thing was sure, Ross would never be able to come
down the draw and get past them. Caution stilled the im
pulse to show herself. Mist swirled low over the water, and
as she moved closer, the men's conversation became audi
ble.

"I'm sure of the location," said Chester. "It's right u
there. A pair of junipers are growing to the right of the nest
I told Professor White that I thought they were hawks, bu
they're peregrines, all right."

"How do we get at them?"

"See that steep trough? It goes almost to the top. It's a
tricky climb, but you can make it. I checked it out myself
There's a flat promontory at the top and a ledge that lead
to the aerie."

She thought she heard someone walking away and was about to follow when the voices continued.

"Where are the girl and Sinclair?"

"Up at the sighting. They're probably still asleep. All cozylike." Chester snickered.

"We'll take care of them. Let's get on with it then."

Corey heard movement and she thought they were leaving, but as she darted a look, she saw Chester and a man standing next to him. She glimpsed a bearded face and a green stocking cap!

Mr. P. Tiercelli!

Her knees were suddenly weak. He actually existed. There he was, brazen as ever. The man who had taken her tiercel and flown it out of Lake City. Ross had not lied to her after all. There really had been a young bearded man wearing a stocking cap. Was he the one who had set the mist net and hit her over the head? Or was it Ross who had trapped the bird and really had been waiting at the water's edge to deliver it to an accomplice in a boat?

She searched her memory of that first day when Ross had carried her into the cabin. He had taken her shoes and left, and when he returned, he had a satchel of food that he could have easily exchanged for the one that had the falcon in it. She could see it clearly now. He had lied about someone shooting at him. Ross and Mr. Tiercelli were the smugglers, and Chester the informer! The funny little man had provided information about the aeries, including this one. As if to confirm her thoughts, she heard Chester whine, "I've done my part. I want my money."

"We haven't got all the birds yet."

"But you said I only had to show you where they were. I've told you about all the sightings."

"I know you have. You've done a good job, Chester."

"The money. I need the money you promised. Pay me now."

"The summer's not over yet."

"I can't do it anymore," Chester said with a rush. "The professor is tightening up the surveillance on all the aeries. After this pair, you won't be able to get at any of the others."

"Then we'll have to change our area of operation."

"I want my money now," Chester whined. "I don't like the way things are going. Somebody's going to find out. I'm not staying here any longer. And if you don't give me my money, I'll—"

"Are you threatening me, you little wimp? All right, have it your way. I'll pay you off. The way I did that greedy aerie warden in Idaho. Remember the one that got himself killed...."

"No, don't!"

Corey was so startled by Chester's frightened cry that her foot slipped and it made a loud crunching sound.

The man swore, "What the—?" He came crashing through the brush toward her.

She had no time to go back the way she had come. There was only one avenue of escape open to her and she took it. She clambered up the rocky draw she had come down just minutes before, this time with the bearded man at her heels.

She gasped for air as he scrambled upward.

He lunged at her. Missed.

She heard him swear, and his breathing was close enough to count every breath he took.

"You!" He lurched out a hand.

She felt his clutching fingers scrape her pants. The dangers of climbing so recklessly were outweighed by the man just behind her. If he managed to jerk her off balance, she would fall. The jagged rocks in the lake waited for her. She had overheard too much, and she knew he would never let her go unharmed.

The advantage was hers because she had been up the steep crevice before. She scrambled upward in a wild rush on all fours, kicking dirt and rocks behind her. "Ross . . . Ross," she cried, praying that he would intervene. The moments they had had together must have meant something.

Then she slipped. Her fingernails bit into the harsh ground as she tried to find purchase for her feet on the slippery rocks, but she kept sliding.

She screamed as he grabbed her. Twisting around, she struck out at the leering, bearded face under the green stocking cap.

He gave her a vicious shove. "Over you go!"

Desperately Corey hooked a leg around his in a kind of scissors hold.

Swearing at her, he jerked his leg free, but the movement left only one of his feet on the steep slope and it began to slip. Frantically he tried to regain his balance—but it was too late. Before she knew what was happening, his hands weren't on her any more. He made no sound as he dropped off into open air.

Corey clawed at embedded stone to keep from falling after him. Looking down, she saw him turn once in the air before he hit the lake. The mist had cleared enough for her to see him go under. She waited for him to come to the surface—but he didn't. Even from this distance she could see circles fanning out and then only slight ripples on the lake's surface as a green cap momentarily floated there. It had happened quickly and quietly.

Horrified, she searched below for Chester but there was no sign of him. He had probably bolted the moment the man had started after her. He would never come to her aid. He must have guessed she had overheard the conversation and was running like a scared hare to save his own hide.

"Well, look who's here," a familiar voice said sociably.

A voice from above jerked her eyes upward. She blinked to clear the hallucination. A man stood there, pointing a gun down at her from a ledge above. His eyes were bright blue, he wore a green stocking cap, and a smile flashed white in his sandy beard.

It couldn't be! She was going crazy! She had just seen Mr. Tiercelli fall to his death and here was another one. This one was alive and smiling.

Comprehension escaped her—and then she knew. She had heard three sets of voices. Two of them had been so much alike that she had been fooled. Two Mr. Tiercellis!

"Which one are you?" she croaked.

In a mocking flourish, he pulled the hat off his blond hair and jerked off the false beard. His white teeth flashed in a grin.

"Guess!"

Chapter Fourteen

Corey felt as if she were in the middle of some diabolical nightmare.

The handsome gunman grinned. "Delvin Cochran, pretty lady."

"You?"

"Surprise! Now get yourself up here." He motioned with the gun and kept it on her as she mounted the jagged, rocky shelves up to where he stood.

"But you can't be Mr. Tiercelli," she stammered foolishly. "The man with a beard and stocking cap left on the plane. And you were at the lodge."

He laughed. "You have to give Ma credit. She knows how to run the operation, all right."

"Trudi?" Corey gasped. That good-natured, friendly woman—running a smuggling ring?

"Too bad you two thought you could horn in. Ma was on to you from the beginning. All that smoke screen you tried to throw up about hunting for Mr. Tiercelli. You wanted a piece of the pie for yourselves. But the party's over!" He gestured with his gun. "Now get over there and join your partner, honey. He's kindly done all the work for us this time. The birds are caught—and ready for delivery."

She turned and saw Ross then, standing just a few feet away. He looked as if he might have jumped Delvin if the gun hadn't been leveled at her stomach. His hands were clenched and she could feel his rage vibrating from every pore. Like a cornered animal, he was waiting for a chance to attack. His eyes flickered over her, but his expression was unreadable.

Her eyes bit into his. "I saw you snare the birds. And I was going after someone to stop you."

"Why didn't you keep going?" Better that she be any place but here, courting bullets from a dangerous gunman. Her presence only added to an impossible situation.

"I heard a boat and then I saw Chester meeting someone. I thought you were going to give them the falcons. I had to find out what was going on," she said stiffly.

"That was your mistake." Delvin grinned. "He ain't one of us. Kind of a lone ranger, I'd say."

Corey knew Delvin's jeer was the truth. Ross wasn't one of the Cochran bunch, but there was no doubt that he was just as guilty. He was snatching falcons on his own. She couldn't bear to look at him. Thieves, all of them! "I get the whole ugly picture now."

Delvin laughed. "A lot of good it will do you, honey, to figure anything out. D.J. will be here in a minute after he disposes of our good friend, Chester."

Corey tried to hide a stiffening she felt inside. He was expecting his twin. Delvin must have left him at the lake, talking to Chester, and climbed up here where he knew the falcons were. Corey kept her face bland. Delvin didn't know that his brother had fallen into the lake and was probably dead.

Corey wished she could use his ignorance to an advantage, but she didn't know how. She wondered if Chester had seen D.J. fall into the lake. Even if he had, there was little chance that the nervous, guilty little man would run for help. He would want to cover his tracks and fast. If only she could tell Ross that the other twin was out of the way.

She moistened her lips. "Very clever—the whole setup. Chester was the informant, wasn't he? I overheard him demanding money. He's the one who's been telling you where the aeries were." She sent Ross a message with her eyes. If they could keep Delvin talking and distracted, Ross might be able to get the gun.

"Yep." Delvin nodded. "For five grand a pair, he was ready to spill his guts about every peregrine in Colorado." He chuckled. "Wimpy little guy. Scared of his own shadow. Must have needed money pretty bad."

"I heard him begging for his money."

"D.J.'s paying him off."

"Why kill him?"

Delvin shrugged. "He outlived his usefulness. We'll be moving on after this pair, anyway."

"You're leaving Colorado?" Ross asked following Corey's lead to keep him talking.

Corey felt the first flicker of hope. D.J. wasn't coming! There weren't two of them anymore. All they had to do was take care of Delvin. Then she'd take her chances with Ross. He was not a killer like this grinning gunman. She'd make some kind of a deal with him. He couldn't get away with the falcons. Not now. She knew him for the deceitful imposter he was.

"Will you be going back to Idaho?" Ross asked.

"Naw, we cleaned that out last year. Besides we had to waste a guy that got too nosy." He grinned. "Just like you two."

"I heard they're paying a hundred thousand dollars a mating pair," said Corey. "That's a lot of money, isn't it, Ross?" Her eyes searched his. *Is that why you did it?* she asked silently.

His face remained stony. Every muscle was tensed and his eyes were fixed on the gunman.

"Yeah, lots of money," agreed Delvin, "but it's getting harder and harder to find the damn birds. We're thinking about—" Then he caught himself. "Smart, aren't you? Pumping me like that. But it won't do you any good. We'll take the birds, and you two can take the fall for this little caper." He looked smug.

"Maybe not," Ross answered grimly.

Delvin laughed. "The sheriff was making inquiries at the lodge about a Ross Sinclair, questioning Paul and Helga about a fake identification card. He said that your pretty little girlfriend was in the office checking up on it."

Corey didn't look at Ross. The secretary in Lake City must have made the inquiry and confirmed her suspicions. The card was fake.

"Couldn't have worked out better," Delvin bragged. "The sheriff won't be looking for us. With a hint here and there, it'll look like you two were doing all the smuggling. Nice arrangement, don't you think? Thanks for getting this pair all ready to go. Hardly seems fair, but that's the way life is," he said. "You win some and lose some, don't you, baby?"

"She's had nothing to do with this. Let her go!" Ross demanded, as if the subject were open to negotiation. "It's me you want for the fall guy."

"Well, now, isn't that gallant? He's trying to protect you, honey. Looks like you've had a nice little love nest here." He smirked knowingly and nodded to the sleeping bags stretched out in front of the fire. He gave Corey a lewd grin. "Can't help but be a little envious. Never have enjoyed such fringe benefits on the job myself. Maybe you'd like to join our outfit so I can—"

"Shut up!" Ross growled. "Keep your smutty trap shut."

Delvin's smile faded. "Who's going to make me? I'm giving the orders."

"If you weren't such a coward hiding behind that gun, I'd take you apart with one hand. You look like a momma's boy to me. Couldn't knock the feathers out of a pillow."

Corey knew what Ross was trying to do, but it didn't work. Delvin wasn't going to prove he could take Ross without the gun.

"Save your breath, big mouth," he snapped. "I've got all the guts I need to pull this trigger and shut it for you."

"But that wouldn't be very smart, would it?" Ross taunted. "If you shoot me, someone will know there's been foul play."

"Not if we stage a murder-suicide. Lovers, you know," he jeered.

"You can't get away with three bodies."

"Of course, we can. Chester was the informer, you two did the snatching and the fourth partner got away with the birds! With a little help, they may even figure out that the one who got away could be your friend Paul." He laughed. "What a great scenario! Wait till I tell D.J." Then he sobered. "I wonder what in the hell's keeping him?"

"Maybe he got detained by the sheriff or the professor?" Corey offered impulsively. "They might be waiting at the bottom of the draw for you to come down. Or maybe Chester got the upper hand." She didn't know where she was going with the taunts, but she could hope that they were putting Delvin off balance. She could almost see his mind working—he didn't want to kill them with witnesses waiting for him when he descended with the illicit birds.

Ross picked up on her lead. "It doesn't take that long to climb up here. Something's gone wrong. You'd better—"

"Shut up! I know what you're doing and it won't work." His voice was strident, as his eyes darted wildly toward the edge of the precipice at the spot where the rocky chute began. He was listening for any sound that would tell him that his twin, D.J., was coming.

Corey exchanged frantic looks with Ross. How could she tell him that D.J. had tried to push her to her death and he had fallen instead? If he knew, he might use that fact to their advantage. Delvin was obviously uneasy about the time his brother was taking. Had her speculations confused him enough to make him wait before carrying out the murder-suicide? In the sudden silence, the absence of climbing feet was ominous. Only she knew that D.J. wasn't coming. How long would his twin wait?

Her answer came a moment later.

"We're going down! You carry the birds," Delvin ordered Ross. "If the authorities are waiting, I'll deliver the culprits into their hands and be a hero."

Corey saw Ross's clenched hands relax, and she knew that he was relieved to have gained some time. He picked up the covered snare, which Corey had seen him use to capture the birds. And then he threw it right into Delvin's face.

Delvin's hands came up instinctively, and Ross leaped for the gun.

They struggled on the edge of the precipice.

A dozen times she thought they were going over.

They rolled on the ground. Closer and closer to the edge. Then the gun spun out of Delvin's hand almost at her feet.

Before she could pick it up, Delvin's hand closed on a rock, and he brought it down on the side of Ross's head. Then he swung toward Corey.

She had the gun. It wavered as she pointed it at him.

He froze.

For a moment, she thought he was going to leap at her.

"I'll shoot. I'll shoot," she warned him.

Suddenly he spun away from her and disappeared down the rocky chute, running away.

She ran to Ross's side. He was trying to sit up. Blood was gushing down his face from a jagged cut. He wiped at it and his expression was befuddled.

"Where is he?"

"He left. I got the gun."

"Let's get out of here." he wavered to his feet.

"You're dizzy. You'll fall if you try to climb down."

He sopped his head with a handkerchief as he went over and picked up the wire snare with the falcons fluttering madly around in it. No time to check and see if they were all right. He'd have to chance it. "Put down the cage!" He turned and saw Corey pointing the gun at him. Her lips trembled, but her eyes were hard like steel.

"Corey, please."

"Let the birds out!" she ordered.

"You don't understand."

"It's pretty obvious even for my besotted brain. You cozied up to me to get your hands on the falcons."

"I have to have these birds." He took a step toward her.

"Stop. Or I'll shoot."

"No, you won't. I love you."

"If you loved me, you would trust me."

"It isn't that. I don't want to ruin your life."

She snorted. "Don't take me for a bigger fool than I am. And don't lie to me. You're doing this for selfish reasons of your own that have nothing to do with me. Why can't you be honest with me?"

"There's too much at stake. I can't take a chance. I don't want you involved."

"I am involved! I think I knew from the first that you weren't what you pretended. But I fell in love with you anyway. How can you leave me without telling me why you have sunk so low as to steal peregrines for money?"

"It's not for money." He took a step toward her.

"Don't!" She poised her finger on the trigger.

"You're not going to shoot me, Corey," he said softly. He ignored the gun, stepped forward and put his hands on her shoulders. "I don't have time to explain. I have to take those birds. And you have to tell the sheriff the truth—you know nothing about me. You'll be safe that way.''

"But I want to know why. You made such an effort to get the eggs to the laboratory. And then turn around and trap two falcons?''

"If the eggs hatch, I will have put some back into the environment for the pair I must steal.''

"Why do you have to steal them? If it's not for money? What could make you do that? Tell me. Now!''

"All right. I don't have time to argue. I have to save my son. It's the ransom I must pay to an Arabian prince.''

She laughed in his face. "You expect me to believe such a tale?''

"It's true!'' There was a dark fierceness in his eyes. "And I don't have any time to spare. My son may be killed!'' He took the gun from her hand. "I might need this. Stay out of this, Corey. Nothing is going to stop me from getting these birds.''

"Ransom? Falcons?'' Such a story was unbelievable. "How gullible do you think I am?'' she taunted.

"Gullible or not, that's the truth. I haven't got much time—so listen! I'm an engineer, and I've been working in Arabia on an irrigation project. The Arabian prince of that province abducted my son and his nanny, and ordered me to bring him two North American falcons as ransom for their lives.''

Her eyes widened and she repeated incredulously, "An Arab abducted your son? And you have to give him a pair of mating peregrines to secure his release? That's crazy!''

"Yes, but if you knew Prince Amund you would know how deadly serious his threats are. He's a fanatic when it comes to falconry. He's decided that he wants to breed peregrine falcons. And he's an impatient man. If he doesn't get what he wants in five days, he will carry out his threats against my son. Nothing, or no one, is going to get in my way. I've got to get these birds to Prince Amund before my time runs out. Now get out of my way, Corey." He picked up the snare.

"Why don't you go to the authorities? Let them handle it."

"Red tape, that's why. I know how the government handles things. Nine times out of ten, they goof up! It takes months, even years, to accomplish anything. My son's life is at stake. I'm not handing his safety over to a bunch of bureaucrats!"

"But what are you going to do?" Her own chest was suddenly tight.

"I have the falcons. I've got to get out of here."

"I'm going with you."

"No!"

"You can't stop me," she flared. If the fantastic tale was true, he needed all the help he could get.

"For heaven's sakes, Corey. I don't want you involved."

"You're an insufferable chauvinist! Keeping this all from me. As if I wouldn't understand. Why didn't you trust me?"

"I couldn't. If something goes wrong, you could be charged as an accessory. Your reputation would be ruined. I couldn't take that chance.

"Well, you don't have any choice now."

"Wait! Corey—"

She brushed by him. "Let's go."

He didn't have time to argue with her. "I'll go first. The twins may be waiting for us at the bottom."

"I don't think so. D.J. fell into the lake chasing me up the draw."

"My God, you could have been killed."

"I wasn't. Now, we only have one to deal with."

They descended slowly. Ross's tense gaze searched below with every step. He had the gun ready, but they reached the bottom without incident.

"The boat's gone," Corey said. "No sign of Delvin—or
D.J." She feared that D.J.'s body might be spread in full
sight at the lake's edge, but it wasn't. A green stocking cap
in some rushes was all that remained.

Gentle water lapped innocently against the shore. The sun
had finally dispersed the heavy morning fog, and visibility
was bright and clear.

"Guess Delvin took off." Ross let out his breath in relief. He had to get the birds to the Bronco as quickly as
possible.

"Chester might have gone for help," Corey warned Ross
as he set a steady pace around the lake's edge.

"I doubt it," Ross said grimly. "He's not going to blow
any whistles on himself."

"What are you going to do now?" she asked as they
worked their way over the rough terrain.

"Take the birds to the Bronco, drive to Denver and con-
tact a man named Kashan. He's a countryman of Prince
Amund and has a private plane that will fly me to New
York. The prince's jet will be waiting there."

Now she understood so much about him. The deep pain
in his eyes, the tension that radiated from him. She felt
guilty for having reported him. But it was his fault. If only
he had been honest with her instead of trying to protect her.
She couldn't help but feel a sense of relief now that she knew
what lay behind the mask he had presented to her. Ross
didn't take any rest stops, and they were both breathing
heavily when they came in sight of the cabin high on the hill.
He suddenly pulled her down beside some rocks.

"What is it?" she gasped.

"We have company."

They could see three uniformed men going into the old
cabin perched above them.

"What'll we do?" she whispered. They couldn't go forward without the risk of being seen. They'd be clearly visi-

ble as they rounded the edge of the lake. If they retreated, they would have to go all the way back and around the other end of the crescent-shaped body of water.

"Damn," Ross swore. "I suppose the ranger's office alerted the sheriff."

"You should have told me," she lashed out.

"No help for it now."

"I'll keep them busy so you can get away," Corey said, quickly making up her mind. "I'm the one who got the authorities involved."

He started to protest.

"Your son, remember?"

How could he refuse her help? Without it, he might be delayed long enough for his plan to collapse. He didn't want her involved, but now he had little choice. "Corey, darling, I—"

"Don't say anything. I want to do it."

"It could ruin everything for you," he warned.

"I can handle it. Don't worry about me."

"You're unbelievably courageous—"

"And stubborn—and a few other things." She put her hand on his cheek. Then she kissed him. "For luck," she said in a husky tone.

"I love you, Tiger," he said.

"I know." Her voice wavered, but she gave him a saucy smile and then walked away.

Ross watched her lithe form move up the hillside. In the next minute, she had disappeared into the cabin. Would she be able to keep the men there long enough for him to get away?

He took a deep breath and spurted around the tip of the lake, running as fast as he could until he reached a band of trees. Once hidden by the thick conifers, he caught his breath and then started hiking upward toward the logging road.

So far, so good. His mind raced ahead. Once he got to the Bronco, he'd take the logging road to the highway, and then north to Denver. As soon as he reached the city, he would alert the prince's contact that he was ready to leave. This part of the plan had been arranged by Amund. The prince told Ross that Zaki Kashan was a merchant countryman whose company had offices in Denver. He would provide a company plane to fly Ross and the falcons to Kennedy airport. From the way Prince Amund talked about his friend, Ross was certain that they had been nefarious partners in similar affairs, which involved circumventing national laws. Birds of a feather, Ross had thought when Amund gave him Kashan's card with a telephone number on it. In New York, Ross would make a quick transfer to the prince's private jet, which had brought some Arabian diplomats to the United Nations. Ross brought his thoughts back to the present. He was glad he had taken the time to hide the Bronco in dense undergrowth. He prayed that the authorities hadn't seen it.

A swift movement through the trees alerted him a second before it happened, but he was not prepared for the commando leap from behind.

"What—?" he gasped as a flying body landed on him. His assailant knocked the bird cage from Ross's hand and pressed his foot against Ross's neck, forcing his face into the dirt. There was no way Ross could raise the gun he had been carrying in his hand. Desperately he pulled up a leg and lashed out with his foot.

He struck soft flesh.

His attacker cried out in pain. The pressure on Ross's neck slackened for a moment.

Ross twisted around. He was halfway to his feet when a boot caught him in the chin. Ross staggered backward. Pain shot from his jaw into his ears. His knees gave way and he went down. A hard object bit into his chest. He had fallen on the gun. He maneuvered an arm under him and grabbed it. He jerked over onto his back and pointed the gun upward, firing wildly.

Delvin staggered back, clutching his arm where the bullet had grazed him. Ross raised himself up on one arm. "Hold it!"

The twin ignored the order, turned and fled into the woods.

Ross staggered to his feet, took one step after him and then stopped. He didn't have time to chase Delvin Cochran. It was a loose end he would have to leave alone and hope that it didn't unravel on him later.

Chapter Fifteen

When Corey came into the cabin, three men were going through the few things she and Ross had left behind. All of them turned toward the door at her entrance, and the expression on their faces was about as reassuring as a wolf pack's would have been.

"Looking for something?" She put her hands on her hips and tried to look indignant. "That's my stuff you're pawing."

A stocky middle-aged man wearing a badge stepped forward. One bushy, unruly eyebrow raised as hazel eyes looked steadily into hers. An ample stomach hung over his western pants, nearly covering a huge turquoise belt buckle fastened at his thick middle. A Teddy Roosevelt mustache should have made him look a little comical. It didn't. There was something poised and waiting about his expression that was not the least bit humorous. "And who may you be?"

"Corinne McCalley. I'm one of the university aerie wardens." She kept a level contact with his unsmiling eyes. "May I ask who you are?" She used her counselor tone, which was polite, firm and businesslike. It certainly didn't reflect the breathless tremors that threatened to catch in her throat.

"Sheriff Wooten. And this is Deputy Diele, and Ranger Emory. Now that the formalities are taken care of, maybe you'll be kind enough to answer some questions."

"On what subject?" she parried, determined to stretch out the conversation as long as possible. She wanted to give Ross as much time as she could to get on the other side of the lake and away in his Bronco.

"Miss McCalley?" A young man wearing a ranger's uniform stepped forward.

"Yes."

"I'm Clyde Emory. My secretary said you were in the office the other day asking about a Ross Sinclair?"

Corey nodded, cursing herself. She should have trusted her instincts about Ross. If only he had leveled with her from the very beginning. But what would you have done? questioned a contrary part of herself. The answer was simple. She didn't know. She probably would have tried to talk him out of going outside the law, but it was too late for that now. Her feelings were no longer detached and rational. She realized that she loved him. She had to protect him at all costs.

"Glad to meet you, Mr. Emory," she said cordially, giving him a warm smile.

The ranger's eyes flickered over her. "Likewise, I'm sure."

Deputy Diele stepped forward. "Hi." Black eyes in a young face smiled at her. "Are you really the daughter of Patrick McCalley?"

She laughed. "Yes."

"Gosh. You've been to the White House and everything?"

"A few times."

The sheriff gave his youthful deputy a silencing glare. He turned to the ranger. "Tell her, Emory, what you found out."

"Oh yes." He cleared his throat. "Well, Miss McCalley, we checked out Sinclair and found out his name is not on the register. The identification card he showed you must be fake. He is not a U.S. wildlife ranger presently assigned to Colorado, or anyplace else. I notified the sheriff, thinking this was something he ought to look into."

"I'm sorry. I made a mistake," she said quickly.

"A mistake?" Emory echoed.

Corey's mind whirled in a devil's wind. Why had she ever gone into that office! This was all her fault. If she hadn't alerted the authorities, these men wouldn't be here. The sheriff was watching every flicker of her eyelashes. She had to be careful.

"What kind of mistake?" he demanded.

Corey took a deep breath. "Well, you see, I misunderstood Ross. He said that he *used* to work for the wildlife service. Now he's a volunteer just like me." She gave an embarrassed laugh. She knew the sheriff would check the statement with Professor White, but it would take some time to find out he wasn't a member of the team, and time was the precious commodity she was trying to give Ross.

"And you've been working with Ross Sinclair?" asked Emory.

"Yes. We had some eggs that we had to get to a laboratory at the university of Colorado. Professor White asked us to take them to Lake City and put them on the plane." Smiling at the ranger, Corey launched into a detailed description of the program to put peregrine falcons back into the wild. She rambled on for several minutes, covering everything from how the eggs were arranged in the incubators to a detailed description of fledgling boxes used to feed young chicks until they were big enough to forage for themselves. She explained that falcons didn't mate until they were three years old. "With the number of maturing falcons we have in our breeding chambers, plus this year's increase in young, we expect to have—"

"This is all very interesting," the sheriff said impatiently, cutting her off. "But where is Mr. Ross now?"

"Oh, he's around the lake somewhere, checking out a sighting. Someone reported the possibility of another pair of falcons near the lake but we haven't been able to find anything," she lied, her mouth dry. "Jake, one of the aerie wardens, told us that Professor White wanted us to search for another aerie. We're hopeful that there may be another pair of falcons nesting in this area. But, of course, the birds that were seen could be hawks or eagles. Ross is checking it out."

"And why aren't you with him?"

"I came back to the cabin for a few things while Ross continued the search."

"I understand that you reported a bird-snatching the other day, Miss McCalley?"

She nodded. Her deeds were coming home to roost.

"How did they do it?" the eager deputy asked, his eyes sparkling with excitement.

"They set a trap, up on the bluff," she said, an idea stirring in her brain. If she could lead these three in the opposite direction from the logging road, Ross would have a better chance of getting away without detection. "The smuggler used a mist net and some pigeons for bait. Let me show you the place. Maybe you can pick up some clues there."

"I think we'd better talk to this Ross Sinclair first," replied the sheriff. He hooked a thumb over his low belt.

"I don't see why. I can tell you everything you need to know," she said with a smile. "Don't tell me, Sheriff, you're one of those males who won't take a woman's word for anything?"

"I've learned to check on everybody's story, Miss Mc-Calley. No offense intended."

"Well, Ross'll probably head back here after he's checked out a couple of spots," Corey responded as casually as she could. "Why don't you take a look on the ridge while you're waiting, Sheriff? The scene of the crime, and all that. I can show you the exact spot. Maybe the smuggler left something behind."

"Sounds like a good idea to me," Emory said.

"Me, too," agreed Diele, smiling at Corey. "We could have a look around and see what we can come up with."

"I'd really love to catch these guys," said the ranger. "We've had warnings to be on the lookout for them, but I never thought they'd show up here in my district."

"How far away is this bluff?" asked the sheriff.

"Just up the side of a hill that slopes down to the lake. Not far."

"You're sure this Sinclair fellow won't be back for a while?"

"I'm sure," she said without blinking.

"All right. Let's have a look. Diele, you stay here in case Sinclair comes back while we're gone."

Diele's youthful face fell. It was obvious he wanted to stay in Corey's company.

"And don't let this Sinclair guy get away," warned the sheriff. "I want to talk to him."

His deputy nodded. "Yes, sir. He won't go nowhere."

Corey gave him a warm smile. "Bye. Tell Ross we'll be back shortly."

"Sure enough, Miss McCalley." The deputy almost tipped his hat.

Corey glanced across the lake as they came out of the cabin. No sign of Ross. He must have made it into the thick drift of trees on the other side. She allowed herself to breathe a little easier.

Chatting away, she began telling her story as they walked. "I was below, watching the nest from a blind, and I saw the tiercel take off. I knew he was going hunting. He disappeared over the ridge above the nest." Talking all the time like a pied piper spinning a tune, she led them away from the cabin and up the hill to the high plateau where the mist net had been set out.

At the top of the promontory, she pretended to lose her bearings and took them in a wide circle for nearly half an hour before she finally led them to the feather-marked spot where the Cochrans had staked out the pigeons and captured the tiercel.

She was complimenting herself on her delaying tactics when the sheriff touched his mustache and settled perceptive eyes upon her. "We stopped at the lodge before we came up here. Paul Hines showed us a mist net that was found half-buried near the stable."

She felt her stomach tighten.

"One of the guests, Trudi Cochran, said she had the impression that you and Ross Sinclair were in some kind of conspiracy together."

"Really?" She gave a false laugh.

"It's funny, Miss McCalley, but you're giving me the same kind of impression."

WHEN ROSS REACHED the Bronco, he transferred the peregrines into two small cages he had ready. The birds seemed to have weathered all the rough treatment without injury. Healthy falcons, he thought with satisfaction as he zipped a cover over them. With good care, they ought to be able to make the journey all right. He knew that they would not eat for a day or two after capture. By that time, he would have them safely in Amund's hands.

Ross sent the four-wheel drive careening down the rough, twisting road, now familiar to him because of his previous trips. One part of his mind tended to the driving while the other wrestled with the problems that lay ahead. He anticipated what he would do once he reached Denver, working the plan through in minute detail.

He worried about Corey. What was happening to her? He knew that she was brave and shrewd—maybe too much so for her own good. He hoped she would be able to keep herself free of any suspicions. It was a good bet that the authorities had arrived to do some investigating.

Suddenly his thoughts were jerked back to the present with a jolt as he glimpsed a movement on the switchback road far below. A glint of sunlight reflected on a windshield. Another vehicle coming up the road toward him. It would reach him in a couple of minutes.

Ross braked to a stop. If he didn't get off the road, he'd meet the other car front to front in just a couple of minutes, a risk he couldn't afford to take. He swore as his frantic gaze swept in every direction. A high bank of dirt on one side of the road and a thousand-foot-drop-off on the other. No way to move off the road in either direction. He was trapped on the narrow shelf of road with scarcely enough room for two cars to pass and no chance of concealment.

Ross looked out the back window and shoved the car into reverse. At a reckless speed, he began backing up. His mind had been so filled with other things that he had been paying only peripheral attention to the terrain. He couldn't remember whether or not the road had widened at any point where he could pull off into the undergrowth. He had to find a hiding place. Any delay now for any reason would be disastrous.

He rounded a couple of curves driving in reverse, but he failed to find a wide spot where he could hide the Bronco in the trees. The logging road clung to the side of the craggy mountain, and its edge was weak and jagged where part of it had fallen away. No place to pull off.

Ross's mind raced and in desperation formed a new plan. He stopped the four-wheel drive in the middle of the road and jumped out. On all fours, he scrambled up the steep cut on the inside of the road and just made it into some thick undergrowth when he heard the approaching vehicle. Whoever it was would have to stop because his Bronco blocked the road. If it was trouble coming up the road to meet him, he would have to jump the driver and any occupants and hope for the best.

An agonizing tick of his watch measured precious lost moments as he waited. A laboring engine and spitting rocks heralded its approach as the vehicle lumbered into view. His heart thumped like an overworked pump. The precious peregrines were in the Bronco. He couldn't give them up now.

An old Ford pickup came into view. Ross peered through the undergrowth. He saw a pickle-faced little man brake to a stop. Obviously puzzled, the driver stared at the Bronco parked in the middle of the road. Then he scratched his thinning sandy hair.

Ross began to breathe again. Cut wood was piled in the back of the pickup. The man must be out collecting firewood. Ross stood up and hurried down the slope to the road. With a smile, he gave a cheery wave to the man. "Howdy! Sorry to block the road. Nature calls, you know."

He saw the man staring at his bloody face and remembered the cut on his forehead.

"Scratched myself on some darn bush."

"You out after wood, too?"

"Nope, but there seems to be quite a bit lying around."

The man nodded his head. "Damn logging outfits. Come in here and strip a forest, they do. Ought to be outlawed. A bunch of money-hungry scoundrels, that's what they are."

"Well, I guess it makes it easy for you to pick up some winter wood," Ross said, trying not to give the impression that he was frantic to be on his way.

"You been fishing?" quizzed the old man, glancing at the Bronco.

"Nope. But I saw some trout jumping in the lake," Ross said in a conversational tone.

The man made a remark about the dry weather.

Ross agreed that the forest was pretty dry. "Well, I'd better be on my way. I'll move my car over some so you'll have room to pass." Ross gave him a friendly wave and climbed back into the Bronco. He moved his vehicle to one side of the road.

The wizened little man gave him a toothless smile as he went past.

Ross was sweating. Unfortunate incident. If someone questioned the old fellow, he'd be able to describe him and the Bronco. Bad luck. What if Corey hadn't been able to handle the authorities. Had she given him away? Could they be on the road behind him already? He pulled his thoughts away from a treacherous quagmire. He took several deep breaths and lectured himself about staying cool.

He drove down the rough road, gripping the wheel and his neck muscles in a tight knot, until he had reached Highway 149 and turned north toward Denver.

About an hour later, he stopped in the small mountain town of Gunnison for gas and cleaned up in the rest room. His luck was holding. It was going to be all right.

Monarch Pass offered a wide smooth highway, and Ross had to caution himself not to exceed the speed limit as he drove up to the summit and down the other side. He didn't want to be stopped for some routine traffic violation, but it was difficult to keep his speed down, especially when he reached the straight, flat road running across South Park where herds of buffalo had once grazed. He met several highway patrol cars, and his chest constricted. Any time there could be an all points bulletin out on his Bronco.

COREY AND THE TWO MEN returned to the cabin. She had kept them away as long as possible. She prayed it was long enough.

"Mr. Sinclair doesn't seem to be back," the sheriff said. "I think we ought to take a look around the lake. You don't mind showing us where he might still be searching for that new nest, do you, Miss McCalley?"

"No, of course not. But I am pretty tired. You wouldn't mind if I took a little rest first?" She gave him a hopeful smile.

"I'm afraid I would." There was a hard edge to his tone. "We might not be able to get a handle on this thing if we let too much time go by."

"You really don't believe that Ross and I had anything to do with trapping a falcon, do you?" she asked with an amused smile. "Why would I get mixed up in anything like that? It's preposterous."

"He could have hoodwinked you," Ranger Emory offered.

The remark was so close to the truth that Corey's laugh was strained.

"That's right," the young deputy agreed, nodding his dark curly head. "You're probably too trusting."

"Do you think this Sinclair fellow is responsible for the snatching, Sheriff?" Ranger Emory asked.

"That's what I'm aiming to find out. Now, Miss Mc-Calley, I'd like to see just where you left your friend."

She shrugged. "If you think it's worth the hike."

"I do."

Corey had no choice but to lead them back around the lake. She was glad the terrain was so rough, because having to climb over all the boulders and narrow rock shelves slowed them down. She was in better condition than the three men and she knew the terrain, but she set as leisurely a pace as she thought the men would tolerate, even contemplating falling into the lake to slow them down.

"Are you sure he went this way?" demanded the sheriff.

She frowned as if in thought. "Pretty sure."

All the time, her mind worked feverishly. No birds would be flying off the high cliff to alert anyone where their aerie had been. It was out of sight from below. How could she keep the sheriff from finding the nest? In the upheaval of events, they had left everything behind, where they had camped on the high ridge: sleeping bags, clothes and foodstuff. If the sheriff found the campsite, he would also be able to locate the violated nest, and it would be apparent that the peregrines had been taken. Maybe she should have told him about the Cochran twins. Now, it was too late to change her story.

When they reached the spot where the boat had been, the sheriff stopped. His sharp eyes spied the crushed grass and muddy footprints. In any case, he never would have missed the spot, thought Corey with sinking despair. A green stocking cap caught in the bushes was like a bull's-eye marking the place.

"A boat was pulled up here," the sheriff said.

"Yeah. Look at how the brush is tramped down. And—!" Deputy Diele raised his arm and pointed excitedly. "There's a body floating a few yards out!"

Corey sat down on the nearest rock. It was all coming unraveled. The whole horrible scenario would come out. Now that they had found D.J.'s body, she would have to tell them she saw Chester meeting here with the smugglers. Once they questioned Chester, he might take the heat off Ross for a while and make the sheriff center his attention elsewhere. Yes, Chester would confirm the twins' presence, and maybe she could still cover for Ross by insisting that Delvin took the falcons that she and Ross were watching. That would keep Ross out of this last bird-snatching if Chester said the right things. Her mind whirled like leaves flying around in the air, falling in a new pattern of half lies and half-truths.

"Would you come here, Miss McCalley?" the sheriff called as the three men stood over the drowned man. "I hate to put you through this, but I wonder if you can identify this man."

Corey got to her feet and forced her leaden body to the lake's edge.

"Do you know him?"

For a moment, her eyes wouldn't focus on the inert, waterlogged body. When they did, she gasped. It wasn't D.J. Cochran, at all.

It was Chester!

Chapter Sixteen

Ross reached Denver at dusk, tired, stiff and anxious. The city lay before him as he came around the last curve out of the Rocky Mountains on Interstate 70. Stapleton International Airport was northeast of the metropolitan area, so Ross kept on the highway until he reached Commerce City, an industrial area of business and small factories. He reasoned that this suburb would provide him with quick access to the airport when the time came to leave. Its working-class population also would give him the anonymity he needed. He chose a small motel with a truck-stop restaurant. He registered under a false name and paid for one night's lodgings in cash, confident he would be long gone by morning. In a few hours he would be in the air on his way to New York City and then out of the country.

He took the cages into the motel room but left everything else in the car. In his wallet, he had a card that Prince Amund had given him. "Kashan Imports, Specializing In Eastern Treasures. 1998 Broadway. Owner, Zaki Kashan." The Prince had told Ross that Kashan was a prosperous merchant who had his own company jet. He had instructed Ross to call Kashan when he was ready to deliver the expected merchandise. It was a simple plan. The Kashan company jet would fly Ross to the Kennedy airport in New

York, and then the Prince's own private jet would take Ross and the illicit birds out of the country.

Ross took a deep breath and dialed the number on the card. He even allowed himself to lie back on the bed as he listened to the ring. When a recording came on, he sat straight up. The offices were closed, said a taped melodious female voice, and would the caller please call back during business hours. Ross slammed down the telephone. There wasn't another number on the card. He grabbed the telephone directory and hunted for Zaki Kashan. He wasn't listed.

Ross paced the motel room. He'd lose a valuable twelve hours by waiting until morning to contact the Arab. He had thought the card contained a personal telephone number where he could contact the merchant whenever he was ready. A simple false assumption had cut him off from his escape route, and time was running out. He couldn't depend on another day's delay. Corey might not be able to keep the authorities off the scent. She had given him this much of a head start, and he couldn't expect any more than that.

Ross began to pace the room, trying to figure out what he should do. Wait for morning to reach Kashan or try to leave now? He finally decided that to change plans and try to get onto a commercial airline would be inviting more risks. Getting the birds unnoticed through the security check would be impossible. That was the advantage of flying on private planes and avoiding the main airport terminals. No, he would have to wait until morning to contact Kashan. He had no choice.

A small restaurant and bar were connected to the motel. He took a shower, changed into clothes he had packed away in the Bronco and went to dinner. In the small café he had a stiff Scotch and soda before ordering a T-bone steak, rare. He knew how tense he was when the waitress touched his shoulder in a friendly gesture and he swung around ready to leap from his chair.

"Sorry, did I startle you?" Her heavy black eyelashes dipped seductively. Full breasts strained at her tight uniform, threatening to pop a button with the next breath. Her plastic name tag said Millie.

"Just tired," he stammered, and gave a wry laugh as he settled back in his chair.

"Well, now, I bet what you need is a good neck rub. Great for relaxing...the way I do it." Millie curved her bold red lips in an inviting fashion.

"What I need is sleep," he answered bluntly. "Uninterrupted sleep."

"Too bad." She gave a disappointed sigh, filled his coffee cup and then gave her attention to two other male customers who immediately responded to her flirtatious banter.

It was pure nerves, he knew, but the unexpected delay had made him feel that the worst was about to happen at any moment. He kept searching the face of everyone who came into the restaurant, prepared to fight his way out if it seemed at all necessary. As the last mouthful of his meal had settled in his tight stomach, he left.

Back in the motel room, he took another hot shower. He had not lied to the waitress, he did need a good night's sleep, but how was he going to get one when he couldn't shut off his mind? He felt a deep ache in his chest as he thought about Corey. Her goodbye kiss lingered in his memory, and he thought of all the things he wished he'd told her. But there hadn't been time. He turned and stabbed his pillow with a hard fist. He hated himself for landing her in the middle of this. No telling what lengths she would go to in order to protect him.

HERIFF WOOTEN had watched Corey's ashen face as she
ressed her fist against her mouth and turned away from
hester's flaccid body.

"I'm sorry, miss. Nasty business. Looks like the fellow
as killed and tossed in the lake. You know him?"

She nodded.

"Who is it, Miss McCalley?"

The shock of finding Chester dead instead of D.J. created
gray fog in Corey's brain, and she couldn't find her way
ut of it. How could it be? She had thought Chester had
otten away when D.J. chased her up the draw. She was
ertain he had run off to save his own skin, but now he was
ead. Who killed him? D.J. had fallen into the lake and
elvin had been holding a gun on her and Ross. None of it
ade sense.

"Is the victim one of the research team?" demanded the
heriff.

She nodded. "It's Chester Carlson, one of the war-
ens." Her voice was scratchy.

"When was the last time you saw him?"

She couldn't answer that without changing the whole
tory. Should she back off the tale she had given the sheriff
nd begin again? The truth would sound like a new pack of
es.

"When was the last time you saw Chester Carlson?" The
heriff repeated.

"I don't remember," she lied. She had to have time to
hink. How much of the truth should she reveal? Now that
hester was dead, there was no one to back up her story
bout seeing him with the smugglers or overhearing the
onversation between him and the twins. She'd bet Sheriff
Vooten wouldn't believe a word of her story.

"I see. You didn't, perhaps, see him having an argument
ith Ross Sinclair?"

"No."

"Could it be that Chester Carlson saw you and Ross Sin clair taking off with some peregrines and tried to stop you?"

"Don't be ridiculous," she managed in what she hope was an indignant tone. "How dare you accuse me of such thing? Maybe Chester fell off a ledge."

"I doubt that the victim would stick a knife in his gut before he fell into the lake."

"He was stabbed?" Her mind whirled, trying to fit piece together.

"Someone murdered him, Miss McCalley. Who?"

"I don't know." That was the truth. She didn't know. No for sure. It must have been Delvin. Chester could have bee waiting at the boat when Delvin came down after the figh with Ross. She and Ross had spent a few minutes talkin after he had bolted. Maybe Chester had told him that hi twin, D.J., had fallen to his death in the lake. He could hav demanded his money from Delvin and been stabbed to keer him quiet.

"Did you think of something?" the law officer proddec

"No." She turned away. She knew she had to keep he wits about her.

"Why don't you sit down, Miss McCalley." Range Emory took her arm and eased her down. "I know this ha been a shock for you."

"Yes." That was an understatement. The one person wh knew the truth was dead. The sheriff wouldn't believe he now if she told him Chester was the informant in the grou and that the Cochran twins were the smugglers he wa looking for. If she had told the sheriff the truth in the be ginning, he might have believed her, but now he would knov she had been lying to him all along. She had not though ahead. Now it was too late. He was watching her expres sion, his unruly eyebrows raised as if perceptive to he thrashing thoughts.

"Why don't you tell me the truth, Miss McCalley? A man has been murdered."

"Ross and I had nothing to do with this," she flared. That much, at least, was true.

"I'm afraid I'm going to have to ask you to accompany me back to Lake City."

"Why?"

"I want to ask you a few more questions," he said smoothly.

She had expected as much. The sheriff wasn't going to let go. He wasn't satisfied with her story. And she didn't blame him. Anyone with a full deck wouldn't deal her out of the game, not yet. It had been a couple of hours since Ross left. He should be well on his way by now. She'd keep the lid on things as long as she could.

SHERIFF WOOTEN left Deputy Diele to take care of the body, and he instructed Ranger Emory to continue his search for Ross Sinclair and to inform the other members of the research team that Chester had been killed. "I'll take Miss McCalley back to Lake City. You two can stay in the cabin. I'll send someone to pick you up tomorrow. Come along, miss, we'd best get started."

Corey had time to think as they hiked around the lake and up to the logging road, but her thoughts didn't bring her any closer to unscrambling the puzzle.

They had left the lake and were climbing the wooded slope to the road when the sheriff suddenly stopped. "What's this?" He pointed to the ground and then leaned down and looked at some dark blotches. "Blood. See, there's a trail of it—disappears into those bushes."

Corey's heart plummeted to the soles of her feet. Had something happened to Ross? Had the same one who plunged the knife into Chester been waiting here to jump him? Maybe Ross hadn't made it away at all.

"What do you think, miss? Looks like there's been a wrestle of some sort here in the dirt. Maybe we ought to take a look around."

She nodded, trying to keep the panic out of her expression.

After a few minutes' search, he said, "No body in the nearby bushes. Whoever was hurt must have made it away."

"Looks like it," she agreed, meeting his eyes with a steady gaze and allowing herself a silent sigh.

On the way back to town in the sheriff's car, Corey was silent. She knew enough from her legal training not to say a lot of things she would regret later. She was sure that the sheriff was going to make a good case against her and Ross. With Chester dead, she had no witness to what had really happened. She wasn't surprised when the officer turned to her and asked point-blank, "Where's Mr. Sinclair?"

"I don't know."

"Would you care to speculate, Miss McCalley?"

"No." It was almost dusk. Had Ross made is safely to Denver? She moistened her lips. "Where are you taking me? To jail? I have to warn you that I know the law. Any false arrest—"

"I'm not arresting you, Miss McCalley." His steely hazel eyes added, *yet*. "It will be more convenient all around for you to stay at the lodge while I do some investigating."

Would Trudi and Delvin still be there? Both of them would blame her for D.J.'s death. Would they fill the sheriff's ears with lies of their own? Already Trudi had expressed her suspicions to the sheriff. If only there were some proof that she and her boys had been lifting the falcons, thought Corey. For the moment, she had to keep silent until she was certain that Ross was safely away.

When they arrived at the lodge, Corey accompanied the sheriff inside. Only Helga was in the lobby. Her eyes widened when she saw Corey in the company of the officer. "Is everything all right?"

"I'm afraid there's been a bad turn of affairs, one of the research team found dead in the lake," Sheriff Wooten told her.

"Oh, my goodness." She put a hand on her heart. "A drowning?"

Sheriff Wooten sidestepped the question. "We need a bit of information, Helga. You have guests write down their license plate numbers, don't you, when they register?"

She nodded.

"May I take a peek at the book?"

She turned a large ledger around on the desk so he could see.

It only took a few seconds for the sheriff to find the name he was looking for. Corey saw his thumb stop at the entry Ross had made when they registered. "Did Ross Sinclair write down this number beside his registration?"

"No. I guess he forgot," said Helga. "Anyway, I noticed he hadn't written it down, and I went out and got the license number myself. Not that we didn't trust Ross," she added quickly. "It's just that I like to have my records complete."

"Good girl, Helga. Good girl." He smiled as he wrote down the number.

Corey was sick to her stomach. It would be only a matter of minutes before every police station would broadcast the license number to its units. She prayed Ross had already left the Bronco and was safely away.

NERVOUSLY ROSS CHECKED on the birds before bedtime. He lifted the cage covers. Eyes like glass balls bordered in brilliant yellow raked his every movement. Every feather was smoothed except for those that flared like a jagged ruff at their necks. The falcons' glassy eyes and half-open beaks made them look fierce and wild. They were young adults, strong and beautiful, Ross decided, and they would be a credit to the long tradition of falconry. What a challenge to train them to ride the wrist until released for the hunt, he thought, remembering the wondrous joy of having a falcon return and settle complacently back on a glove, when the bond was greater than the instincts of nature. "First the hawk, then the horse, then the hounds, then, and only then, the humble falconer," he quoted to himself as he covered them again.

Tomorrow they might be settled in enough for a little food, he thought as he went to bed. Soon he'd be home and have Robin safely in his arms. His life would begin again in some other country—but not the United States. Once it was known that he had broken the law, the authorities would be waiting to pick him up. He could never come back.

Ross couldn't stop thinking about Corey. Wonderful, brave, beautiful Corey. In the beginning she fought him with every fiber of her being, but in the end, because she loved him, she had put her own principles aside to help him. If only he had had the courage to trust her earlier. But he had been afraid. For himself, and for her. His life was already mixed-up, and he wouldn't have willingly involved her in unlawful smuggling, but the choice had been taken out of his hands. He remembered how Delvin had threatened them. The handsome, smiling murderer had been ready to kill them both. Thank God, he'd jumped Delvin, and Corey had gotten the gun. After that, he'd had no choice but to tell her the truth. Now he knew that she truly loved him. She had shown it by covering for him and allowing him to escape. It was unlikely that he would ever see her again, and he felt a deep loneliness that he knew would be with him always. A bitterness swept through him. He had found the woman to share his life with—only to lose her.

Dozing fitfully, Ross listened to the highway's rumbling noises all night long. He couldn't settle into a refreshing sleep. Once, he jumped to his feet when someone stopped at his motel door.

Tensely he waited, ready to lash out at anyone easing it open.

After a long moment he heard the person fumble his way into the unit next door. He went back to bed, rigid, heart pounding and wide-awake.

He was up early and on the phone precisely at eight-thirty, when the recording had instructed him to call back.

"Kashan Imports."

Ross lessened his grip on the receiver. "I would like to speak with Mr. Kashan. This is Ross Sinclair—he's expecting a call from me."

"I will connect you with his secretary."

There was a buzz and then some syrupy music came on. Tension climbed up the nape of his neck like the trek of a soft-footed centipede. Come on! Come on! He kept glancing at his watch. One, two, three, four minutes. Blast it all!

"Hello, Miss Lamsi speaking, may I help you?" A mature voice broke off the musical recording.

Ross repeated his name and the fact that Mr. Kashan was expecting a personal call from him.

"I'm sorry, Mr. Sinclair, but Mr. Kashan isn't in right now. Would you care to leave your number?"

"No, I don't want to leave a number. It's important that I speak with Mr. Kashan right away."

"I'm sorry, but that's impossible," she said with even, mechanical politeness. "He's not available to the phone right now."

"I must speak with him."

Her pleasantry acquired a rough edge. "Mr. Sinclair, if you will leave your number, I will deliver your message to Mr. Kashan when it is appropriate."

"And when will that be?"

"I'm not certain. I have not confirmed his itinerary for the day."

"Then he hasn't arrived at the office yet?"

She hesitated. "No."

"Then I would like his home phone number."

"It is not our policy to give out his private number to anyone. You would have to get that from him."

"How can I, when I can't even speak to him?"

"If you care to leave a message." Her tone was final.

Ross's hand tightened on the receiver. "All right. Here's my number—" he read it off the motel phone "—and as soon as he steps inside that office, you give it to him. Understand?"

"There are already people waiting to see him, I'm afraid. Telephone messages do not have top priority, Mr. Sinclair."

"This one better have," he said evenly but with force. "I'm certain that Mr. Kashan will not be pleased if he doesn't speak with me immediately." With that warning, he hung up, and not too gently.

Ross waited. No telling how early Zaki Kashan got to the office, but if people were already waiting for him it was a good sign that it wouldn't be long. Ross kept looking at his watch as the minutes kept slowly ticking by.

Kashan wasn't going to return the call, Ross thought, trying to keep down a rising panic. Maybe the autocratic secretary hadn't even given him the message. Ross waited for forty minutes before he phoned again. This time he didn't get past the switchboard operator. He was told that Mr. Kashan and his secretary were in a meeting. She was sorry, but she had been instructed to hold all calls to his office. If he would care to leave a message...

Ross swore silently and hung up. For a moment he just sat there on the edge of the bed, staring at the faded tweed rug.

Then he got up, packed his personal things, picked up the bird cages and loaded the Bronco. He was courting danger by leaving the sanctuary of the motel, but he had no choice.

The mile-high city of Denver stretched along the foothills that rose in undulating folds along the front range of the Rockies. A few skyscrapers were etched against a periwinkle sky at the city's center, and the gold-covered dome of the state capital gleamed in the morning sun. The Kashan Imports had a Broadway address, and Ross knew that busy street cut diagonally through the downtown district. When he reached it, he was relieved to find that he was only a block from the address on the card. He decided to leave the birds in the Bronco. He would be too conspicuous carrying them into the ultramodern building that housed Kashan Imports.

The lobby was all glass, polished chrome and speckled black-and-white marble. Ross read the directory and found the office he wanted on the forty-fifth floor. The elevator hummed quietly as it went upward. He was glad he had left a tweed jacket in the Scout, as well as a beige sports shirt and matching tailored slacks. He probably wouldn't have made it past the doorman, in faded jeans and a sweatshirt. The elevator doors swung silently open, and a hushed elegance greeted him.

Gold-leaf letters on a pair of glass doors identified the import company. All merchandise must be kept somewhere else, thought Ross, for the suite of offices appeared to be strictly management. Ross knew that Arabians, like Orientals, could not be hurried through polite rituals, and he lectured himself not to leap at Kashan with all the raw tension that had been building to explosive levels.

"May I help you?"

He recognized the smooth, efficient and cold voice of Kashan's secretary. Miss Lamsi, a well-groomed, dark-haired woman in her early forties, was seated behind an impressive executive desk. Her sharp eyes registered Ross's presence even as a polite curve of her lips waited for his response.

"Good morning," he said smoothly, quickly calculating that either the meeting was over or she had lied to the switchboard operator. He guessed that the latter was true. The spacious outer room was empty. If anyone had been waiting for Kashan, they were gone now or had been dismissed. The woman played God, thought Ross, and made the rules in her little professional empire. He would bet that his telephone message lay ignored on her desk until she was good and ready to deliver it.

"I hope I'm not late," said Ross apologetically.

"Late?"

"For my appointment with Mr. Kashan."

"I make all his appointments, and his calendar is clear this morning."

"Oh, he didn't tell you then. I'm Ross Sinclair, the one who called earlier."

Her eyes narrowed with the recognition. "Oh, yes, Mr. Sinclair, and I told you—"

"Yes." He cut her off. "I know, but you see I was able to get in touch with him before he left home and he told me to come right down." He gambled that such a thing had been possible. "Please tell him I'm here and that Prince Amund sent me."

He could see her mind rejecting his story, but she couldn't be certain whether or not he told the truth. She gave Ross a look that threatened to melt him down to an ugly spot on the rug. Then she stood up. "One moment."

Ross let out the breath he'd been holding as she disappeared through a carved door that led into a private office. He hadn't decided what he would do if she came back and dismissed him from the office. At this point he was only acting instinctively as the need arose. He had lied glibly without knowing what the next line in the script might be.

He stiffened when she came back, and then felt a flicker of victory. She wasn't smiling—and Ross took that to be a good sign.

Miss Lamsi gave a curt nod toward the door. "He'll see you, but only for a few minutes."

"I'm sure that will be sufficient. Thank you." He could afford to be generous. A heavy load had floated off his shoulders—the next leg of his journey had begun. Time was running short, but with Mr. Kashan's cooperation, he would make it to Robin in time.

Zaki Kashan was a small round gentleman with large dark eyes and a white smile below a thick black mustache. When Ross greeted him with the traditional, *"Salam 'alaikum,"* he smiled broadly and responded, *"Wa 'alaikum as-salam."* Then he motioned to a chair near the window. Apparently he had been enjoying a cup of the strong, cardamom-flavored coffee preferred by Arabians and reading several foreign newspapers instead of attending any meeting.

The Arab offered a small cup of the strong brew, and Ross politely accepted. Mr. Kashan asked about his friend, Prince Amund, and Ross gave calm responses even though they nearly choked him. He knew he couldn't bring up the purpose of his visit until his host was ready. For nearly fifteen minutes, they talked about Tasir Province and Ross's work there. All the time, Ross was afraid the dragon secretary in the outer office would come in and demand his departure.

Finally Mr. Kashan set down his cup. "Now, how can I be of service, Mr. Sinclair?"

"I believe the prince contacted you about using your company plane to fly me and some merchandise to Kennedy airport."

"Ah, yes, I had forgotten."

"We appreciate your time and consideration," Ross said politely.

"Yes, of course. Glad to be of help. When would you desire to make the trip?"

"Now. This morning."

He was visibly startled. "But how very sudden."

"Yes. Time is of utmost importance."

The Arab frowned. "I would have expected the arrangements could be made more leisurely."

He doesn't know about the falcons, Ross thought, a little perplexed. The prince hadn't told Kashan what it was that needed to be smuggled out of the country.

"The merchandise is perishable," Ross said evenly. "And I didn't know exactly when it would be ready. I have it in the car. I could drive directly to the airport and board immediately."

"But, Mr. Sinclair, how unfortunate. You see the company plane is not even here. It is in Hawaii. There will be an extended delay before its return. I am so very sorry."

His quiet words rose like a hurricane's surf in Ross's ears.

Chapter Seventeen

Ross set down his small cup carefully. He mustn't let the juice of panic rise to the surface.

"I am sorry to inconvenience you," apologized Mr. Kahan.

Ross nodded thoughtfully and looked politely at the man who had just dashed his plans to tiny, jagged shards. No company plane! No way across the country. And no time left! His mind scrambled for an avenue of escape. If he ruled out commercial flights, he would be reduced to a rented Bronco, with two illegal birds in his possession, and a whole continent and ocean between him and his destination. He could be easily traced and followed if he tried to drive across the country. Even now, he feared trouble awaited at the car rental office for him when he tried to return the Bronco. Besides, he had no ready cash or credit to buy a car, and that left stealing one. Ross had never been a man to put himself on the wrong side of the law, but in the present circumstances, he might not have a choice. His options were few. Time was running out. The prince had promised his private jet would be at Kennedy, waiting for Ross and the falcons, but how to get there? "I need to get to New York as quickly as possible."

"It is unfortunate." Kashan nodded. "I didn't realize your request would be so urgent or perhaps I could have made some adjustments."

"I understand," said Ross smoothly. "My apologies for the intrusion."

"Not at all." His smile was equally polite, but cold. For the first time, Ross wondered if Kashan was trying to out-maneuver his old friend Amund in some way. As if to voice Ross's thought, the Arab said, "Perhaps, if I knew exactly what the merchandise was, we could make some other arrangements...." Kashan's voice trailed off softly.

Now Ross got the picture! The greedy desert fox, he thought. Kashan wasn't about to let any treasure of the prince's slip through his pudgy hands. If the merchandise was so valuable that it must be taken out of the country in such a devious manner, he wanted to make certain his share had not been overlooked.

"My apologies," Ross offered smoothly. "Of course, it is only prudent that you know what is being carried on your plane. I'm certain the prince kept his silence only to protect me. He is such an honorable man," Ross lied with a false smile. "The truth is that during my three years in Tasir Province, the prince and I hunted falcons many times. He has a fondness for the blue-black peregrine falcon, which he hopes to breed along with his desert hawks. He *persuaded* me to bring him back a pair." Ross almost choked on the word, but he kept his polite smile even.

"I see," Kashan said thoughtfully.

"The U.S. government has a law against such raptors being taken out of the country," added Ross, "but that's the merchandise I wish to fly to Kennedy airport as soon as possible. I have a pair of peregrines in my car in the parking basement of your building, if you would care to see them."

The Arab folded his hands over his fat stomach, which shook with suppressed laughter. "Birds! I never would have guessed." He laughed deeply as if he'd been on the end of a good joke. "My good friend, the prince, is a boy at heart, isn't he? So much money that he must amuse himself in some fashion. Falcons!" He laughed again. "Well, now, I can see what you meant by perishable merchandise."

"Yes, there is always danger that the birds will not survive, and it's important that I deliver them healthy and fit."

"I see. Well, we mustn't let the prince's gift tarry too long, must we?"

Gift! Bile soured Ross's mouth, but he kept his counsel. It would do no good to tell Kashan the truth, that the falcons were a ransom payment he was making. The knowledge might make the Arab hesitate to get involved. Ross forced himself to lean back in a relaxed manner. "You can see my quandary, now that your company plane is unavailable."

"Yes, yes. Well, now that the situation is clear, perhaps there is something I can do for you, after all." He rose from his chair and with short smooth steps went over to his black-enameled desk. He flipped an embossed leather-bound book and scanned the pages. Then he nodded and smiled across the room at Ross. "Yes, just as I remembered. A private jet owned by a California subsidiary company of mine is due to interrupt its flight in Denver about midnight, day after tomorrow. But it will only be on the ground long enough to pick up some material from me. If you could be ready to board her, I'm certain we could get you and your merchandise aboard. Would that be of help?"

Two days away. Two days waiting. Two days of hiding. The delay would bring him right up against the deadline that the prince had set. If the plane was delayed even another day—his son could be killed. Anger, frustration and fear swept through Ross.

Kashan watched his face. "Would that be of help, Mr. Sinclair?" he repeated.

Ross knew that in the precarious circumstances, he didn't have any other option. "Yes. A very great help."

"Good. Now, how can I be of further assistance?"

"Could you notify the prince's private jet in New York to be ready for me to board the night of my arrival."

"Certainly, certainly, and now, Mr. Sinclair, you must let me extend my hospitality for the rest of your stay. I don't think it wise for you to be in public places while waiting for the plane. My home would be more discreet."

"Thank you very much," Ross responded with relief. He hated to think about hiding out in a motel for two days.

Kashan smiled. "I suggest that I have someone here return your rented car, say, at the end of the week, when you are far away. For now, it would be my pleasure if you would allow my chauffeur to take you and your cargo to my home, where you will be both safe and comfortable."

"You are most kind."

"It will be a pleasure to have you as my guest."

Ross murmured his thanks and wondered why the tension was still in the back of his neck? Was he was getting paranoid? The unexpected hospitality seemed suspect. Why should Kashan take such a personal interest in him? Was he being deftly manipulated?

"I'll make the arrangements, Mr. Sinclair."

"Thank you, again," said Ross, smiling. "I'll get the falcons from the parking garage."

"My car will be waiting out front for you." Kashan pushed an intercom button and Miss Lamsi entered with her usual brisk efficiency.

"Yes, sir?"

Kashan instructed her to arrange for the chauffeur to take Mr. Sinclair and his things to his home.

"I'll tell my wife you are coming." He shook hands with Ross. "See you this evening."

As Ross went by the secretary, he smiled politely. "Have a nice day, Miss Lamsi."

"Thank you." Her unsmiling eyes told him she had not appreciated his high-handed tactics. He felt her dagger eyes in his back as he left the office. An enemy? The muscles in his shoulder blades tightened.

He took the elevator down to the parking garage. People kept getting on and off the elevator as it crept down from the forty-fifth floor. Nervous sweat coated the palms of his hands, and his mind whirled with nettled speculations. Was Kashan being honest with him? Was he caught in some kind of rivalry between two Arabs? He hoped he was doing the right thing by going to Kashan's house. But what choice did he have? The answer was clear—none.

In the parking garage, Ross deftly lifted out the leather-covered cages, stuck his small suitcase under one arm and walked toward the outside entrance. He had taken only a few steps when a police car with two officers in it drove through a nearby entrance. His heartbeat quickened when he saw they were driving slowly—looking at license plates.

Ross didn't know whether to stop and find cover in the parking garage, keep walking or make a quick retreat to the elevator. In another minute they would be at the Bronco. Would they guess that he had just left it? And more important—was the Bronco's license number on their sheet?

Ross increased the length of stride, measuring the distance to the outside entrance with his eyes. It was closer than the elevator. He shot a glance back. His worst fears were confirmed. The patrol car had stopped at the Bronco. If they had seen him taking things out of it, they would be after him before he could exit the garage.

He quickened his steps, expecting a shout of "halt" before he reached the exit, but none came. Kashan had said the car would be waiting at the front door. Ross reached the corner of the building at the same moment he heard a car barrel out of the parking garage. In the next second the car was upon him—and then roared on by. A green Mustang with a redheaded woman at the wheel passed him without notice.

Ross shot a glance over his shoulder. No sign of the police car yet. Resisting an urge to break into a run, he walked at an even pace toward the entrance. He saw a black limousine waiting at the curb. A chauffeur opened the door as Ross approached.

"May I take those, sir?" The swarthy-faced man nodded at the leather satchels and Ross's small suitcase.

Ross handed him the suitcase. "I'll keep these with me."

"Very good, sir."

Ross put the covered birds inside the limousine and then sank back into the cushions. The chauffeur got into the front seat and closed the door just as the police car came around the corner to the front of the building.

Ross looked straight ahead as it passed, not breathing until it disappeared in traffic. It was a good thing he was sitting down, Ross thought wryly. His legs were too weak to hold him.

COREY CAME DOWNSTAIRS to the lobby about noon, wondering how long it would be before the sheriff brought her in for more questioning. She found Trudi Cochran sitting on the couch, talking to the officer in her neighborly fashion. "I knew there was something strange about them, but I couldn't quite put my finger on it, Sheriff. What is this all about? I'll be glad to help if I can."

Helga had told Corey last night that the Cochrans were still at the lodge, and Corey wondered what their next move would be. Maybe Trudi and Delvin didn't know about D.J.'s fall into the lake. Maybe his body hadn't been found yet. They might be waiting to hear from him.

Corey watched Trudi give the sheriff her friendly smile. How cunningly she hid her true nature under a folksy veneer. Trudi Cochran was about as simple as a coiled snake ready to bury its fangs in soft flesh. Sheriff Wooten saw Corey and stood up, waiting for her to join them. She wasn't ready for the confrontation she knew was coming. Worry, sleeplessness and indecision had stretched her nerves to a snapping point. All night she had hashed and rehashed the events of the day. And in the middle of a sleepless night, she had figured out how the Cochrans had fooled her and Ross. During their stay at the lodge, they had never seen the twins together. It was either D.J. or Delvin—never the two of them! A change of clothes and different outward behavior was enough to fool everyone. Only one twin remained at the lodge while the other one posed as Mr. Tiercelli. He took the bird out on the plane and delivered it to someone. Trudi's homespun friendliness masked a mind as treacherous as a scorpion. Corey braced herself as she walked across the lobby.

"Well, now, look who's here." Trudi's friendly laugh was the same, but her eyes were blue chips of hard steel. "We were just talking about you. Funny business, all of this."

"Yes, isn't it?" Corey returned sweetly.

"Good morning, Miss McCalley. Won't you please sit down?" The sheriff offered her a chair. She thought he smiled, but his black mustache drooped over the corner of his mouth, hiding any welcoming curve that might have been there.

"Thank you." Corey shifted her gaze from him to Trudi, keeping her gaze level and what she hoped was an unreadable mask on her face.

The officer sat back down at one end of the couch and placed his hands comfortably on a stomach that hung over his tight pants. "My deputy came back to town early this morning with some interesting information, Miss Mc-Calley."

Corey's stomach twisted into a tight knot. "Oh?" she said in an unconcerned tone.

"While Diele was waiting at the lake for the coroner to come and pick up the body, he did some nosing around the spot where we found poor Chester Carlson. Guess what Diele found?"

She waited for him to tell her. At this point, she didn't know what might have come to light, and she certainly wasn't going to offer any information.

"My deputy found a woman's boot without a heel at the bottom of a steep water chute. Looked like somebody had done some climbing on it."

Corey swore silently at herself. Carelessly tossing the boot away had brought attention to the draw. She couldn't have marked it better with a sign.

"Deputy Diele made a little climb and guess what he found? The other boot and a pup tent. And a couple of sleeping bags. One of them with your name on it."

Corey tried to keep her expression bland.

"And that's not all. Diele found an empty peregrine nest. And signs of violation. Like the birds had been snatched. You know anything about that, Miss McCalley?"

There was a satisfied gleam in Trudi's eyes as they flickered from Corey's face to the sheriff's.

"The way I see it," continued Sheriff Wooten as Corey remained mute, "you and Mr. Sinclair were in the process of lifting the falcons when Chester Carlson came upon you. He tried to stop you and was killed, accidentally or otherwise. Your accomplice got away with the falcons. You stayed behind to muddy up the waters as much as possible. Isn't that the way it happened, Miss McCalley?"

Motive and opportunity. The circumstantial evidence was mounting. Corey knew that it was time that she told him what had really happened. She had given Ross as much lead time as she could. Her voice seemed to be detached, coming from some point beyond her own mouth. "We didn't kill Chester. Delvin and D.J. came across the lake in a boat. Chester met them. I overheard him demanding money for telling them where the aeries were located. They refused to pay him."

Trudi looked horrified. "Did you ever! Well, if that don't beat all. Trying to lay the blame on Delvin and D.J. My boys would never get mixed up in anything like that, Sheriff."

Corey ignored her interruption. "One of the twins, D.J., is still in the lake. He fell. I saw him go under the water. I thought it was his body that had washed up when you asked me to identify it, not Chester's."

"What a crock of lies. Sheriff, just turn around and lookee there. See who's coming down them steps right now. Land's sake! Now how in the world could D.J. be in some lake when he's waltzing in here this minute as handsome as could be?"

"Howdy," the twin said in that quiet way of D.J.'s. He wore the same faded jeans and an open-necked shirt. "Nice to see you again, Corey," he said politely.

"That's not him," Corey said flatly. "It's the other one, Delvin. He's pretending to be D.J. They do it all the time. That's how they give each other alibis. D.J.'s dead. He fell into the lake. I saw him. Send for Delvin, you'll see!"

"Go get Delvin," Trudi readily told her son.

"No, keep him here," protested Corey. "So he can't switch and come back pretending to be the other one."

The sheriff's eyebrows matted together. "All right. Where's your twin brother?"

"He's—"

"Have a look-see, Sheriff." Trudi pointed toward the coffee shop and cackled. "If that ain't my boy, I'll eat a coon's tail for breakfast."

Corey's eyes froze in disbelief. It couldn't be! The second twin sauntered toward them.

"Someone looking for me?" Delvin's broad grin stretched widely across his handsome face.

Corey felt the floor dip dizzily under her. She looked from one twin to the other, and from far away she heard Trudi's deep laughter.

Chapter Eighteen

Zaki Kashan lived in a walled Moroccan-style home at the edge of southeast Denver. It was only one-story high but spacious, with several wings stretching out from a center court. Pristine white walls, ruddy ceramic tiles and sculptured greenery trailing over covered walks hinted at a quiet oasis in the urban sprawl. A private gate opened at their arrival, and the chauffeur drove forward around a circular driveway to the front of the house. Fountains and plumage birds kept the air in motion in a lush garden, and Ross had a momentary sense of displacement, as if he were already back in Tasir Province.

Apparently Kashan had called ahead and informed someone of his arrival, for a houseboy in a white jacket and black pants was ready and waiting to take Ross and his belongings to a spacious suite in the guest wing of the house. The houseboy led the way, carrying Ross's suitcase, while Ross followed with the birds.

"The dinner hour is at eight, sir."

"Thank you."

When the young man politely asked if there was anything more he could do, Ross said, "Yes, I would like several small pieces of red meat."

The servant did not blink at the request, but only gave a slight bow and left the room.

Ross had to smile. The unruffled Eastern composure always surprised him. He was certain that he was the first guest to make such a request, but the servant acted as if Ross had asked for a pitcher of iced water.

In a moment the boy was back with rich chunks of red meat in a covered container. Ross thanked him and waited until he was out of the room before lifting the covers on his birds. Once more the feathers around their faces stood out like a sunburst. This time they screamed at him as he poked the meat through the mesh and replenished their water.

A slight brush of moving air on his neck made him turn around. A slender boy, about twelve, stood in the doorway of the bedroom, his eyes fixed on the peregrines. He wore jeans and a sloppy T-shirt. Ross cursed himself for not locking the door. "Yes?"

"May I come in?" the boy asked politely. "I'm Yomen, my father's second son. I came to welcome you to our house." His eyes flitted back and forth from Ross's face to the caged birds, who were beginning to react to the light.

"Thank you. The pleasure is mine." Ross didn't like the covetous expression on the boy's face. He hurried to finish putting the meat in place.

"No, no, don't cover them up. Let me look at them. They are magnificent." The boy's face was flushed with excitement. "The coloring is so different from our brown hawks." His broad nostrils quivered, and Ross saw his eyes widen with pleasure. "I have never seen such a handsome pair." Ross cursed himself. It was obvious that the boy was mesmerized by the falcons. Every flicker of his dark eyelashes registered envy. There was probably little that the boy didn't have, but a pair of peregrine falcons might be the exception. Ross felt an arctic coldness rush through his veins. He didn't know how dangerous this new situation might prove to be.

"You like to hunt the falcons, then?" he asked casually as he covered the birds again.

"Not here in America, but in my homeland. I trained my first hawk when I was only eight," the young Arab bragged.

Without an invitation, Yomen sat down on the edge of the bed and eagerly told Ross about his struggle to raise the young fledgling to be a loyal and successful hunter. "I miss him. I wish I had a pair like that to train." He looked at Ross with a placid, sweet face, as if he were used to having such a request being honored immediately.

"I am truly sorry. This pair is spoken for," Ross answered firmly. "I must take them back to Tasir Province to a friend of your father's, Prince Amund."

Yomen smiled, nodded. "I am sorry, also." The boy walked to the door and then turned back. "We shall see." His smile was broad, and he was gone as quickly as he had come.

Ross swore silently.

For several moments, he wandered nervously around the room. Then he lay down on the large silk-draped bed and stared at the ceiling. He was desperately tired, every nerve thin edged and vibrating. The minutes crept by. Two days of waiting. He'd go mad.

He was worried about Corey. He had left her in a terrible situation. By now she must have told the authorities everything, but she had given him the time edge he'd needed. He just hoped that he didn't lose his head start during this forced wait. He was certain the police officers who were checking the garage had had the Bronco's license number. They would have radioed its location back to Lake City. Thank God, there were hundreds of offices in that building.

He wondered if the Cochrans had been arrested yet. The whole story must be known by the authorities. Very clever the way the Cochran family worked their smuggling ring.

Once the police questioned Chester, he would spill his guts, and the story would be out.

He glanced at his watch. It had been over twenty-four hours since he'd left Corey to face the authorities. She was probably settled back into her warden duties. At the end of the summer, she would go on with her career as if they'd never met. He groaned with the aching loss. She had saved his skin. Guilt that he had used her affections and loyalty to make his escape, left a bitter taste. He wished there had been some other way. For most of the afternoon Ross examined his situation from every direction he could. Kashan had agreed to fly him out of the city, but it would mean nearly a three-day delay. He was still unsure that the Arab had been telling the truth. Had he only pretended his company jet was in Hawaii to delay Ross's departure? Maybe the Arab knew all along that the merchandise that Ross was taking the prince was a pair of peregrines. Maybe he thought it would be a good trick on the prince to snatch them for his own son. Ross didn't understand the Eastern mind. He was always surprised by their religious and family devotion, and by their cruel and often barbaric treatment of others. Prince Amund's abduction of Robin for a pair of falcons defied a civilized mind, as did Zaki Kashan's unexpected hospitality.

When it was almost eight o'clock, Ross took his last clean white shirt, dark blue pants and wheat-colored jacket from his suitcase. After he had showered and shaved, he re-packed everything and set the bag by the door as he left the room for dinner.

Kashan and his wife were waiting in a spacious, pearl-and-silver-decorated salon with accents of gleaming brass. Flecks of silver sparkled underfoot in a mosaic pattern, and velvet pieces of deep blue furniture were like peacocks against the pearl-luster walls.

"Good evening, Mr. Sinclair. May I present my wife."

Ross bowed politely. Mrs. Kashan was an attractive matron wearing a black sheath dress, black hose and high-heeled sandals. Her smooth ebony hair was drawn back on her head in a thick twist, and diamond earrings were her only adornment. She smiled and nodded, but added little to the conversation.

None of the children, of which there were five, Ross learned, joined them for dinner. It was a quiet, serene affair that decried the tense churning in Ross's stomach. The main dish was *kipsa*, a favorite dish made with lamb, rice, cucumbers, raisins and tomatoes. Ross had seen large community pots of it, with Arabian men reaching in with their hands to eat the food as they sat on the ground. Apparently Kashan had brought the favorite recipe to America, but he had adopted the foreigner's elaborate table settings of silver and china.

Kashan was a perfect host. "Have you been working long in my native country, Mr. Sinclair?"

"About four years." He told him about the irrigation system his company had been developing.

For most of the dinner, they exchanged polite conversation. His host seemed bent on entertaining him. Ross forced himself to ask questions about Mr. Kashan's business, and he complimented Mrs. Kashan on her household. He knew the social rituals that were a part of the Arabian culture.

"It is a pleasure to have you in our home," his hostess quietly assured him.

Ross ate as much as his tight stomach would allow and followed the polite conversation as best he was able. He knew that Kashan would bring up the peregrines, for it was too much to hope that his son had not followed through on his smug, "We'll see."

The subject came up after dinner when the men had retired to a small sitting room, which was quite Western in its decor. Leather furniture, built-in television, stereo, VCR and even a movie screen. All the comforts of the rich, thought Ross.

Kashan settled in a deep chair to enjoy his ritual cup of cardamom coffee, which Ross knew was traditionally followed by a sweet green tea. The Arab offered his guest a small cup of the bitter brew and said casually, "My son, Yomen, tells me that you graciously showed him the falcons."

Ross kept his expression bland as he sipped the strong liquid. He nodded, but did not respond in any other way. Here it comes, he thought. Ross felt the cords in his neck stiffening.

"He was quite impressed by them, in fact." Kashan smiled. "My older son has never taken to the hunt, but Yomen is very good." Pride crept into his voice. "That boy can train the most aggressive of raptors." He then repeated the story his son had told Ross about catching his first hawk. "It has been a disappointment to leave that bird behind, but now his loneliness could be lessened."

Ross forced himself to look directly into those ebony eyes. "Yes?"

"It's about the peregrines. My son would very much like to have those falcons, Mr. Sinclair. I am willing to pay handsomely."

"I'm sorry, sir, but this pair is not for sale at any price." He couldn't negotiate politely as was expected.

Kashan's lips quivered. "I have never known that to be the case, Mr. Sinclair." His eyes hardened. "May I remind you that you are my guest, and your safety at the moment resides with me. Even with my help in getting you to the New York airport, it is very unlikely you can successfully get through customs with two illegal birds. Everyone coming and going is carefully watched, and anything suspicious is examined."

"I am well aware of that." How many sleepless hours had he lost thinking the same thing? "I'm eternally grateful for your help at this end and I would like very much to repay that kindness at some future date, but I cannot let these birds go. They must be delivered to Prince Amund."

"I will pay you much more."

"It is not a matter of money."

Kashan smiled thinly. "You take me for a fool, Mr. Sinclair—"

"No, I do not. I take you for a father who loves his son as I love mine."

The answer brought a puzzled lift to Kashan's black eyebrows. "And what does that have to do with the situation, Mr. Sinclair?"

Ross gambled on the only thing he had left—the truth. "I have a son, too. He's only three years old and I love him dearly. Prince Amund has taken him into protective custody." Bitterness coated the word. "Robin will be returned to me when I have delivered the peregrines into Amund's hands. You see, sir, it is not a matter of money. It is a matter of my son's life."

Kashan's pudgy hand rested on his stomach. In the silence, a mocking voice taunted Ross that the Arab had known about Robin's abduction from the beginning. He couldn't tell what the man was thinking. The prince could have told him everything. All along Kashan could have known that Ross was no more than a thief taking contraband out of the country. He could have decided to keep the birds for his son and he had cleverly brought Ross to his house for that express purpose. The whole thing could have been a setup.

Ross tightened his jaw against a rising flood of anger and helplessness. Every muscle in his body was tense, like a cornered animal ready to spring.

Kashan set down his cup and looked into Ross's guarded face. The Arab was not smiling as he stood up. "Would you like to take a turn in the garden, Mr. Sinclair? It's a lovely evening and I will join you in a few minutes."

Ross was at a loss to read the Arab's mind. What was he planning? Why did he want him out of the house? Ross had no choice but to wait and see. "Yes, thank you. A breath of air would be refreshing," he agreed, setting down his cup.

Kashan opened a glass door, and Ross stepped out onto a stone terrace that formed an inner court. For a moment he stood there, his ears alerted to the fact that Kashan had left the room. Where had he gone?

Ross made his way across the court to the guest wing. Was Yomen lifting the birds from his room even now, he wondered with a spurt of panic. As Ross moved closer to one of the bedroom windows, he could clearly see inside. A small bed lamp illuminated the interior.

The tension in his chest eased. The room was as he had left it. No sign that the birds had been disturbed. Ross leaned up against the wall outside the bedroom window and waited. He expected to see Kashan enter any moment and removed the falcons for his son. He waited for several minutes. Nothing happened. Then he heard Kashan calling his name.

Ross returned to the terrace door opening into the small sitting room. The Arab was smiling broadly. Fear lurched up into Ross's throat. He looked pleased. What had happened?

"I have made a telephone call for you, Mr. Sinclair. Someone is on the line waiting to speak to you." He turned his broad back and led Ross across the hall to his study.

Ross picked up an ivory-and-gold telephone with moist hands. "Hello," he said, puzzled.

"Daddy, Daddy." There was a childish giggle. "I hear you, Daddy...."

"Robin." Ross choked on the name. Joy shot like a gey-
er through him. "Are you all right?"

"I miss you. Please, Daddy, you come back now." His
ittle voice sounded so close.

"Yes, yes, I'm coming back. I love you, Robin."

"You come kiss me night, night, Daddy?"

"Yes, I will, son. Soon, soon."

"Bye, Daddy." The connection was broken. Ross stared
t the phone. He blinked against a swelling fullness in his
yes.

"I apologize for my countryman," Kashan said in a
veighted tone. "A man's son is not for barter." He held out
is hand. "Good luck, Mr. Sinclair. I hope you make it."

Chapter Nineteen

The sheriff's office in Lake City was located on the bottom floor of a two-storied brick building that looked like a renovated warehouse. The rooms were all pigeonholes and crowded wall to wall with desks and records. Corey sat on a hard-backed chair in front of a battered desk and told her story for the hundredth time to a disbelieving sheriff.

They had been at it all day. She didn't know how much longer she could keep spinning the same story. "I tell you I saw D.J. fall into the lake. I watched the water, and only his hat came up. I thought he had drowned. Obviously he didn't. Maybe Chester rescued him and got killed for his trouble. I only know that D.J. tried to shove me off that cliff and fell himself."

"Tell me the scenario again. This time, I'd like to hear about Ross Sinclair. You've talked all the way around his part in this. According to you, he was nowhere around when all this happened. Don't you realize how serious this situation is? He's disappeared. The falcons have disappeared. A man has been murdered. And yet, you keep lying!"

"I'm not lying. Chester was the informant. Delvin or D.J killed him. One of them was the Mr. Tiercelli that snatched my peregrine and flew it out of here. You can check with the pilot. They both were at the lake yesterday morning ready to snatch the second pair."

"Their mother says they went horseback riding."

"She's lying."

"You and Ross Sinclair took those birds off that hill, idn't you?"

Corey kept her gaze steady and didn't answer. She had een watching the news. Nothing about a man being ar-sted smuggling a pair of falcons. Maybe Ross was already ut of the country. She knew that the Denver police had und the Bronco in an underground parking lot and were sking all the people in the building about him. She prayed e hadn't left any trails that would lead them to him.

Sheriff Wooten chomped down on an unlit pipe. "I nought as much. While this Sinclair fellow got away, you ept us busy wandering all over the place. You're an ac-omplice, Miss McCalley, to a very serious federal offense. Vhy don't we start over and you tell me the truth this time?"

"What good would it do? I've told you that one of the ochran twins murdered Chester, and then ran off, but you on't believe me." She set her chin.

The sheriff sighed. "There is no evidence that the Coch-ans had anything to do with this, Miss McCalley. The facts ld up quite differently." He leaned across the desk. You're the one with the opportunity, and you've been lying me since the first moment we met. You and Ross Sinclair e in this together."

If she told him why she had helped Ross break the law, it ouldn't change anything. Ross was still a fugitive. His otive wouldn't count for anything. Once the U.S. govern-ent got involved, the mills of litigation would begin to ind slowly. She was enough of a lawyer to know that.

"Tell me where we can find Sinclair and those falcons."

"I don't know."

He sighed. "You leave me little choice. I'm going to have arrest you for the murder of Chester Carlson. I think you

and Ross Sinclair killed him when he caught you lifting the
birds.''

She had seen it coming. She couldn't blame him. His
version made more sense than the real one.

''Do you know a good lawyer, Mis McCalley?''

''They run in the family,'' she said with a wry smile. ''I
want to call my father from the privacy of a telephone
booth.''

The sheriff nodded his head in relief. Now they were getting somewhere.

Corey put in a call to Patrick McCalley in Washington.
There were delays. He was in conference with the president.
When she finally reached him, she swallowed her pride and
told him the whole story. As expected, her father was furious. He swore at Corey for getting into such a mess. ''Why
have you been lying for this guy?''

''Because I love him.''

''Love him? Use your brains! The no-account has got you
taking the rap while he gets off scot-free.''

''He's only doing it to get back his son.''

''Don't be such a fool, Corey. Ransom, my eye. He's lin-
ing his pockets. That's what he's doing. Told you some sob
story and you fell for it. Well, he's not going to get away
with it. No daughter of mine is going to be taken for that
kind of ride.''

''Dad, please.''

''I'll take care of this. My way!''

Corey hung up. She leaned her head against the telephone box. She never should have made that call. She knew
that the worst thing she could have done was to bring her
influential hard-nosed father into the situation. He would
send out a dragnet that would cover the whole United States.
She prayed Ross was already out of the country.

AFTER NEARLY TWO DAYS of waiting, the expected jet arrived on time. Ross had allowed Yomen to help him care for the falcons. A mutual friendship had developed between them. When it was time for Ross to leave for the airport, the boy gave him an affectionate and reluctant goodbye. He touched both cheeks to Ross's. "Someday we hunt together, Mr. Sinclair," he promised.

"I would like that," Ross lied. He never wanted to fly another falcon. The memories were too bitter, the heartache too strong. His joy in the beautiful soaring bird had been ruined forever. How could he forget the glow on Corey's face or the luminous shine in her eyes as she watched the peregrine's flight?

Kashan accompanied Ross and the falcons to Stapleton airport even though it was after midnight. "You must be careful, my friend. What you are trying to do is very risky, very risky, indeed. There is always tight security at the Kennedy airport. I hope you make it through without detection."

"I will." He had come too far to think about failure now.

"I pray to Allah that you find your son well."

Ross's jaw hardened and he didn't answer. He didn't want to think about Amund carrying out his threat against Robin.

Everything went smoothly at Stapleton. Kashan personally saw him aboard the private jet and exchanged pleasantries with the other two passengers, two Oriental gentlemen who were also going to New York.

"May Allah be with you." Kashan had given Ross the traditional embrace on both sides of his cheeks and assured him that the prince's plane had been alerted to his arrival. "They told me that there is extra security at Kennedy because of a bomb threat. It couldn't have come at a worse time for you," Kashan had said regretfully. "They will be looking into anything that looks suspicious, especially at the international terminals. I have arranged for your personal baggage to be transferred, but you will have to get the birds aboard yourself."

"Thank you very much. I shall always remember your kindness," said Ross with matching Eastern dignity.

He couldn't believe that he was really safely away until the jet had circled the glittering city of Denver and headed east on its projected path at thirty thousand feet. Not until then did he let his thoughts run ahead to the last and most precarious part of his mission—leaving the country! If for any reason he was stopped at the New York airport and found with two illegal falcons in his possession, he would be immediately charged with smuggling. His motivation would count for nothing. He could argue and plead, but he knew that the peregrines would be confiscated immediately and he would be taken into custody. Nervous sweat beaded on his forehead. He mustn't let that happen! Success was too near. The ordeal could be over in the next twenty-four hours and his precious son in his arms again. Any delay would put him over the time limit that Amund had set.

Ross tried to relax. He had to be alert and at his best when the plane landed at Kennedy airport. One false step could mean disaster. He stretched out his long legs as much as possible and closed his eyes, listening to the airplane's drone. His luck had held this far. Even though he had been detained in leaving the state, there had been no sign that anyone was on his trail. Corey had handled everything beautifully and had kept him out of the law's clutches. She was a fighter, he knew that. And loyal. And smart. He hoped everything went well for her in the future.

He dozed fitfully during the three-and-a-half-hour flight that seemed like ten. The jet circled out over the Atlantic and then came down like a soaring bird ready for nesting. The sky was just getting light. Buildings and towers were gray specters without color and distinct form. Airport lights smudged by early morning fog lent a haunting macabre atmosphere to the scene as the plane taxied to its terminal.

The two Oriental businessmen left the plane ahead of Ross. A male attendant told Ross that he would arrange for his luggage to be transferred to the Arabian jet. Ross gave him his small suitcase, but he kept the leather-covered cages.

The heavy gloom of the airport did nothing to alleviate Ross's mounting anxiety. He needed a bright sun overhead, not shadows, gray mist and the muffled drones of unseen planes. His heart was hammering loudly as he left the plane. It was starting to rain.

Ross walked across a wide strip of concrete, carrying the quiet peregrines in their tote-bag cases. Look casual and relaxed, he schooled himself. After all, he could be carrying something as innocent as camera equipment. Keeping an even stride, he walked from the plane to the main terminal. He read signs that indicated a covered walkway led to another building where private international jets were boarded.

Inside the terminal, even at this early morning hour, the airport swarmed with travelers, attendants, workers and airline staff arriving or leaving. Ross kept a measured pace in harmony with a moving line of people going from one concourse to the other. Families, business men and groups of young people surged through the terminal.

"Pan Am Flight 304 now boarding at Gate 5."

"Would Mr. Joseph Andrews please contact the United ticket agent."

Every time the loudspeaker bellowed forth, he nearly jumped. An impelling need to move as fast as he could was an urge he had to firmly control. He must blend in unnoticed with the crowd. His height gave him an advantage. He could see what lay ahead over the heads of the people in front of him. All the individuals coming toward him seemed innocent enough. Most of the travelers wore frowns and anxious expressions. He couldn't see anyone showing interest in a man carrying a couple of leather cases.

As Ross passed through a doorway, a uniformed guard locked eyes with him and Ross's heart lurched wildly like a runaway truck.

"Good weather for ducks," the man said with a grin.

"Sure is." Ross nodded and stopped breathing until he was past him. He knew that his nerves were taut enough to pop like guitar strings. Steady. Don't panic, he told himself. The hardest part was over. He had the falcons. Now, all he had to do was make it safely to the prince's private jet.

The terminal used for international private jets was filled with diplomats, foreign magnates who had their own planes and other travelers affluent enough to bypass commercial transportation. Ross hoped that this elite environment would help him slip through without inspection. There wasn't a gauntlet of custom officials to get by when departing from Kennedy, but Ross knew that anyone without the protection of diplomatic immunity could be searched at any time. U.S. laws against private search and seizure did not apply to customs officials. If someone wanted to stop him, they could, on any pretext whatsoever.

A squawking loudspeaker, ringing telephones, motorized carts and raised abrasive voices made a cacophony of noise that vibrated in his ears. He had been in this terminal upon arrival in the prince's jet. At that time, he had made mental notes about the best route to take to avoid congested areas, in order to reach the proper loading gate.

Ross started across the terminal, knowing that he was within a few short minutes of victory or defeat. *Easy, easy. Don't look around. Don't be fooled by that prickling on your neck. It's just nerves. Keep walking. You're going to make it.* He kept trying to move forward, but suddenly he was clogged in a slow line of people that was barely moving.

What was the matter? Ross craned his neck. He swore when he saw that the departure gate had been narrowed by a sliding iron grid. Two officials stood there. Were they searching carryon bags and parcels? Ross couldn't tell exactly, and he couldn't gamble on staying in the line until he found out. He moved out of the line and abandoned the crowd trying to go through the gate. Zaki Kashan had warned him about the bomb scare. Was that what this was all about? He couldn't tell, but it didn't matter. He couldn't take a chance on anyone looking under the leather covers of the cages. He would have to reach the prince's jet by some other route. He turned around and froze. Almost eyeball to eyeball, he looked into the faces of two uniformed men wearing identifying badges of the U.S. Customs.

The immediate, overwhelming instinct was to bolt. Only some detached inner control kept him rooted to the spot. The possibility that the encounter was perfectly routine kept him role-playing the innocent traveler. The guilty run quickly, someone had said. He knew he mustn't draw attention to himself. These officers might not be specifically interested in him at all. The hope died with their greeting.

"Mr. Sinclair. Ross Sinclair?"

His nod was almost imperceptible.

"We'll take those for you, Mr. Sinclair." They reached for the leather satchels.

If he was going to bolt, it would have to be now. He clenched his fists on the handles, his muscles were poised to run, but the reality of the situation made such a flight hopeless. There wasn't a chance of getting away. The men took the bird carriers from his hands. He wanted to bash in their smiling faces, but he knew that he'd never accomplish anything in an open fight. He had lost possession of the falcons—that's all he could think about. His own safety at that moment was of little consequence.

"Please come with us, Mr. Sinclair."

Their polite, matter-of-fact manner was a contrast to the havoc that raged inside Ross. He had failed! Never had Ross felt such diabolical anger and such hopelessness as he did at that moment.

On the outside, he remained stiff and controlled while his mind raced to find a way to get back the falcons. The officials escorted him down a long corridor and then ushered him into an ordinary-looking room with tables and upholstered chairs. Ross's gaze swept around the room, noting a row of windows on one side and a closed door on the other. Two people sat in chrome-and-leatherette chairs at the far end. As one of them stood up to face him, the floor dropped like a runaway elevator.

Corey!

As he stared at her, the truth roared and crashed inside his skull. She had betrayed him after all! Her sense of morality had won over any feelings she might have had for him. What a fool he'd been. Everything was brutally clear. Customs had been alerted and they were waiting to pick him up. All this time he had believed that she was protecting him.

"Hello, Ross." She smiled at him, those lovely azure eyes working their magic.

"A welcoming committee, I see," he responded bitterly. "I suppose I have you to thank for the reception." He recognized the man at her side from a picture in a newspaper. Patrick McCalley. She had used her father to have him arrested. The knowledge was like bile in his throat.

"Ross," she said in that gentle voice of hers. "This is my father. We were afraid we had missed you."

"Really?" he managed in an even tone. "I wish I could have disappointed you."

"Now, young man, no need to be discourteous. You've been courting considerable trouble for yourself. Going against the law. Trying to flaunt the laws of the U.S. government."

"Daddy," she murmured, her gaze still fastened on Ross's stony face.

"All right, Corey. I'll forgo the lectures. Now, Mr. Sinclair, my daughter tells me Prince Amund is holding your son until you present him with two peregrine falcons. Is that correct?"

"I told him what you'd said," Corey said quickly. "It is true, isn't it?" She held her breath.

"Yes, it's true," he said in a weary tone.

"And you chose to ignore the proper channels and try to smuggle these birds out of the country," Patrick McCalley snapped in a censuring tone.

"Yes, that's also true, but I had no choice."

"There is always a choice, young man! You have acted stupidly and put my daughter in great danger. It's no thanks to you that she isn't in jail right now, charged with the murder of Chester Carlson."

"Chester?" His startled glaze swung to Corey.

"He didn't run away after D.J. fell," Corey said quickly. "We think Chester dived into the lake and pulled him out. And got killed for his heroic act."

"But how do you know that? I mean, with Chester dead—"

"Exactly, young man! No one believed my daughter's story about the Cochrans, and Sheriff Wooten was about to charge her with the murder when she had the good sense to call me and tell me the story."

"No one believed me," Corey said. "But there was one witness we didn't think about until my father heard what had happened."

Ross looked at her blankly. "Who was that?"

Her pearly teeth parted in a broad laugh. "Papa Cochran, bless his heart!"

For a moment, Ross still looked blank. "Papa Cochran?"

"He was the one who received the falcon and was preparing to deliver it for a payoff. D.J., as Mr. Tiercelli, flew the falcon to his father in New York while Delvin stayed behind at the lodge and pretended to be both twins. After I told my father about the Cochrans, he made a few phone calls to the federal law enforcement officials." She chuckled. "Sure enough, they tracked down Papa Cochran. Trudi lied about her husband being dead. Papa Cochran still had the tiercel in his possession. He confessed to everything, implicated the whole family. Trudi is ready to peel the skin from his bones. They've all been arrested."

Ross had been under tension too long to feel any sudden relief. Corey leaned up and kissed his cheek. "It's all right, Ross, darling. Really it is."

He swallowed hard. "Corey, I never meant to get you in the middle of this," he began. "I never dreamed you might be charged with anything like murder. If I had known—"

Patrick McCalley cut him off with a wave of his hand. "My daughter flew to Washington yesterday. Since she is bullheaded enough to get herself involved in this affair, I had no choice but to intervene on your behalf." Corey sent Ross a triumphant look as her father reached into his pocket and pulled out a piece of crisp vellum paper with the president's letterhead on it. "I was able to secure this for you. It's a letter to Prince Amund from our president, advising him that it is our government's pleasure to send him a gift of two peregrine falcons to be personally delivered by our special envoy, Ross Sinclair."

Ross stared at the paper in his hand. The letter looked authentic. His forehead furrowed. A gift! From the president of the United States. He looked at Corey. "Is this for real?"

"It's all legal, darling. Take two lawyers' word for it," Corey assured him. "The law says that it's illegal to take raptors out of the country—except for special reasons!"

Mr. McCalley cleared his throat rather pompously. "My daughter convinced me and I convinced the president that this is a special reason. He is making a gift of the peregrines that you have in your possession. You can present them to him without fear of reprisals from our government.

"You're no longer a fugitive," Corey assured him, smiling.

Her father turned to the Customs officials. "Better get those birds aboard and alert the pilot that Mr. Sinclair has arrived."

"Yes, sir." The men left with the precious leather cases. Mr. McCalley gave Ross a wry smile. "I guess my daughter has made up her mind about quite a few things."

Ross blinked. This whole confusing scenario was a figment of his imagination. He had pushed too hard, too long. He couldn't believe what was happening.

Corey laughed at his bewilderment. "I've decided I want to be involved in environmental issues. From the other side, of course. Sound like a good idea?"

He smiled at her. She was in charge of her future now. At least, the whole stupid mess had crystallized her own thinking. Whatever they might have had together was gone. Corey was back in her own world now. "I think it's great."

Ross held out his hand to Patrick McCalley. "Thank you, sir."

"Thank my daughter," he answered briskly. "She seems to have some notion that you're worth it."

Urgency was upon him again. Every minute counted. The birds were aboard, waiting. "Will you walk as far as the gate, Corey?"

"Sure." Her eyes twinkled as she leaned up and kissed his cheek. "I'm going with you."

Chapter Twenty

Ross leaned back in the plush chair of the luxurious jet cabin and laughed deeply, joyously. Corey had never heard him laugh like that before. A wonderful, infectious sound that made the brooding shadows in his eyes disappear and erased the tense lines around his mouth. "Corey, my love, you are an angel sent from above."

"An angel?" she teased, laughing with him.

"What else? An angel with friends in high places. The president of the United States, no less. I still can't believe it." Then he sobered. "Darling, I never dreamed you'd be accused of murder. I thought you would tell them about Chester and he would verify the truth about the Cochran twins."

"So did I. You can imagine my surprise when they pulled him out of the lake instead of D.J."

He put his arm around her shoulders, pulled her close and leaned his cheek against hers. "I never dreamed that I'd left you to dance on hot coals."

"It was a little steamy at times," She admitted frankly. "Especially when both twins showed up grinning like Cheshire cats at me. D.J. must have been a good enough swimmer that he made it out of the lake, with or without Chester's help, and then killed him."

"So Chester was the informant."

"I never would have guessed. He seemed like such an innocuous kind of guy."

"Not very smart if he expected to be paid big money for acting as an informant," Ross said.

"I really felt sorry for Professor White when he found out. He had become quite fond of the funny little bird-watcher. Never suspected anything."

"I thought it was Bill," Ross admitted. "But then jealousy could have had something to do with my choice.

"Jealousy? I told you that Bill and I are just old friends."

"Back there at the airport, you said that you'd decided what kind of law you were going to practice," Ross said, taking his arm away from around her shoulder. Just because she was here with him didn't mean he should jump to any conclusions.

"Definitely. This whole thing has made me decide to take charge of my own life and follow my own ambitions. Of course, the cure was pretty drastic." She laughed. "There's nothing like being arrested to make a gal take a good long look at her future. Now, I know what I want. I'm *not* going to work in some corporate law office like my father wants. I'm going to take on some legal environmental issues."

"I think that's wonderful," he said honestly, but with a tinge of regret. She was the kind of woman who would fill her own life very adequately.

"I think I'd be good at that kind of law, don't you?"

"I think you'd be great at anything you set your mind to, Tiger."

"I'm glad to hear you say that," she said solemnly. "I have one other goal—and I may need your help."

He looked puzzled. "What's that?"

"The fact that I'm here with you should be a pretty good clue. That is, if you don't mind having a lawyer in the family."

Did she really mean it? Hope sprang into his eyes. "Corey, you've given me so much already. I love you more than I thought I could love anyone, and I want the best for you always."

"Does that include you and Robin?" she asked boldly.

The lonely ache that had been with him disappeared in the warmth of the lips she raised to his. He kissed her and was filled with possessive desire that made his voice husky. He whispered, "We'd love to marry you, Corey McCalley."

She raised her lips for another kiss. "Proposal accepted."

HOURS LATER, Ross peered out of the window and saw the shadows gliding upon the sienna sand dunes. His heart had begun to beat faster on their descent to the small desert airport at Kasardi. The end of his journey was near, and new apprehensions tightened his chest. Had the falcons survived? He knew that birds died in captivity for no apparent reason other than they couldn't stand being caged up.

"What's the matter, darling?" Corey took his hand, which was suddenly sweaty.

"Just worried about the birds. They've been in those cages a lot longer than I had planned. Extra days in Denver may have put too much of a strain on them."

"Oh, Ross, you don't think—? No, I'm sure they're fine."

"I can't help but worry about a lot of things. Robin, for instance. Is he still all right? Maybe I took too long and Prince Amund became too impatient to wait."

"Ross, don't torture yourself so." There was a tremor in her voice that betrayed her own nervousness. She put her head back against the seat and closed her eyes. Please, please let it be all right, she prayed. How could Ross survive the heartbreak of losing his son, now, after all that had happened? She was afraid he might throw his own life away seeking revenge.

The jet touched down and taxied to a hanger. "Well, we have company," said Ross, looking out the window. His voice was tight, his jaw set.

"Who?" Her own stomach tightened in nervousness.

"An official jeep, soldiers and a black limousine."

"The pilot must have called ahead," she said.

"Yes. I'd say we're expected." His voice was cold.

"It's going to be all right." She kissed him quickly.

The plane touched the ground and rolled to a stop at a private hangar.

"Look!" Corey pointed out the window as Ross unfastened his seat belt.

"A welcoming committee," Ross said, recognizing the royal uniforms.

The falcons had been placed near the pilot's cabin, and before Ross and Corey could get out of their seats, the bird carriers were already being taken off the plane by two men in palace uniforms.

Ross rushed down the aisle. He lurched through the open cabin door. "Wait. Those birds are still my property! I'll take them to Prince Amund myself. I have this letter for him."

A swarthy-faced man motioned for the two men carrying the leather-covered cages to continue. He turned to Ross. "His Royal Highness has ordered that you remain here and await his pleasure." He took the letter from Ross.

"Await his pleasure! I want my son back—now!"

"You will obey His Highness, Mr. Sinclair."

"No!" Ross started for the birds.

The uniformed guard whipped out a gun. "Don't be foolish. You will do as you are told or I will shoot you." The dispassionate tone left no doubt about the sincerity of his threat.

Corey came down the steps and stood at Ross's side. "What's happening?"

"They've taken the birds. I'm supposed to await Amund's pleasure." Fury blazed in his eyes. Ross swore as he watched a jeep take off with the birds.

The man's face remained passive. "There is a car waiting, Mr. Sinclair," he said politely, and motioned with the gun for them to walk in front of him.

Corey saw a black limousine was parked near the gate. "What's going to happen? she asked, fright causing tremors to race up her spine.

"I don't know. You never know with Prince Amund. He's half-mad with power."

Two armed men were posted at each end of the limousine. One of them hurried to open a door as Corey and Ross approached the car. After they were seated in the back seat, the guards remained at each door, their rifles ready for any trouble Ross might give them.

No sign of a driver. There was nothing Ross and Corey could do but sit there and wait.

She slipped her hand into his and squeezed it tightly. Thank heavens, she had come with him. She knew he was shaken by the delay. In a firm voice, she tried to reassure him. "The prince isn't going to insult someone bringing a gift from the president of the United States," she assured him with as much firmness as she could manage. "Even if the birds are dead, he'll have to pretend appreciation. He wouldn't dare do otherwise. He'll have to release Robin in any case."

Ross turned anguished eyes upon her. "Maybe it's too late. Maybe he's arranged an accident. My son could already be dead."

"You mustn't think like that."

A muscle in his cheek quivered. "Why didn't they take us to the palace? Why keep us waiting here like sitting ducks? I don't like it. I don't like it at all!"

Neither did Corey. She gazed out the window at the alien landscape. A few buildings dotted a landscape of smooth, rippling sand dunes that stretched away as far as the eye could see. No familiar signs of home. They were Americans in a strange and hostile land. Her father's influence couldn't help them now. They could be taken hostage or disappear without a trace. It had happened to others just like them. Their stories were in the papers every day—American hostages held in captivity and the U.S. government unable to do anything but protest.

"Scared?" he asked, reading her thoughts.

She nodded.

"You shouldn't have come."

"All right, I'll go home—if you'll go with me." She managed a smile.

"Agreed," he answered with a grin, but the stiffness in his body did not slacken.

They both jumped when the car telephone rang.

One of the guards reached in and took it. His dark face was expressionless as he listened. Then he hung up and motioned for the other guard to get into the back seat with Corey and Ross.

"Where are we going?" Ross demanded. "Where are you taking us? I demand to see my son."

The guard sat on a jump seat facing them, with his rifle ready in case they made a hostile move. The man's dark eyes did not change expression, nor did he answer Ross's demands. The other guard climbed into the driver's seat. With a shift of gears, he drove the car through a high gate onto a straight road cutting across the barren landscape.

Corey stared out the window as the black limousine hummed on the newly built highway, a sign of Western civilization. Modern traffic whizzed by in both directions, and, in contrast she saw a caravan of camels just arriving from the desert.

Corey's heartbeat quickened as the strange landscape flowed by the windows. Were the guards going to take them out on the desert and dump them? "Are we heading toward town?"

Ross nodded. "But not toward the palace," he said a few minutes later as they entered the outskirts of Kasardi.

"Do you think they're going to hold us as hostages?" whispered Corey. A prisoner could be hidden forever behind high walls and windowless buildings.

Ross frowned.

"What is it? Do you know where we're going?"

They had entered a maze of streets and high walls, and the limousine stopped at a flight of steps leading up to a modern apartment dwelling.

"What is it?" She searched his face, not daring to believe the sudden joy that registered there.

"They've brought us home." His thoughts raced. Could it be?

When the car stopped, their guard slipped out and held the door open for them.

The moment Ross and Corey stepped out, a small blond-haired boy came bounding out the front door of the house.

"Daddy! Daddy! You're back!"

"Robin!"

Ross bounded up the steps and caught the boy in his arms, hugging, kissing and twirling him around. A small, veiled woman watched from the doorway, her eyes sparkling.

"Daddy, did you bring me something from your trip?"

"I sure did." Ross turned and grinned at Corey. "Something very special."

Corey blinked rapidly to keep back the warm tears in her eyes. Then she ran lightly up the steps to meet her new son.

Harlequin Intrigue™

COMING NEXT MONTH

#145 SOUTHERN CROSS by Jenna Ryan
At NORStar Space Park, fantasy became reality.
There, dreams came true . . . but so did nightmares.
Especially for Kristian Ellis, who witnessed a murder
but couldn't prove it. Only one man could help her—
Tory Roberts, part-owner of the space park, the man
determined to become a permanent part of her life.

#146 DIAMOND OF DECEIT by M. L. Gamble
Bank exec Emma Kingston was vacationing when the
vault blew up. A man was killed—his identity
strangely obliterated—and a king's ransom littered
the floor but not a thing was stolen. Philip Rowlands
had an explanation: after years of hunting down
Coop, Emma's fiancé, Philip tracked him to the
bizarre break-in. Did Emma have something that
belonged to Coop? She claimed she had nothing but
memories that had turned bitter two years ago when
Coop was presumed dead. Was Philip the answer to
an imperiled woman's prayers? Or the deluded
prisoner of an obsession?

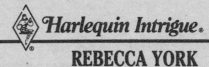

Harlequin Intrigue®

REBECCA YORK

Labeled a "true master of intrigue" by *Rave Reviews*, best-selling author Rebecca York makes her Harlequin Intrigue debut with an exciting suspenseful new series.

43 Light St.

It looks like a charming old building near the renovated Baltimore waterfront, but inside 43 Light Street lurks danger...and romance.

Let Rebecca York introduce you to:

> *Abby Franklin*—a psychologist who risks everything to save a tough adventurer determined to find the truth about his sister's death....
> *Jo O'Malley*—a private detective who finds herself matching wits with a serial killer who makes her his next target....
> *Laura Roswell*—a lawyer whose inherited share in a development deal lands her in the middle of a murder. And she's the chief suspect....

These are just a few of the occupants of 43 Light Street you'll meet in Harlequin Intrigue's new ongoing series. Don't miss any of the 43 LIGHT STREET books, beginning with #143 LIFE LINE.

And watch for future LIGHT STREET titles, including #155 SHATTERED VOWS (February 1991) and #167 WHISPERS IN THE NIGHT (August 1991).

HI-143-1

HARLEQUIN
American Romance®
THE LOVES OF A CENTURY

Join American Romance in a nostalgic look back at the twentieth century—at the lives and loves of American men and women from the turn-of-the-century to the dawn of the year 2000.

Journey through the decades from the dance halls of the 1900's to the discos of the seventies... from Glenn Miller to the Beatles... from Valentino to Newman... from corset to miniskirt... from beau to significant other.

Relive the moments... recapture the memories.

Watch for all the CENTURY OF AMERICAN ROMANCE titles in Harlequin American Romance. In one of the four American Romance books appearing each month, for the next nine months, we'll take you back to a decade of the twentieth century, where you'll relive the years and rekindle the romance of days gone by.

Don't miss a day of A CENTURY OF AMERICAN ROMANCE.

A CENTURY OF
AMERICAN ROMANCE
1920ˢ

The women... the men... the passions... the memories...

If you missed #345 AMERICAN PIE or #349 SATURDAY'S CHILD and would like to order them, send your name, address and zip or postal code, along with a check or money order for $2.95 plus 75¢ postage and handling ($1.00 in Canada) *for each book ordered*, payable to Harlequin Reader Service to:

In the U.S.
3010 Walden Ave.,
P.O. Box 1325
Buffalo, NY 14269-1325

In Canada
P.O. Box 609
Fort Erie, Ontario
L2A 5X3

CAR-1RR